GET A FREE BOOK!

I'm a pretty nice guy once you look past the grisly images in my head. Most of all, I love connecting with awesome readers like you.

Join my VIP Reader Group and get a FREE serial killer thriller for your Kindle.

Get My Free Book

www.danpadavona.com/thriller-readers-vip-group/

trembling with both arthritis and unease. She hesitated for a moment, letting her thoughts wander to the deputies. Had they left her this?

Perhaps it was a prank. Even in the wilderness, kids terrorized people after dark. Her fingers fumbled with the knot, a task more difficult than it should have been.

"Old bones, old hands," she said, cursing as she loosened the knot. The burlap fell open.

The smell hadn't hit her until now. She recoiled.

A dead crow lay before her, its black feathers matted and sticky with a red substance that could only be blood.

"Dear God."

Panic welled up inside her. What sort of twisted soul would do this?

As she lost her balance, the contents of the sack scattered across the wooden porch, the lifeless bird tumbling out in an omen.

She crashed against the porch, wrenching her back. She couldn't rise. But there was no one to help, no one to deliver her from the corruption that had found its way to her doorstep.

Patricia's eyes detected movement in the shadows. A figure lurked. The dying porch light flickered, drawing obscene patterns on the figure's obscured face.

"Please, help me," she said, though she doubted this person was here to offer aid.

The figure lunged. A gloved hand clamped down on her mouth as she was about to scream. The other hand brandished a rusted hook, its cruel curve glinting in the light.

The cold leather of his glove pressed over her mouth and cheeks. Squeezing. Suffocating.

"Please," she tried again, tears streaming down her face as she fought back the urge to retch from fear. "Why are you doing this?"

His breath was hot on her face as he stared at her from the shadows of his hood. The wind caught her muffled scream and shredded it into something incomprehensible. To anyone listening, it might sound like an animal moaning.

The echo ricocheted off the farmhouse as he plunged the hook into her belly. The pain was blinding. Blood bubbled out of her mouth and nose as white-hot agony tore her to pieces.

And as her life slipped away, the wind carried her last whispered plea on its mournful wings. The porch light, like a dying firefly, revealed the blood pooling on the wooden slats and dripping through them. With a sputter, the light extinguished itself, plunging the farmhouse into an abyssal darkness.

As the March wind rushed through the trees, a lifeless body lay crumpled upon the porch, the victim's once kindly eyes forever glazed with terror.

The killer, hidden by the darkness, stood silent and motionless over his victim. His breath was heavy, carrying a perverse satisfaction.

A crow, its wings beating against the gale, soared across the sky. Its silhouette momentarily blotted out the pale glow of the moon. As it passed, the killer raised his head, his eyes following the bird's path. A smile tugged at the corners of his mouth.

Death had come to Wolf Lake.

2

In the heart of the farmhouse, darkness crept from the closets, the basement, the empty rooms and hidden spaces. The killer swayed. An ancient grandfather clock, its chipped and weathered face corrupted by the passage of time, chimed with midnight's arrival. Each hollow note rang through the home.

As the last chime sounded, the killer's breath quickened. He tore his gaze away from the lifeless body sprawled on the porch that no longer captured his fascination. The evidence of his brutality was stark against the leather of his gloved hands. The dull sheen of the rusted hook, once a tool, had become an instrument of death.

Satisfaction rose inside him, tainted by a nagging sense of unease that refused to be silenced. The thought of being discovered, of losing everything he had worked so hard for, plagued him. Even as he reveled in his newfound power, he knew it was only a matter of time before the law came calling.

Time to move on.

The crow lay beside the woman's body, its black eyes unblinking. Once a symbol of approval for his task, it seemed to accuse him. Every instinct cried danger, urging him to flee from the judgment in the bird's eyes.

He looked around the forgotten landscape that framed the farmhouse. He was an outcast, banished from society because of the gravity of his actions. The isolation, the sting of pariah-hood, granted him strength. This desolation was his dominion, a place where he felt in control.

The night's chill crept into his bones. Ancient wood groaned around him, as though mourning the loss of its caretaker.

His thoughts were a maelstrom of rationalizations that drowned out any semblance of remorse. The cold followed him inside as he closed the farmhouse door. He paused, taking in the scene that unfolded before him. The old record player sitting on a dusty side table caught his eye, stirring something inside him.

He placed the worn vinyl on the player, watching as it settled into place. The disc's grooves seemed to hold memories of countless nights spent spinning, echoing the tunes that had filled the room he now stood in. As he lowered the needle, a soft crackle rushed like fire through the home, a prelude to the mournful dirge about to fill the air.

As the first notes of "Gloomy Sunday" began, goosebumps broke over his skin. Billie Holiday's voice filled the space, adding to his melancholy. He let the music take him and cleanse his soul. His eyes drifted back to the closed door, beyond which lay the ruined form of Mrs. Hudson.

He stood beside the player, the silhouette of a man lost in his own monstrous nature. Yet, as Billie Holiday's sorrowful tones reverberated off the walls, he felt as if he'd crossed a line from which there was no return.

He had to leave before law enforcement arrived, but the song held him captive, forcing him to confront the reality of what he'd done. With each note, the darkness beyond the living room stirred.

Enough. He tore himself away from the melody. With a sudden jerk, he ripped the needle from the record. Silence fell, broken only by his ragged breathing. He stared at the player as it slowed to a stop.

As he stepped into the night, leaving the farmhouse and his sins behind, "Gloomy Sunday" lingered in his mind. Stalking across the floorboards of the front porch, he approached Mrs. Hudson's lifeless body. Her blood loss had slowed, but the slats were forever stained. He kneeled beside her, his gloved hand hesitating for a moment before reaching out to trace the line of her jaw.

"I could have learned to love you. Forgive me, yes?"

His words revealed a glimmer of remorse. Yet there was no going back. Death now resided in this home, and he was its architect.

"It wasn't your fault," he whispered, almost as if seeking absolution.

He opened the pocketknife. His fingers trembled as they dislodged a single silver strand from her head.

Tucking the hair away, he rose to his feet and glanced around the yard, searching for witnesses. His senses were on high alert, attuned to every small noise in the night. He needed to stay focused.

Without another glance at the house, he reached down to hoist the woman's lifeless body into his arms. Her lightness startled him, a cruel contradiction to the weight of her absence.

He maneuvered through the darkness, tripping over ruts as he hauled his burden towards the tree line at the edge of the property. The gargantuan watchers of the forest closed around him, their shadows dancing on the ground in the faint moonlight. The woods were a natural fortress that provided sanctuary from prying eyes. Every rustle of leaves underfoot, every crack of a twig made him clench his jaw.

Several steps into the woods, he dropped the woman on an earthen ground devoid of snow and ice. His hands worked quickly, scraping a shallow grave into the soil. It was haphazard and dug in haste, inadequate for its purpose. But he was out of time.

Laying Mrs. Hudson to rest in her makeshift grave, he covered her body with soil and leaves. The wind would blow away her cover, but he couldn't concern himself with that.

With a groan, he rose to his feet. The darkness would shield him for now, but the looming threat of discovery was too great to ignore. As he hurried away, his mind churned, planning his escape even as his heart mourned the innocent life he'd taken. The chilling satisfaction he'd felt earlier was now a frozen stone in his stomach. Yet his journey was just beginning.

Before guilt could wrap its spindly, clawed fingers around his heart, he turned toward his vehicle, which he'd concealed behind a stand of pines across the road. He felt the dead eyes of the farmhouse window following his retreat.

In the distance, a dog howled. This was his domain now, a place where he wielded power without fear of retribution.

She was not the first, and she wouldn't be the last.

3

On a dreary March morning, Raven Hopkins sat in the leather-bound confines of a chair, inside a high-rise office in the center of Harmon. The floor-to-ceiling windows offered a sprawling vista of the city. Across the polished mahogany desk sat tycoon Franklin Devereux, his eyes sharp as he studied her. He had asked her to meet with him this morning, and she'd spent all week wondering what he wanted.

"Ms. Hopkins, I've been following your work with great interest. You've solved some of the most high-profile cases in the county. Law enforcement relies on you, and you attract clients to your private investigation firm."

"Thank you, Mr. Devereux, but I can't imagine you brought me here just to compliment me."

She was aware of the man's power and influence, and she wondered about his intentions.

"Your skills are commendable, but I must point out the risks involved." He drummed his fingers on the desk. "You've nearly lost your life several times, and I can't imagine your work adequately compensates you. Are the risks worth it?"

Raven hesitated, her eyes drifting towards the window.

She knew the dangers of her profession all too well; she bore the scars both visible and hidden. But there was something about the thrill of solving cases, the satisfaction of bringing justice to those who needed it, that kept her going despite the risks.

"Mr. Devereux, my work means a lot to me. It's true that I've faced life-threatening situations, but the people I've helped make it worthwhile."

"Interesting. But consider this: Are your personal sacrifices necessary? Is there not another way you could contribute to society without putting yourself in harm's way?"

What was he suggesting? Certainly, he wasn't offering her a job. This was Franklin Devereux. She was shocked he even knew her name.

She thought about her brother LeVar, who'd turned his life around and now worked as an unpaid intern for Wolf Lake Consulting. Then there was her mother, Serena, with whom she'd reconnected after years of estrangement. And of course there was her partner, Chelsey, the one person who understood the complexity of her life.

"Mr. Devereux," she said, her voice firm yet respectful, "I appreciate your concern and the opportunity to discuss my work with you. But I enjoy private investigation and the people I work with. They're like family."

"Ms. Hopkins, I believe your skills and dedication could be put to better use. Allow me to make you an offer."

Raven raised an eyebrow, intrigued but wary. It seemed he really was offering her a job. Whatever he intended, she had no intention of starting at the bottom and—

"Head of security for my corporation." The corners of his mouth lifted in a smile. "A position that comes with a salary far beyond what you're currently earning. You'd have access to cutting-edge resources, the prestige that accompanies working for a renowned company like ours, and the financial security you're seeking."

His words hung in the air like a tantalizing scent, and she felt her pulse quicken. Financial stability, something she'd never known, now dangled just beyond her grasp. All she had to do was reach out and take it. She couldn't deny the allure of the opportunity, the ease it would bring to her life. Head of security? She had never dreamed this was possible.

"Mr. Devereux, that's quite an offer," she said, struggling to keep her emotions in check.

"You'd no longer need to put your life on the line every day, Ms. Hopkins. Instead, you would protect a local empire, ensuring its continued success as we expand into a national power. Your talents would not go to waste. Let me tell you about our package and the vacation time."

As Devereux detailed the benefits of the position, Raven's mind kept drifting back to Chelsey. Their bond, forged over countless cases and late-night stakeouts, was more than just professional. Chelsey was her best friend, her anchor in the often chaotic world of private investigation.

"Think of the life you could lead," Devereux said. "The freedom from financial worry; the ability to focus on what truly matters. More time to enjoy the finer things in life."

Raven's fingers tightened around the arms of her chair. The image of her friends filled her thoughts, their laughter echoing through the office at Wolf Lake Consulting, the way they celebrated each solved case.

"Imagine the connections you'll make. The people you'll meet, the opportunities that come with working in such a prestigious company."

She nodded, but her thoughts remained on Chelsey. Their partnership was more than solving cases side by side. It was a bond forged by shared fears and hopes, laughter, and tears. The memory of Chelsey's smile after cracking a tough case danced in her memory. She couldn't imagine trading those moments for anything, even a life of luxury and security.

"Your skills would be invaluable to us," Devereux said, gesturing to the cityscape outside the window. "You could help shape the future of this corporation, and with it, your own future."

She took in the view of Harmon's busy streets, their shimmering surfaces reflecting traffic lights and the gray sky above. The city's business district seemed so far away from her desk at Wolf Lake Consulting. A part of her imagined sitting in an office like this, with a commanding view of the skyline stretched before her.

And she'd grown up here. Well, not in the business district, but Harmon had been her home until she turned eighteen. She could return as a conquering hero and make a difference in her home city.

As much as Raven tried to envision herself in this opulent world, her thoughts returned to the work yet to be done. The thrill of chasing leads and piecing together evidence was a passion to her. The trust and camaraderie she'd forged with her coworkers was priceless, something no amount of money could replace.

"Ms. Hopkins?" Devereux said, pulling her back to the present.

"Sorry. It's just that you're giving me a lot to think about."

"Of course." He considered her with a thoughtful expression. "I understand completely. Just remember that this isn't an opportunity that comes around every day."

Raven nodded, weighing the promise of security and prestige against the life she loved. As the conversation continued, she felt torn between the desire for a secure future and the loyalty she had for Chelsey.

Devereux stood and extended his hand, a signal that their meeting had ended. As Raven shook his hand, the executive's voice lowered, adopting a more serious tone.

"Take your time, Ms. Hopkins. But choose wisely. There are dozens of candidates interested, but I'm giving you the opportunity to skip the line and claim what's yours."

"Thank you, Mr. Devereux. I'll give it some thought."

She donned her coat and walked toward the exit. The door opened with a soft hiss as she passed the administrative assistant's desk and stepped into the hallway.

Outside, the city was alive with energy, despite the dreary weather. Raindrops clung to the glass panes of high-rise buildings, their surfaces shimmering in reds and greens as they caught the lights. The streets teemed with people huddled beneath umbrellas, scurrying about their days.

"Magnificent view, isn't it?"

Raven turned to see a female executive admiring the cityscape.

"It always is."

Vehicles raced past. Horns honked as commuters vied for position.

"But it's easy to get lost in a crowd," the woman mused before walking away.

As Raven descended the concrete steps to the parking garage, Devereux's words played inside her mind. The job offer was tempting, promising stability and a life free from danger. But the thought of turning her back on her friends—the people who had been her rock during countless cases, late-night stakeouts, and moments of self-doubt—made her wonder if the money was worth it.

She drove through the heart of Harmon with the windshield wipers swiping the weather aside. The chill in the air mirrored the cold uncertainty knotting in her chest. She looked out at strangers passing by, wondering how many others faced similar life-altering decisions.

This was her day off, but as Raven made her way home, she passed Wolf Lake Consulting, her second home, the place where she'd found a sense of belonging. She stared at the converted house. Chelsey's green Honda Civic sat in the parking lot. A wave of nostalgia swept over her. She remembered the first time she'd walked into that building, how welcomed she'd felt. It was easy to recall solving her first case, the thrill of the chase, the satisfaction of helping someone. She remembered the late nights, the takeout meals, the laughter

The grand office and impressive title offered by Devereux could never replace the fulfillment she found in her work. But fulfillment didn't pay the bills, and it sure would be nice to have more vacation time. Plus, her wealth could ensure LeVar and her mother never struggled.

Wolf Lake Consulting faded from her mirrors. How soon before it faded from her life?

4

The mid-morning light was gray against the shattered glass and discarded wrappers littering the cracked pavement of the parking lot. Chelsey Byrd sat in her green Honda Civic beside LeVar Hopkins, their breaths visible in the air as they observed Reginald "Reggie" Barkley from a distance. Reggie sauntered out of his apartment building, unaware of their presence.

"Thanks for stepping in today, LeVar," Chelsey said as she focused the binoculars on their target. Her dark wavy hair framed her face, and the black leather jacket, open at the zipper, rubbed together as she shifted position.

"Bet," LeVar said, his black dreadlocks swaying. "You know I got your back, Chelsey. Always happy to help."

"Raven's really thrown off our rhythm, you know?" Chelsey continued, the binoculars never leaving their subject. "I don't know what's been going on with her over the last several days."

"Maybe it's just stress."

He cocked his head, trying to get a better view of Reggie through the windshield.

"Maybe." Her thoughts drifted back to her partner Raven and

the strange behavior she'd exhibited of late. Chelsey shook her head, forcing herself back to their surveillance. "Now let's see what our target is up to."

As they watched, the suspect approached a beat-up truck parked across the street from his apartment. The bed took up half of a handicap parking spot. She groaned, looking for an excuse to bring Reggie down. Reggie made a habit of defrauding insurance companies, and they suspected he was up to no good this morning. His demeanor seemed casual, but there was a predatory glint in his eyes that gave away his true intentions.

"Got your camera ready?" Chelsey asked, her fingers tapping on the steering wheel.

"Yep," LeVar replied, holding up a Canon with a zoom lens, poised to take pictures if necessary. "We need solid evidence on this guy."

Reggie fumbled with something in his pocket before producing a set of keys and unlocking the truck's door. The investigators exchanged glances.

"Maybe he'll slip up today."

Her attention wandered to the rearview mirror, where she caught a glimpse of herself. She looked weary, the dark circles under her eyes betraying the hours spent on this case. Her knees bounced with anxiousness as she glanced over at LeVar.

"Anyway, Raven has the day off," she said, hoping LeVar knew what his sister's secretive plans were. "She had to go somewhere this morning but didn't say where."

LeVar rolled a knot out of his back, trying to find a more comfortable position. "Yeah, I heard. Whatever it is, she didn't fill me in."

"No big deal."

Except it felt like a big deal. Despite her imposing and athletic frame, Raven was as easygoing as they came. The concern for her friend was an unrelenting itch.

"Looks like Reggie's getting ready to leave."

LeVar pointed towards the man as he stepped into his truck.

"Stay alert."

Her fingers drifted to the key dangling out of the ignition. She intended to follow Reggie, but not yet. It was better to wait until he turned the corner before showing her hand. They watched as Reggie cranked the motor. For a moment, everything seemed normal, just another day on the stakeout.

Until Reggie's eyes met Chelsey's in the mirror. A wild expression twisted his features, his eyes widening in shock and fear. In that instant, he recognized them as threats. It didn't take long for the shock to turn into anger.

"Damn, he spotted us."

Adrenaline flooded her system. Her instincts screamed at her to act, to do something before Reggie could slip through their fingers.

"What is he up to?"

Reggie threw his truck into gear, tires screeching against the worn pavement. With a guttural growl of the motor, he aimed the vehicle straight at her Civic, hell-bent on crushing them.

"Chelsey, move!" LeVar braced himself against the dashboard.

The truck bore down on them, but her training kicked in. Years of honing her skills as a private investigator had prepared her for moments like these. Her hands flew over the steering wheel, shifting gears and slamming down on the accelerator. The Civic lurched into motion just in time.

Tires squealed. The truck hurtled past, missing the car by a hair. A sickening crunch resounded through the parking lot as the vehicle slammed into a dumpster, its metal twisting and groaning under the impact.

Inside the pickup, an airbag pinned the suspect's head

against the headrest. Stunned by the collision, he shook his head, trying to regain his bearings.

"Bastard tried to kill us," LeVar said.

"Guess we shouldn't invite him to dinner."

"Stay here." He flung open the door and sprinted toward the battered truck.

"LeVar, don't!"

She always worried about LeVar, though he was the most qualified member of her team. As a deputy with the sheriff's department, he was trained to handle violent offenders.

LeVar rushed to the dazed man, who attempted to clamber out of the wreckage. Ignoring the white powder coating his clothes and face, Reggie stumbled onto the pavement, his eyes darting around for an escape route.

Chelsey hurried out of the car. LeVar could handle himself, but concern for her friend lingered.

LeVar closed the distance between them, his speed propelling him forward. He grabbed Reggie's arm, twisting it behind the man's back with the deftness of an experienced fighter. The fraudster yelped, his feeble attempts at resistance snuffed out.

"Oh, does that hurt?" LeVar asked, his voice low and dangerous. He secured Reggie's wrists with zip ties, ensuring the man had no chance of slipping free. "Too bad. That's what you get for trying to kill us."

"Get off me!" Reggie spat, attempting to wrench his arms away. His face contorted with frustration as he realized the futility of his actions.

Chelsey kneeled beside them. "You made a big mistake today."

"I was just driving away."

"Then you suck and need lessons. The village won't be happy that you murdered their dumpster."

"Whatever. I didn't do anything." His bravado faded. He looked from Chelsey to LeVar, realizing how much trouble he was in. The suspect's face reddened as he strained against the bindings, a vein bulging in his forehead. "You can't do this. I'm gonna call the sheriff's department on you."

LeVar smirked and pulled out his badge, brandishing it before Reggie's eyes. "Go ahead. I'm a deputy."

"Aw, hell."

Chelsey smirked while she dialed the number for the sheriff's department. Pressing the phone to her ear, she walked away from the others, drawing her leather jacket together as the late-winter wind shoved her around.

"Thomas," she said, "it's Chelsey. We got Reggie Barkley. He tried to crash his truck into us but ended up hitting a dumpster instead. Yeah, we're fine. Can you send someone to pick him up?"

As she spoke with Thomas, Chelsey wondered about Raven again. Her partner would have handled Reggie as well as LeVar had. She wished she knew what was going on with Raven, but now wasn't the time to dwell on the subject.

Thomas told her a deputy was on the way.

"Thanks, Thomas. See you soon."

She hung up the phone and returned to LeVar and their captive.

"Backup's on the way," she informed LeVar, who nodded in response.

"Good." He kept a firm grip on Reggie's arm. "This fool ain't goin' anywhere."

Reggie cursed and squirmed. A few blocks away, a siren rose.

Chelsey inhaled, the March morning filling her lungs.

Thomas wouldn't be happy when he saw that dumpster.

5

Raven approached the ranger's cabin, shaking the dampness from her coat. She took in the familiar comfort of her home nestled in Wolf Lake State Park. The foggy morning had left everything drenched, but inside awaited the warm embrace of the crackling woodstove.

Pushing open the door, Raven sniffed burning maple and fresh coffee. Darren, with stubble on his face, sat at the small kitchen table and read the newspaper. He looked up at her arrival, happiness turning to concern when he saw her expression.

"Hey, you're soaked," he said, taking her waterlogged jacket and hanging it beside the fire. "How did it go with Devereux?"

Raven hesitated, her fingers tracing the edges of her sleeve. "He kinda made me an offer."

"An offer?"

"He wants me to work for him. Full-time, good money, benefits, access to resources we could only dream of at the office."

Darren stared at her. "You're kidding. Franklin Devereux? I mean, you're totally qualified, but how did he even get your name?"

"Good question." Raven bit her lip, unsure of how to proceed. "I didn't know what to say."

"Wow. That's . . . big." He rubbed his chin, processing the news. "What are you thinking?"

She shrugged, taking a seat next to him at the table. "I don't know. It's all so sudden."

He reached over and squeezed her hand. A knot formed in her stomach. The decision before her was monumental, and the thought of all that could change left her unsteady.

Darren gestured toward the mugs of coffee on the table. "Maybe it will help to talk it through."

"Maybe." She took a cautious sip of the hot brew, wincing at the bitterness but welcoming the warmth as it spread through her chest. He always made his coffee strong, a habit she had grown to love.

"Okay, what are the benefits of working for Devereux?"

"Financial stability, for one. Better pay than I could ever hope for in private investigation."

"Amazing technology too, I bet. The stuff we only read about in journals."

"Exactly. And there's the prestige that comes with working for a renowned corporation like Devereux's. It would open doors for me."

"True." He rubbed his chin. "But what about the other side of the coin? What would you be giving up if you took the job?"

She thought of her colleagues. "I'd be leaving Chelsey and the team. I love them. They're like family to me. And well, LeVar *is* family."

"Would you be able to keep in touch with them?" he asked, his eyes searching hers.

"Of course." She sounded more confident than she felt. "But it wouldn't be the same. We wouldn't be solving cases together, sharing the thrill of a breakthrough or celebrating our successes as a team."

"Is that something you're willing to give up?"

His question hung in the air, heavy with implications.

"I don't know. I've worked so hard to get where I am today, and this opportunity feels like everything I've ever wanted."

"Then maybe it's worth considering. You deserve to have your dreams realized, Raven. You've earned it."

"But at what cost? Am I willing to trade my relationships and the camaraderie I've built for financial security and professional advancement?"

"Only you can answer that question. Whatever you decide, I'll support you." In the silence that followed, the fire seemed to crackle more loudly. "Have you thought about what this could mean for your mother?"

The question caught her off guard, making her jump.

"Ma's been through so much. Addiction nearly destroyed her life, but she fought her way back to sobriety. I'm so proud of her."

"Think about the extra income from this job. It could offer her a level of comfort she's never known. It could change her life too."

"She does well working at Shepherd Systems."

"But not like this."

Raven chewed her lower lip, considering the possibility. The allure of the money was strong, and images of her mother never going through need flashed through her mind.

"The final decision must be about you and your happiness," he said.

She knew Darren would always have her back, no matter what path she chose. But as the heat of the woodstove sheltered them from the March cold in the cozy cabin, she felt a deep-rooted sense of loss.

"I don't know what to do."

"Take your time. You don't have to decide right now."

As the rain continued to patter against the cabin windows, Raven stared into the dancing flames inside the woodstove, her thoughts a whirlwind of conflicting desires and dreams. Her decision would not only impact her own life but also the lives of those she loved, especially her mother.

But when faced with the choice between the comfort of her current life and the allure of a prestigious opportunity, one question lingered in her mind: What did she truly want for herself?

Before she could decide, her phone rang. She glanced at the caller ID. "It's Chelsey," she said.

"She didn't find out about Devereux's offer, did she?"

"I can't imagine how."

She answered.

"Hey, Raven," Chelsey's voice came through the speaker. "I realize it's your day off, but we've got a situation. A woman outside of Wolf Lake hasn't been answering her phone, and the sheriff's department needs our help."

Darren was already retrieving a dry jacket for her from the closet.

"Give me the address. I'll head over there as soon as I can."

"Thank you, my friend. I owe you one."

After ending the call, Raven stared at her reflection in the cabin window, the world outside obscured by the rain-drenched glass. Guilt settled in her stomach. The idea of leaving her team behind, trading their tight-knit friendships for a life of luxury, gnawed at her conscience.

"What did Chelsey want?" Darren asked.

"The sheriff's department needs us. A woman outside the village hasn't answered her phone all day, and the department is worried."

"Then you should go. I know how much your work means to you, and to those you help." He read the conflict on her face. "Raven, it's natural to feel torn, but remember that you have to do what's best for you. You're allowed to be conflicted, but don't let guilt hold you back from making the right decision."

A gust of wind tossed the rain against the window.

"I'll keep that in mind."

She pulled on her coat and prepared to face the chill, the unforgiving weather, and the even colder reality of the choice fate had offered her.

6

Sheriff Thomas Shepherd pulled his silver Ford F-150 to a stop in front of a quaint little house two miles outside Wolf Lake. The chilling March breeze rustled the trees, making him lower his head as he stepped out of the cab. Chelsey, his fiancée and partner in crime-solving, followed suit, the dark waves of her hair fluttering in the wind.

"Beatrice should be able to help us," he said, adjusting his jacket collar against the biting cold. "She's the woman who called me."

"Who's this woman that isn't answering her phone?"

"Patricia Hudson. We'll stop by her house next. It's just down the road."

They approached the front door. A birdfeeder hanging off a hook swayed. Before Thomas could knock, the door opened, revealing a silver-haired woman with sharp eyes that seemed to take in every detail.

"Hello, Sheriff. I'm Beatrice, the one you talked to on the phone. Come in out of the cold."

Thomas and Chelsey stepped inside. The interior was so

warm that perspiration broke out on his back. They followed Beatrice into the living room, where she gestured for them to sit.

"Patricia and I talk every day," Beatrice said, her fingers working at a frayed spot on her sleeve. "It's not like her to not answer her phone or just leave town without telling me."

"Has she been acting unusual lately?" Chelsey asked.

"Nothing out of the ordinary. We mostly talk about our grandchildren and the weather."

"Could she have gone to visit family?" Thomas asked.

"Patricia's not the type to do that. We tell each other everything. That's why I called you."

Thomas exchanged a glance with Chelsey, noting the worry in her eyes. He knew she was thinking the same thing he was. Something had happened to Patricia Hudson. The widow lived alone outside the village. If she injured herself and couldn't reach the phone, there were no neighbors to help.

"Thank you for letting us know," Thomas said, standing up. "We'll check on Patricia and make sure she's safe."

"Before you go," Beatrice said, her eyes narrowing, "there was a man who mowed Patricia's lawn last week. Something about him didn't sit right with me."

Thomas faced her. "Why did he make you nervous?"

"I saw him lurking around the property even when he wasn't working. He was in that truck of his a few days ago, parked by Mrs. Hudson's property for no reason. It gave me the creeps, but I don't remember his name."

"Can you describe him?"

"Mid-forties, I'd say. Tall, thin, and scruffy looking. He drove an old, battered pickup truck. The paint was peeling, and it had a distinct rattle when he pulled up."

"Make and model?"

"Sorry, but I'm not a truck expert. There was mud covering his license plate too."

"Thank you, Beatrice. We'll look into it. If you see this man again, call me."

After they headed back to the vehicle, Thomas reached for his radio, calling back to the station as Chelsey slid into the passenger seat.

"Hey, Lambert, it's Thomas. I need you to run a background check on the guy Patricia Hudson hired to mow her lawn. We don't have a name, but he's in his mid-forties, tall, thin, and drives an old pickup truck."

"Got it, Thomas," Lambert said. "I'll call the bank and see who cashed Mrs. Hudson's checks. Give me a few minutes."

Thomas observed the wilderness through the window while they waited. It was dark beyond the treeline. Chelsey remained silent, lost in her own thoughts.

"Thomas," Lambert said after two minutes. "His name is Phillip Space. He's a local with a sketchy past and an assault record."

"Thanks, Lambert. We'll stop by Mrs. Hudson's property to investigate."

As they drove away from Beatrice's house, Thomas replayed the conversation in his mind. The details about Phillip Space were troubling. He glanced at Chelsey, sensing she shared his concern.

Her phone buzzed, and she looked down to read the text. "Raven's on her way," she said as Thomas parked in front of the missing woman's house. "She'll meet us here."

"Good. We could use a second set of eyes if this woman is lost in the wilderness."

He studied the farmhouse. There was a blackish discoloration on the porch, but he was too far away to see what it was. They stepped out of the car and approached the porch. Chelsey shivered, and it wasn't because of the March wind.

When he climbed the steps, he stopped short. Dried blood spatters marred the paint and crusted between the slats.

"Blood," she whispered, unable to finish her thought, her eyes wide with horror.

He removed his gun. "I'll call it in."

As they surveyed the porch, he wondered about Phillip Space, the man with the sketchy past and an assault record. Stepping around the stain, Thomas rapped his knuckles against the door.

"Patricia Hudson? It's Sheriff Thomas Shepherd."

Nobody answered.

"Thomas," Chelsey said behind him, "is this . . . Patricia's blood?"

"I can't wait. We're going in."

He braced his shoulder to break open the door, but when he touched the knob, it turned without resistance. Unlocked.

With Chelsey on his heels, he entered the house. He called out again, but no answer came. There were no signs of a struggle downstairs. For unknown reasons, the record player in the corner drew his attention.

Together they moved from room to room without finding Patricia. It took him five minutes to clear the house. Nobody was there.

The porch squealed under his feet as Chelsey followed him outside. The wind shifted, carrying a foul odor that hit him like a slap in the face. He paused and looked toward the stench.

"What the hell is that?" Chelsey didn't answer. She didn't need to. He had a sick feeling he already knew what the source of the odor was. Once you smelled death, you never forgot. "Follow me."

They approached the edge of the property. As they neared the woods, flies rose in anger and buzzed at their faces. Dread coiled in his chest like a venomous snake.

They stepped through the trees. Both stopped in their tracks as the gruesome sight appeared. Mrs. Hudson's mutilated body lay sprawled on the ground.

"Dear God," Thomas breathed, his expression a mixture of revulsion and sorrow. He hesitated for a moment before moving closer, careful not to disturb the evidence.

Chelsey tried to steady her trembling hands, but the grisly scene was too much for her. She turned away, bending over and retching.

He divided his attention between calming her and focusing on the body.

"You all right?"

She straightened, wiping her mouth with the back of her hand.

"Sorry," she said, her voice raw. "It's just . . . too much."

"Take a moment."

She nodded, closing her eyes as she fought to regain her composure.

He turned back to the grisly scene and kneeled before the body. They had to find Phillip Space.

7

Chelsey's breath came in ragged gasps as her eyes darted from one shadow to another. The woods around the property seemed to close in on her, branches reaching out like the tendrils of some unthinkable beast.

"Come on, we need to get away from here," Thomas said, his voice calm despite the gruesome scene they had just uncovered. He touched Chelsey's arm and steadied her. "I'm going to call for backup."

He pulled out his radio and pressed the send button. "Control, this is Sheriff Shepherd. We have a 10-54 at Patricia Hudson's property. I need Deputy Lambert and Aguilar on scene, along with the forensics team. Over."

"Roger that, Sheriff. Alerting them now," the dispatcher replied.

Thomas tucked the radio into its holster and wrapped an arm around Chelsey, guiding her away from the crime scene. "You're safe now. I promise."

"What if the killer is still nearby?"

"Look at me," Thomas said, tilting her chin up so that their eyes met. His certainty instilled a sense of safety that only he could provide. "The body has been here for several hours. The killer is long gone."

She breathed, her heart rate beginning to slow as she allowed herself to trust in Thomas's words. But the image of the lifeless, mutilated body remained at the forefront of her mind.

"Let's wait for backup, all right?"

"Sure. I'm okay now," she said, allowing Thomas to lead her away. As they walked, her thoughts raced, trying to make sense of what had just happened. Who could have done such a thing?

He remained silent as he guided her, his presence a reassuring anchor in the stormy waters erupting around them.

They reached the edge of the woods, and she finally felt the knot in her chest loosen.

"Who would do this, Thomas? Who would murder a widow and dump her body in the woods?"

"I don't know, but we'll find out. Could be a robbery gone wrong."

Distant sirens cut through the air. Within minutes, Deputies Aguilar and Lambert arrived, followed by the forensic team. Medical examiner Claire Brookins led the group, her russet hair pulled back into a ponytail.

"Thomas, Chelsey," Deputy Lambert nodded to them as he approached, his buzz-cut and tall stature lending him an air of authority. "We heard you discovered the body. What a terrible thing. Are you okay?"

Chelsey nodded and leaned her head on Thomas's shoulder.

The woods buzzed with activity as the investigators combed the area for evidence and documented the scene.

Chelsey watched the flurry of activity from a distance, her mind whirling with fears. The image of Patricia's gutted corpse dominated her thoughts, and the knowledge that someone capable of such brutality was still out there didn't help.

"I had a terrible feeling when we arrived at the house," she said, absently twisting the hem of her shirt between her fingers. "What kind of burglar would do something like that?"

Thomas looked toward the body. "Someone sick."

She knew she should leave and give herself some distance from the horror, but her duty to catch the killer kept her rooted to the spot.

"Chelsey," he said, bringing her back to the present. "You don't have to be here. My deputies can work with Claire."

As if she'd heard her name, the medical examiner approached.

"Thanks for getting here so quickly," Thomas said, nodding in appreciation. "I'll brief you on what we know."

"Thank you, Thomas."

He turned to Chelsey. "Stay here."

Chelsey shook her head. "I'd rather come with you."

As they walked towards Patricia's body, Thomas shared the limited information they had gathered so far. Chelsey stayed a few steps behind, struggling to compartmentalize.

"Her name is Patricia Hudson," he told Claire. "She's a widow, lived alone. No known enemies, no reason anyone would want to hurt her, though a neighbor mentioned a man named Phillip Space watching her house. We're running checks on him now."

Claire absorbed the details.

"The killer gutted her," he continued. "It's not pretty, Claire."

"I'll do my best to figure out what happened here."

With that, Claire took charge of the scene, directing her team. Thomas returned to Chelsey's side.

"Claire's going to take it from here. Let's get you away from all this."

Before she could respond, a familiar black Nissan Rogue pulled up and Raven stepped out. Her long dark braids swayed as she hurried towards them.

"Thomas, what's going on?" she asked, breathless. "I got a text from Aguilar. She said something terrible happened."

Thomas guided Raven aside to brief her on the situation. He didn't want Chelsey to overhear, but she did. "We found Patricia Hudson's body. It's bad. Chelsey's pretty shaken up."

"I've got this," Raven said, her eyes darting to Chelsey with a mix of worry and sympathy. "Maybe I should take her home. Give her a chance to breathe."

"Sounds like a good idea." Thomas turned around. "Raven can take you home. What do you say?"

"I guess," Chelsey stammered. "This isn't like me. I never react like this at crime scenes."

"This is no ordinary crime scene."

"Let's go home," Raven said, an arm wrapped around Chelsey's shoulders as they headed towards the Rogue.

Chelsey slid into the passenger's seat. Even with the doors closed, she could hear the wind shrieking through the trees. The engine started and they drove away from the farmhouse in the direction of the lake road.

The rattling of Raven's Nissan Rogue made Chelsey wonder if the SUV was on its last legs. She stared out the window, her thoughts a whirlwind of confusion and fear. Why had she embarrassed herself by losing her cool?

"Thank you for coming. I'm so sorry I ruined your day off."

"Don't even think about it," Raven said, her eyes never leaving the road. "You're my friend; you needed me. That's what matters."

Guilt weighed on her. Raven deserved time away from the office, and God knew Chelsey didn't pay her friend enough to work overtime. She leaned back in the seat and closed her eyes, trying to force the images from her mind. As they pulled up to the A-frame, she felt a small sense of relief.

Home. Familiar and safe.

"Come on," Raven said, guiding her out of the car and into the house. "Jack and Tigger can't wait to see you."

Inside, the comforting scent calmed her nerves. She sank into the couch; its embrace offered a respite. Tigger, her orange tabby, seemed to sense her distress and hopped onto her lap, purring. Jack rested his head on her knee, his warm eyes filled with concern.

"Thank you," Chelsey whispered to Raven, who was watching her with worry. "I don't know what I would have done without you showing up."

"Hey, we're partners," Raven said, taking a seat next to her. "It's not like you haven't done the same for me."

Chelsey managed a smile and petted Tigger, drawing more comfort from the steady rhythm of the cat's purring.

"Can I get you anything, Chelsey? Coffee or tea?"

"The last thing I need is caffeine, but thanks."

"Something to eat?"

"I wouldn't keep it down."

Raven stood and approached the window, where she stared at the gray clouds racing across the sky.

Chelsey crinkled her forehead. "You seem distracted."

"Nah, I'm fine," Raven said, her back still turned. She appeared stiff. Her beaded hair threw shadows on the A-frame's wooden floor like a net ensnaring her thoughts.

"Is it because of what happened?"

"That might be it. Until the sheriff's department catches whoever did this, we have to watch each other's backs."

8

Raven squinted at the empty driveway where Phillip Space's truck should have been parked. She stood on the sidewalk, hands on her hips, as she surveyed his small, one-story house. It was crucial that she find him and talk to him about Patricia Hudson's murder case. But it seemed he had other plans.

Back at the A-frame, Chelsey was taking a nap with Jack snuggled beside her. Thomas and his deputies scoured the countryside for Phillip Space, but he was nowhere to be found.

"Excuse me," she called out to a man across the street who was watering his plants. Burt Johns, she remembered from her earlier inquiries. She jogged over, catching his attention.

"Can I help you?"

"Hi, I'm looking for Phillip Space. Do you know where he might be?"

"Phillip?" he asked, lowering the hose and scratching his head. "Haven't seen him today. Why do you ask?"

"His safety might be in danger," Raven said. With Phillip a murder suspect, she had to tread lightly.

"Is that right? Well, I don't know where he is."

"Are you sure? It's really important I find him."

"Like I said, I don't know. Maybe he's out working or something."

He turned away, continuing to water his plants as if she were no longer there.

"Listen, I understand you don't know where he is. But if you see him later, could you please ask him to call me?" She held out a business card, the Wolf Lake Consulting logo gleaming in the gray light.

Burt eyed the card for a before taking it. "Yeah, I can do that."

He pocketed the card and returned to his gardening.

Raven checked Phillip's property again, then walked back to her vehicle. She opened the door as an SUV pulled up. The window lowered, revealing a middle-aged man with a scruffy beard.

"Hey," he called out. "Are you the one looking for information on Phillip Space?"

"Who's asking?"

"Someone who knows things." An untrustworthy glint lit the man's eyes. "But it'll cost you."

"Oh yeah? How much?"

"Two hundred," he said, never breaking eye contact.

"You have to be kidding me."

"Do you want the story on this guy or not? You think he murdered that lady, right?"

"What do you know about the murder?"

"I know Phillip Space is capable of murder, and I can prove it."

Raven didn't trust this man. "Not interested."

As she lowered herself into her vehicle, he persisted. "I was kidding about the two hundred. Ten bucks. That's all I ask. Gotta pay the bills."

"Sorry, I'm not giving you ten dollars."

"If you don't like what I have to say, you can have the money back."

"So this is like a money-back guarantee."

"Yup."

Raven hesitated, weighing the risks. Her bank account was already stretched thin, but this could be valuable information. Deciding it was worth the gamble, she nodded. "Deal."

She handed over the ten-dollar bill. The man grinned and pocketed the money, then he removed a smartphone from his jacket pocket and showed her a picture of Phillip Space attacking another man outside a bar. Raven studied the image, trying to commit every detail to memory.

"What's going on here?"

"Phillip Space has a violent streak. He attacked this guy outside a bar for no reason."

"AirDrop that picture to me."

"Sure thing."

The photograph appeared on Raven's phone.

"And you just happened to be there to catch it on camera?"

"Call it a stroke of luck."

"Who are the other people in the picture?" she asked, hoping for more information.

"Sorry, sweetheart. That's all you get for ten bucks."

"Wait," she said as the man raised the window. She snapped a picture of his license plate, making a mental note to have Darren look into him later.

"Nice doing business with you," the man said before driving away.

Raven sat there, watching the SUV disappear down the street. He'd played her, but at least she had something to bring back to the office.

After a short drive into the village, she pulled into the parking lot of Wolf Lake Consulting. Stepping out, she glanced at the converted two-bedroom house that served as their office. This was her second home. It would be difficult to give it up.

"Hey, Raven," LeVar greeted her as she walked in. He sat behind Chelsey's desk, his black dreadlocks pulled back into a neat ponytail. "Find Phillip Space?"

"Maybe something just as good." She removed the phone from her pocket and showed him the picture of Phillip Space mid-fight outside the bar. "Guy in an SUV sold me this for ten bucks."

LeVar studied the image. "That's definitely Phillip, but it doesn't prove he killed Patricia Hudson."

"True, but it might lead us somewhere. I'll call the sheriff's department and see if they know anything."

He smirked. "You really gave a random dude ten bucks for a picture?"

"What choice did I have?"

Raven dialed the number for the Nightshade County Sheriff's Department and spoke with Deputy Lambert. She explained the situation and sent him the picture, waiting while he examined it.

"Yep, that's Phillip Space all right," Lambert confirmed. "He's been arrested twice for DUI and once for assault. This picture confirms what we already know. He's an unstable individual with a short fuse. Let us know if you find anything else."

"Will do." She hung up and turned to her brother, who was biting the end of a pen, deep in thought. "Lambert confirmed Phillip's been arrested for assault before. It could be relevant."

"Sounds like it is," LeVar said, looking up from his notes. "I've only got an hour before I need to head to the community college for class. Think you can handle things here?"

"Sure. Focus on your studies."

He hesitated before speaking again. "You've been acting kinda strange lately. Is something up?"

She looked away, unable to tell him about the job offer she'd received. It would mean leaving Wolf Lake Consulting and her friends behind, but it was an opportunity that could change her life.

"Nothing's wrong," she said, forcing a smile. "Just really focused on this case, that's all."

"*Aight.* I'd better hop."

He grabbed his bag and headed for the door, but not before planting an awkward kiss on her forehead.

Sitting alone in the office didn't feel right anymore, as if the walls sensed her impending decision and were turning against her. She headed to the sheriff's department, hoping to discuss the findings with Thomas and Lambert.

Upon arrival, she spotted Deputy Lambert at his desk, sorting through paperwork.

"Hey Lambert," she said, casually leaning against the edge of his desk. "How's the investigation going?"

"Slow and steady," he said, looking up from his papers with a half-smile. "These things take time. You couldn't wait to see me after our phone conversation?"

She snickered. Lambert could always lighten the mood in the room.

"Actually, I was hoping to speak with Thomas. Is he around?"

"Thomas is still at the crime scene with the forensic team. They're combing the area for any evidence they might have missed."

"Ah, I see." Raven bit her lip, wondering if she should wait for Thomas.

"Did you want to talk to him about the fight?" he asked, nodding towards the picture.

She valued Thomas's advice and wanted to talk to him about the job offer. He would know what to do. But would he tell Chelsey?

"Just show him the picture when he returns."

"Will do. Is something else on your mind?"

"Not really. I'd better join the team and help them look for Phillip."

As she turned to leave, her thoughts drifted to the mysterious SUV driver who had sold her the photograph and the license plate number she had recorded on her phone. She paused, debating whether to share the information with Lambert. He looked busy. Maybe she should let Darren handle the identification.

"Raven, before you go," he said, "I just wanted to say how much we appreciate your help and Wolf Lake Consulting's expertise. We'll crack this case soon. I'm sure of it."

"Thanks, my friend," she said, offering a tight smile.

Keeping secrets from her friends and colleagues was a betrayal, but what choice did she have?

She stepped out of the sheriff's station, squinting against the clearing sky. Conflicting loyalties warred inside her as she fumbled with her phone. A notification from the bank caught her eye, and she winced as she read the message. Her account balance was dangerously low, and she wondered if she'd be able to make ends meet this month.

"Wonderful," she grumbled, wondering how her account could be so low when she shared living expenses with Darren. Though they saved money by living together, she still had that loan for her Nissan Rogue to worry about.

Needing his advice, she dialed Darren's number as she paced in front of the station. He answered, his voice a welcome balm to her frayed nerves.

"Hey, Raven. What's up?"

"Darren, I need you to do me a favor. I also need to talk to you about my bank account."

"Uh, okay. I'm a financial planner now?"

"Don't joke at my expense. It's been a long day."

"Tell me what you need."

"First, I have an SUV driver's license plate number. Could you look into it? Find out who the driver is?"

"Sure thing. Send me the details, and I'll get on it."

"Thanks. And the other thing." She rubbed her temple. "My bank account's running low. I'm worried I'll bounce a check."

"Raven, we'll figure it out. We can go over your expenses later, see where we can cut back."

"That would mean a lot to me."

"Anything else I can help with?"

"Could you check on Chelsey when you have a moment? Just make sure she's doing okay."

"Don't worry, I'll look after her."

"Thanks, Darren."

"Hey, that's why you love me, right?"

"Oh, it's not the only reason," she said, purring into the phone.

"I'll keep that in mind for later."

Raven hung up the phone and headed back towards Wolf Lake Consulting. She couldn't afford to let her personal life distract her from the work. There was still so much to uncover about Phillip Space and his potential involvement in Patricia Hudson's murder. She needed to find the truth—not just for the sake of justice, but for her own peace of mind as well.

9

As Thomas traveled home, the chilling scene he had just uncovered played like a horror movie in his mind. Patricia Hudson dead in the woods just steps from her yard, the lifeless body sprawled on the ground and half-covered in leaves and brush. And the crow—that damned crow—lying next to the victim with its black feathers matted in gore. He shuddered, trying to concentrate on the road ahead.

Forensics had found no fingerprints, no signs of forced entry at the house. Had Patricia opened the door willingly? Had she known the man who murdered her?

He needed to check on Chelsey. As he stopped in their snow-covered driveway and rounded the house, he spotted Chelsey outside on the back deck. She'd bundled herself in a heavy winter coat, but seeing her out in the cold made him anxious. Jack bounded through the snow, barking at the falling flakes.

"Chelsey." Thomas hurried up the deck. "You shouldn't be out here in this weather."

She looked up, her dark wavy hair peeking out from under her hat. "I needed fresh air. I'm okay, really."

"You'll catch the flu. Come inside, please."

She acquiesced, her breath visible in the freezing air. "Jack. Come on, boy."

The dog was rolling around in the snow and grinning, so Thomas left the deck door open.

He guided her into the warmth of their home. Inside, the two settled into the living room, the fire crackling in the hearth. She stared expectantly, waiting for him to tell her about the investigation.

"After the team removed the brush, they found a dead crow beside the body."

"God, Thomas. This wasn't a robbery gone wrong. The crow must be the killer's calling card."

He sighed, rubbing his temples. "Phillip Space remains a suspect, but we don't have a shred of evidence against him. Not yet. We're still trying to piece everything together."

"You're doing your best. That's all anyone can ask for."

"It's you I'm concerned about."

"Raven stayed with me until I took a nap. I still can't believe I reacted like that." Their conversation was interrupted by Jack bounding into the house, shaking snow from his fur. "Jack, no."

Thomas couldn't help laughing as the dog rubbed against the couch.

"All right, buddy," Thomas said, ruffling Jack's ears. "Let's get you dried off."

As Thomas tended to Jack, his thoughts swirled like the snow outside. The haunting image of the crime scene lingered. He wondered about Phillip Space and the disturbing symbolism of the crow.

In the kitchen, he prepared hot chocolate. The steam rising from the mugs brought a sense of comfort to the room. He handed a drink to her, their fingers brushing.

"This will hit the spot," she said, cradling the mug in her

hands. She sipped the hot liquid as Thomas regarded her with concern.

"Hot chocolate helps, right?"

"Yes, but I'm fine. Really, Thomas, I appreciate your concern, but I wasn't out there long enough to catch the flu. Which is a myth, by the way."

"Humor me. It's what my mother always told me."

As they sat together, sipping their drinks in companionable silence, the wind howled outside. March could be cruel in Upstate New York, promising nicer days as it blasted the landscape with winter's last breath.

Tigger hopped onto her lap and curled into a ball. Thomas watched her for a moment before excusing himself.

"I'll be back in a few minutes."

"Take your time," she said, her eyes following him as he climbed the stairs to the second floor.

Once inside the bathroom, he closed the door and leaned against the wall. The memory of the investigation left him feeling dirty, corrupted. He wasted no time shedding his clothes and stepping under the spray of hot water. The water ran down his body, banishing the contamination that had clung to him since discovering that poor woman's body.

As the spray pummeled him, his thoughts drifted to the killer's bizarre signature—a dead crow. What message did the murderer intend to convey? The cryptic nature of the symbol hinted at a disturbed mind. One that took pleasure in taunting those who sought to bring him to justice.

Despite the mounting suspicion, solid evidence against Patricia's lawn-care worker remained scarce. Was he wasting time by having his deputies scour the village for the missing man?

The sheriff relaxed under the steady flow of hot water that

loosened his knots of tension. Refreshed, he dressed and descended the staircase.

"Feeling better?" Chelsey asked as he entered the living room.

"Much." He took a seat on the couch beside her.

"Good. I could tell you needed to relax."

Thomas hesitated, debating whether to burden Chelsey with the details of the investigation. But he knew her keen intuition and sharp mind could prove invaluable.

"Are you all right discussing the case?"

"You don't have to handle me with kid gloves. I threw up, that's all. What's on your mind?"

"Phillip Space. Ever since the neighbor told us about him watching Patricia Hudson's house, I've had a sick feeling about the guy. Your team is doing an excellent job investigating, especially Raven."

"Now that you mentioned Raven, have you noticed her acting weird?"

"Weird how?"

"Secretive, withdrawn," Chelsey explained. "I don't want to jump to conclusions, but I'm worried there's something going on that she doesn't want to discuss."

He trusted Chelsey's instincts, and if she sensed something amiss with Raven, he couldn't ignore her concerns. "I'll monitor her behavior and see if there's anything I can do."

"I just want to make sure she's okay."

"Can you be more specific about how she's been acting?"

The fire crackled in the background. Reflected light danced across the walls.

"Sure," Chelsey said, her fingers tracing the rim of her mug. "The other day, I walked into the office while she was on the phone with someone. As soon as she saw me, she quickly ended the call, saying she had to go. And today, after she drove me home, she just stared out the window, lost in thought."

"Anything else?"

"Then there was Monday morning. I needed her help to put away some case files, and when I approached the kitchen I could hear her whispering to someone. But when I entered, she was alone and acted like nothing happened."

"Maybe she was just talking to herself, working out a problem. Or she could have been on the phone with LeVar or Serena."

"Thomas, I've known Raven for years. This isn't normal for her. I can feel it. Something's off."

Chelsey wasn't one to make baseless accusations, and he knew better than to dismiss her intuition. Still, he worried they were reading too much into Raven's actions.

"She'll talk when she's ready. In the meantime, I'll watch her."

10

Alone inside Wolf Lake Consulting, Raven ran a background check on Phillip Space. The familiar hum of the office printer disappeared under the noise of snow and rain pelting the windowpanes. She felt a pang of nostalgia as she remembered the hours working alongside Chelsey. Betraying her friend was the last thing she wanted to do.

The sound of the door opening drew her attention to the hallway. Scout Mourning entered, her hair damp from the elements. She shook herself like a wet dog, sending droplets across the room.

"Hey, Raven," Scout said, pushing her glasses up the bridge of her nose. "Thought I'd come lend a hand with the investigation. I heard Chelsey had a rough morning and wasn't coming in today."

"I'll take all the help I can get. Have a seat and make yourself comfortable."

The teenage intern was another person Raven would miss if she accepted Devereux's offer.

Scout pulled out a chair and settled in. "You know, I was

just talking to my guidance counselor again. She came up with a plan so I can graduate early and go to Kane Grove University."

"What do you think about that?"

The girl pondered over the question, her gaze shifting outside. "I don't know. Sometimes I feel like I'm ready to move on, but then I think about everyone I'd be leaving behind in high school. It's not a simple decision."

Raven nodded, understanding the teenager's dilemma all too well. "It never is. But whatever you decide, remember to follow your heart."

Watching the young sleuth work stirred a pang of doubt within Raven.

She shook her head, dispelling the distracting uncertainty. Instead, she focused on the pride welling up inside her as she observed Scout's dedication and talent. The girl had overcome so much—a devastating car accident, spinal surgery, learning to walk again—and yet here she was, using her skills and passion to solve a murder case.

Thomas stepped inside, his sandy hair tousled from the wind. "Raven, got a moment?"

"Of course, Thomas." Raven tore her gaze from the screen, her attention shifting to the sheriff. "What's up?"

"Here's what I found on Phillip Space. He's been working for Patricia Hudson for some time now." Thomas handed her a file.

"Over a decade. But why would he kill her?"

"That's a good question. We pulled his prints off the doorknob at Patricia's house."

"But if he worked for her, it would make sense that he entered the home now and then."

"Maybe." He eyed her. "You seem a little tense today."

"I'm just trying to juggle everything."

As they discussed the case, Raven's thoughts drifted to her

loan payments on the Nissan Rogue. The shocks needed replacing. It was another expense she couldn't ignore.

She would figure out everything. The question was how. She loved living with Darren at the ranger's cabin, and goodness knew it was nice to share expenses with someone she loved, but there had to be something more.

The phone vibrated on her desk, the screen displaying a text from Franklin Devereux. Her thumb hovered over the screen. She couldn't bring herself to read his message yet.

"All right, I'm heading out," Thomas said, straightening his hat. "I'm going to check the places where Phillip Space hung out. If any news breaks, I'll get a hold of you." He turned to Scout. "Thanks for helping."

The teenager waved and returned to her work. The door closed, but not before letting in a gust of chilly, damp air.

"It's great that you're filling in for Chelsey," Raven said. "You'll go far in whatever you choose to do after school. Your work ethic is amazing."

The girl blushed. "I can't even think about it yet. Not until I finish high school and college. Then there's graduate school. Who knows where it will lead?"

"What does your mom say?"

"That I need to think things over and not rush into a decision."

"Wise words."

"Yeah, I suppose. She's been pulling out her hair over finances all week."

"Why's that?"

"The village," Scout said. "They're raising taxes again."

"Wait, what? I hadn't heard that."

"Yeah, it's all over the news," Scout said, scrolling through her phone. "It's putting a lot of pressure on business owners. Some are considering leaving the village."

She wondered if the new tax rates would affect Wolf Lake Consulting.

"I hope it doesn't come to that."

The text from Franklin Devereux remained unread. Why was she thinking about another job when Chelsey was home, recovering from a traumatic event? She dialed and waited for her friend to pick up.

"Hey, Raven," Chelsey answered, her voice sounding stronger than it had before.

"How are you feeling?"

"Better, actually. I'll be able to come back to work tomorrow."

"Good. We could use your help here," Raven said, glancing over at Scout, who tapped away at her keyboard. "I've been working with Scout on Patricia Hudson's case. We found out that Phillip Space has multiple arrests on his record."

"Interesting. Do you have any leads on where he is?"

"The sheriff's department is looking for him. Thomas just stopped by, in fact." She wasn't sure how to broach the next subject. "Listen, Chelsey. I heard about the village raising the tax rates. Is everything okay financially?"

"Ah, yeah, it's not ideal," Chelsey said, her voice wavering. "But we'll manage. Wolf Lake Consulting will find a way."

"Just let me know if there's anything I can do to help." Before they could continue their conversation, Raven's phone beeped, signaling another incoming call. "Hold on, Chelsey. I have another call coming in. It might be important."

"Go ahead, take it. I'll see you tomorrow."

She switched lines.

"Raven, it's Thomas."

"News?"

"We spotted Phillip Space on the outskirts of the village. I'm headed there now."

Thomas read her the address.

"Got it. I'm on my way," she said, adrenaline surging through her veins. Hanging up, she turned to the teen. "Scout, Thomas found Phillip Space. I have to go. Can your mother pick you up?"

"If she can't, LeVar will give me a ride."

"Perfect. Sorry I have to leave like this. Listen, I'll lock the door on the way out. Don't open it for anyone until someone picks you up."

"Got it."

She grabbed her coat and rushed out to her Nissan Rogue. Wolf Lake Consulting vanished from her mirror as she navigated a hairpin turn. Five minutes later, she spotted the sheriff's cruisers along the roadside.

Raven pulled up behind the cruisers. Stepping out of the vehicle, she surveyed the scene: Aguilar had Phillip Space face down on the gravel shoulder, his wrists locked in handcuffs. Thomas stood nearby, his arms crossed, watching as Lambert searched the suspect's truck.

"Thomas," Raven said, squinting against the sun's glare. "What happened?"

"Phillip Space tried to make a run for it when he saw Aguilar. We caught him before he escaped the county. Raven, we found a knife under the seat. There was blood on it."

"Get off me!" Phillip shouted, his voice muffled by the ground. "I won't say a damn thing without my lawyer."

"Easy, Space," Aguilar said, pressing a knee into Phillip's back. "You're not helping yourself here."

"Anything else interesting in there, Lambert?" Thomas asked, looking towards the truck.

"Nothing yet, boss man."

Thomas assessed the captured suspect. She knew that beneath that quiet exterior, his mind was working overtime, analyzing every detail and possibility.

"Mr. Space," Aguilar said. "If you didn't kill Patricia Hudson, help us understand why you ran."

"Lawyer," he said, refusing to look at her.

Aguilar sighed, hauling him to his feet. The handcuffed man glared at Raven, his eyes full of defiance.

"Take him in, Aguilar," Thomas said. "We'll question him once his lawyer arrives."

"Got it, Thomas," Aguilar said, shoving Phillip towards her cruiser.

As they loaded the suspect into the backseat, Raven's phone buzzed with a text. LeVar had picked up Scout. She released a breath, thankful the girl wasn't alone anymore. One unread message sat in her inbox.

Aguilar hadn't driven off when two TV news vans whipped around the curve. Someone had tipped them off about the arrest, and now they swooped down like hawks hungry for a story. The vans blocked the road, preventing the cruiser from driving away.

Raven cursed. Phillip Space's arrest was about to become a circus.

11

The cruiser's flashing lights threw a harsh red and blue glow over the scene. Aguilar sat inside the vehicle, as she watched over Phillip Space, whose pale features contorted in fear. Raven couldn't help but feel uneasy as she noticed the news team's camera lens focused on the suspect. What if he wasn't guilty? The media had already convicted him of murder.

"Phillip Space, why did you kill Patricia Hudson?" a reporter asked, thrusting a microphone toward the closed backseat window.

The sudden barrage of questions from the media caught Thomas off-guard, but he regained composure and placed himself between Aguilar's vehicle and the news crews.

"Step back," he said. "There will be an official statement once we have all the facts."

"Come on, Sheriff Shepherd, give us something," a mustached reporter said.

"Give us some space."

Raven moved to join Lambert and the other deputies as they

formed a human barrier between the reporters and Thomas. Her muscular frame commanded respect.

"Thank you," Thomas said, giving Raven a nod of appreciation before addressing the crowd again. "As I said, there will be an official statement later. For now, please allow us to do our job."

"Did you find any evidence linking Phillip Space to the murder?" a persistent woman asked, refusing to be deterred.

"Excuse me, but that information will come out when it's time. Let us handle this."

How would Phillip's life be affected by the media circus, especially if he turned out to be innocent? As the questions continued to fly, Raven wondered what secrets his past might hold, and whether there was more to the story than met the eye.

"Everyone, clear out," Thomas said, gesturing to the news vans. "You need to move so we can take the suspect in."

Aguilar turned the key in the ignition, her eyes darting from Thomas to the crowd of reporters.

He turned to Lambert. "Get the suspect back to the station with Aguilar and make sure he stays safe from this mob."

"Got it," Lambert said, moving toward the cruiser where Phillip was waiting, a mixture of fear and confusion on his face.

As the crowd backed away, Raven approached the sheriff. "Are you sure he did it?" she asked.

"That knife Lambert found under the passenger's seat. If Phillip is innocent, why did he flee, and why was he carrying a knife with dried blood on it?"

She watched as another deputy searched Phillip's truck, each piece of evidence collected and cataloged.

"Thomas," she said, hesitating as she tried to put her thoughts into words. "What if he didn't do it? What if this is all just a huge misunderstanding?"

"Raven, we have to follow the evidence. I know it's hard, but our job is to find the truth."

"Right, but what if the truth isn't as clear-cut as we think?"

"Then we need to dig deeper," Thomas said, his gaze meeting hers. "I trust you, Raven. If you think there's more to this story, then I want you to find out what it is."

With the suspect gone, the news vans retreated. She studied the worn-out truck, its faded paint and rust spots betraying years of hard work. She felt a pang of guilt for helping to paint Phillip in a violent light. With his arrest, he was at the center of a media frenzy, and she wondered if she had played a role in condemning an innocent man.

"I feel like I may have rushed to judgment with that photo."

"We can't ignore evidence," Thomas said with understanding. "But it's good to question ourselves. Keeps us sharp."

"His truck. It doesn't look like he has much money. How will he pay for his defense?"

"Public defender, most likely. But let's not get ahead of ourselves. We still have a long way to go in this investigation."

"Phillip did yard work and repair jobs. Owning a knife isn't unusual for someone like him."

"True, but why hide it?" Thomas asked, crossing his arms.

Raven bit her lip, unable to come up with an explanation. She tried to balance her instincts with the facts in front of her. Thomas was a good sheriff, dedicated to finding the truth, but she also knew that even the best could make mistakes. Something was off about this case.

"Maybe he panicked."

"I know you want to help, but we have to focus on what we know. If there's more to this story, we'll find it."

Her eyes remained locked on Phillip's truck as the deputies removed a toolbox. She stepped away from the others and pulled out her phone. She needed to talk to Chelsey, who might offer a different perspective. Dialing the number, she paced back and forth.

"Hey, it's me," she said when Chelsey picked up. "Thomas arrested Phillip Space. I think we might be making a mistake here."

Chelsey's tone was cautious. "What do you mean? He messaged me that Phillip fled after spotting Aguilar's cruiser, and he had a bloody knife under the seat."

"Why would he drive around with a murder weapon in his truck? If he really killed Patricia Hudson, wouldn't he have gotten rid of the knife?"

"People don't always think clearly in those situations."

"He's just a guy who does yard work and repair stuff. It's not strange for him to have a knife. I don't know what to believe anymore."

"Raven, it's okay to question things. That's part of our job. But remember, sometimes people make mistakes. Desperation can lead to poor decisions. Perhaps Phillip thought hiding the knife was his best option."

Raven stared at the ground. "I hear you, but I think we're moving too fast. What if we've got the wrong guy?"

"Then the facts will prove he's innocent. We'll work on this night and day."

"I hope so," Raven said, releasing the tension from her shoulders. "Thanks, Chelsey. I needed to hear that."

"Anytime. We'll discuss this further at work tomorrow morning."

Raven hung up. She couldn't let her doubts cloud her judgment when lives were at stake. She had run a background check earlier, but now she felt compelled to find any details she might have overlooked.

"Thomas," she called out, catching up to him as he started back toward his truck. "I want to question Phillip at the station."

He paused and turned to face her, his expression a mixture of surprise and hesitation. "Question him? You're not part of the sheriff's department, Raven."

"I know, but I fed you the evidence that made him a suspect."

Her eyes met his, refusing to look away.

Thomas rubbed the back of his neck. "All right, I'll let you sit in on the interview. But we'll have to do it in the presence of his lawyer. No exceptions."

"I understand."

As she drove back to Wolf Lake Consulting to gather the background check, she considered the questions she might ask during the interrogation. She needed help—a legal expert who could provide guidance on Phillip's defense. It was then that she remembered Franklin Devereux. She pulled over and dialed his number, her hands shaking.

"Mr. Devereux, I need your help."

"Ms. Hopkins, how can I assist you today?"

"The sheriff's department just arrested Phillip Space."

"Does this have anything to do with the murder investigation?"

"It does."

"Careful, Ms. Hopkins. Crossing the sheriff won't win you any favors."

"I know, but I need someone who can help with the legal side of things for Phillip Space. He doesn't have any money, and I don't trust a public defender to stand up for him."

"Give me some time to check around and I'll get back to you. Just hang tight, okay?"

"Thanks, Mr. Devereux. I appreciate it."

If there was even a shred of doubt that they had the wrong person, she couldn't let this go. She owed it to herself, to Thomas, and to Phillip Space to find the truth.

At the office, she snatched the background check off her

desk. As she scanned the various entries, a pattern emerged. Years ago, Phillip had been caught up in a web of alcohol abuse, leading to a string of petty crimes. It seemed he had spent some time in rehab, trying to turn his life around.

Continuing her search on the internet, she found an article detailing how Phillip had pulled himself out of the darkness and started his own business, often volunteering at local events and offering free services to older residents who couldn't afford them.

"Seems like you've done your best to change," Raven said, leaning back in her chair. "So why are you driving around with a bloody knife?"

Her phone buzzed on the desk, breaking her concentration. It was a text from Devereux.

I found someone who can help. Will call you shortly.

She couldn't ignore Phillip's troubled past, but the man she read about seemed different from the one Thomas had arrested. It wasn't uncommon for people to change after they'd hit rock bottom. Her mother had.

But was Phillip's past enough to convict him in the eyes of the law?

12

The glow of the outdated television set spread shadows on the walls. His bloodshot eyes were glued to the screen, watching as the local broadcast unveiled the breaking news of Phillip Space's arrest. A smirk crept across his face as he took in every detail of the unfolding scene.

"Phillip Space, a forty-five-year-old lawn care worker, has been arrested in connection to the gruesome murder of Patricia Hudson," announced the prim news anchor.

On the screen, Deputy Veronica Aguilar held Phillip in a cruiser. Despite the grainy footage, he could see the confusion and fear on the arrested man's face. Phillip squirmed like a worm on a hook.

He shook his head in amusement, reveling in how easy it had been to misdirect and manipulate the entire sheriff's department. They had fallen for his ploy like complete amateurs, blinded by their own desire for justice.

Too bad for Phillip. Collateral damage.

He considered Sheriff Thomas Shepherd. He knew about Shepherd's Asperger's syndrome and wondered if it played a part in the sheriff fixating on the arrested suspect. No matter, he thought. It only made his game more enjoyable.

The satisfaction of seeing his plan unfold emboldened him. He could do this forever. Kill and blame others. Leaning back on his worn-out couch, he was the puppet master pulling the strings, staying one step ahead, once again outsmarting the authorities. Getting away with murder.

On the TV, Sheriff Thomas Shepherd stood tall, his sandy hair ruffled by the wind. The green-blue of his eyes shone on the old screen, his unwavering determination to bring justice to Nightshade County obvious. The sheriff addressed the press gathered around him, his voice steady despite the chaos unfolding in the background.

"We are confident that we're close to solving Patricia Hudson's murder," he declared, nodding at Deputy Tristan Lambert, who stood nearby, solid as a rock. "Phillip Space has been taken into custody, and our investigation is ongoing."

He couldn't help but chuckle at Shepherd's misplaced confidence. His boldness grew at each passing moment, and with it a new sense of invincibility. Watching them flounder in their pursuit, he knew he was untouchable, free to indulge in his darkest desires without fear of capture.

Nightshade County was his. He couldn't wait for his next kill, the anticipation already growing inside him. The time was coming, and the thrill of the chase would soon be his once more.

With a disdainful shake of his head, he found the off button on the TV remote. The screen went black, but the images danced in his mind like malevolent ghosts. The springs of the couch groaned as he rose; he crossed the room to where a hidden panel lay nestled in the living room wall.

Time for a trip down memory lane. He eased the panel open, revealing the small, aged wooden box concealed behind it. Old and weathered, the box might have looked like an unremarkable relic if not for the tender care with which the killer treated it. His fingers traced its edges before lifting the lid to reveal the memorabilia it contained.

"Hello, my darling," he crooned, his voice low and reverent. "Have you been waiting for me?"

His fingers avoided a burned-out match and hovered over the hair that had belonged to Patricia Hudson. The memory of the kill returned to him. He brushed the hair, lost in the dark remembrance.

But even as he savored the satisfaction of his deed, something shifted in him. The gratification brought by the broadcast was slowly receding, replaced by an itch, a burning need. The anticipation was building, a thrilling crescendo that begged for completion.

Hunger clawed at his stomach. He paced across the worn wooden floorboards. It was reckless, he knew. With Phillip's arrest dominating the headlines, the town would be on high alert. But the exhilaration he'd felt watching the broadcast was a thrill that he hadn't experienced until today.

The logical part of his mind knew caution was paramount, that he had to let the heat die down and allow Phillip Space to take the fall. But logic warred with the hunger, a primal force. His mind teetered between reason and impulse.

Yet the hunger remained, a constant presence that refused to be ignored. It chipped away at his resolve.

The anticipation, the danger. It invigorated him, breathing life into his solitary existence. His eyes scanned the county map pinned to the wall, illuminated by the weak glow of a single lamp in the corner.

Somewhere secluded. He needed privacy to work.

As he pondered his options, a new excitement built, a heady mixture of adrenaline and pleasure. He could taste the fear of his next victim, feel the warmth of their blood on his hands. It was intoxicating, overwhelming, and he reveled in it.

Control. He needed to maintain control.

With regret, he placed the hair back into the box. As he closed the lid, he felt a strange sense of finality, a chapter closing in the story of his life. But another was beginning. He slid the panel into place.

Just then, a crow landed on a branch outside his window, its black eyes staring straight at him, unblinking and unnerving. It cocked its head to one side, as if waiting for him to speak, to acknowledge its presence.

The crow let out a single guttural caw, as if in agreement with his decision to kill. He smiled with renewed purpose. Nothing would stand in his way, least of all the bumbling fools at the sheriff's department. Let them chase shadows.

But what to do now that Phillip Space was in jail? He needed someone else to blame for the murders.

And with the crow as his witness, he vowed to exercise his power over life, a promise sealed in blood and darkness. Carved into the fabric of the night.

13

As dawn broke over the village, a pale light filtered through the office at Wolf Lake Consulting. Raven rubbed her tired eyes, having spent the night poring over every detail of Phillip Space's past, trying to find some connection that Thomas might have missed. The room was cluttered with papers and case files strewn about her desk.

Could he really be innocent? She considered the photo of the man fighting, his face contorted with anger. But the picture proved nothing about Patricia's murder.

She needed to visit Phillip's house and find clues that were overlooked during the initial investigation. Before leaving, she picked up her phone and dialed Darren's number. "Hey, Darren. Any progress on tracking down that guy in the SUV?"

"Working on it, Raven. There's an issue at the park. The wind knocked a pine tree over, and it's blocking the ridge trail. Gotta clear that first. I'll let you know as soon as I find something."

"I'm headed to Phillip Space's place to look around. Call me if you learn anything new."

"Will do."

She grabbed her coat and keys, her thoughts lingering on

Phillip's possible innocence. Sometimes people were wrongly accused, but she'd given information to the sheriff's department that led to his arrest.

The neighborhood seemed asleep when she pulled up to Phillip's house. The place was rundown, paint peeling and shutters hanging at odd angles. Phillip led a tough life, and apparently his lawn care business wasn't making him rich.

A weathered barn towards the back of the property caught her attention; its wooden doors were ajar. As she approached the barn, the smell of motor oil and damp earth filled her nose. She hesitated, then pushed open one of the doors and stepped inside. Tools, spare parts, and other miscellaneous items coated in a layer of dust cluttered the interior.

Her eyes fell on a pile of wood near the back wall, and she moved closer for a better look. Several pieces of a broken fence lay amongst the debris.

"Hey!" a voice called out, making her jump. "What are you doing in there?"

She whirled around. "This is Phillip Space's barn, correct?"

"Yeah, it is," the stranger said. "Who are you?"

"Raven Hopkins. I'm a private investigator working with the Nightshade County Sheriff's Department."

"Good luck with that." The man snorted.

"I just thought I might find something here that could prove his innocence."

"Is that so? Well, you better be careful poking around other people's property. You never know what you might find."

"Thanks for the warning. May I ask your name?"

"Ray Cassillis. I live next door, not that it's any of your business. Whatever you do, stay off my property."

The man stalked off. She stood for a moment, contemplating her next move. The barn held no answers, but the house might. She knew breaking into Phillip's home was risky and illegal, but there was more to the story than met the eye. Huddled against the chill, she approached the back door and removed a hairpin from her braids. With practiced ease, she inserted it into the lock and wiggled it around until she heard a click.

The interior smelled of stale cigarettes and cheap beer. The living room held a worn-out couch, and a table dominated the dining room. A few dishes lay in the kitchen sink, but other than that, the place was orderly.

She crept down the hallway, pausing at each door before reaching Phillip's bedroom. The room was just as modest as the rest of the house: a simple bed, a nightstand, and a faded dresser against one wall. Raven approached the dresser and searched through the drawers.

Her fingers brushed against a small cardboard box tucked away in the back of one drawer, and she carefully pulled it out. Inside, she found a collection of old photographs.

A much younger Phillip grinned back at her, his arm wrapped around a beautiful woman who bore a striking resemblance to Patricia Hudson. A little girl with golden curls and a mischievous smile clung to Phillip's leg, her eyes full of adoration.

She couldn't reconcile the man in these photographs with the one sitting in a jail cell, accused of murder. A worn leather journal lay beneath the box of photographs. Curiosity piqued, she pulled it out and carefully opened to a random page. Scribbled words lined the paper, as if Phillip had been in a hurry to get his thoughts down.

Raven flipped through the pages, finding entry after entry detailing Phillip's struggle with alcoholism and his overwhelming guilt for past actions. Raw emotion filled every word, the desperate longing for change and redemption. He had been working hard to turn his life around, and it only made her more determined to help him.

She took one last look around the bedroom before making her way to the back door. As she stepped outside, her resolve hardened. Leaning against her SUV, she dialed Franklin Devereux's number and tapped her foot as she waited for the man to answer.

"Raven, how can I help?"

"Have you found that lawyer friend of yours? The one who might take on Phillip's case pro bono?"

"Actually, yes. Her name is Sandra Ford, and she's agreed to meet with you to discuss the details. And don't worry, she's good. One of the best."

"Thank you, Mr. Devereux. I appreciate it."

"Anything to help, Raven. I don't want an innocent man to go to prison."

As they hung up, unease settled in Raven's stomach. By accepting Franklin's help, she was inadvertently putting herself in debt to him. Would he expect her to accept his job offer in return for his assistance? She pushed the thought from her mind for now, knowing she had more pressing matters to attend to.

Back at the office, she drummed her legs under the desk as she stared at the corkboard on the wall. Newspaper clippings, photographs, and scribbled notes covered the board, a spiderweb of information she hoped would lead her to the truth about Patricia Hudson's murder. A photo of Phillip Space stared back at her.

"All right, Sandra Ford. Let's see if you're as good as they say."

She dialed the number.

"Ford and Associates, how may I help you?" a receptionist answered.

"Hi, my name is Raven Hopkins. I'm calling to speak with Sandra Ford about the Phillip Space case. This is in regard to Franklin Devereux's call."

"Please hold."

A few moments later, a voice came on the line. "Sandra Ford speaking. How can I assist you, Ms. Hopkins?"

"Franklin Devereux recommended you for the Phillip Space defense. I've been looking into his background, and I believe there's a strong possibility he's being framed for Patricia Hudson's murder. I need someone who's willing to fight for him."

"Sure, Ms. Hopkins. Franklin mentioned your call earlier. He seems to think highly of you. Tell me what you know."

Raven briefed Sandra on the facts she'd gathered so far, outlining her suspicions about Phillip's innocence. She could hear pen scratching paper through the phone as Sandra took notes.

"Very well, Ms. Hopkins. I'll meet with Mr. Space and hear his side of the story. In the meantime, keep digging. The more evidence we have, the better."

"Thank you, Ms. Ford. I appreciate it."

"Of course. And call me Sandra. My office will be in touch."

As Raven hung up, she felt a modicum of hope. Perhaps they could prove Phillip's innocence. She dialed Chelsey's number. Her friend's voice brought relief.

"Hey, Raven," Chelsey said, sounding more like herself. "What's the latest?"

"Phillip Space might be innocent. I've got an attorney on the case, and I'm going to keep digging."

"I trust your instincts. If you think he's innocent, then you're probably right. And I'll be back at work this morning just as soon as I take care of Tigger and Jack."

"Are you sure you're ready?"

"Absolutely. We've got a case to crack, and I want to help."

"Great. I can't wait to see you. But Chelsey."

"What's wrong?"

"Defending Phillip Space. Will Thomas be angry with me?"

"I admit it places us in a precarious position, but Thomas wants the truth. He's not interested in arresting innocent people."

"Thank you, my friend."

After working with Chelsey all morning, Raven drove to the ranger's cabin for lunch to see how Darren was progressing with the fallen tree and his own investigation.

As if her thoughts had summoned him, the phone rang. Darren's name appeared on the dashboard.

"Raven, I traced that SUV to a man named Eddie Monroe," Darren said.

"Who is he?"

"Just a guy who lives a mile outside the village. Couldn't find a connection between him and Phillip Space. But I agree with you. It's worth paying him a visit."

"Thanks for your help. How are things going with the tree?"

"Got it off the path and reopened the ridge trail, but that December blizzard is still causing issues. The weight of the snow weakened the root systems. I'm afraid this won't be the last tree to fall before spring."

"That sucks. Hang in there, Darren. I'm on my way home for lunch. Talk to you in a second."

As she drove back to the ranger's cabin, she worried about the killer still being loose. Every tree lining the road appeared sinister.

She glanced at the rearview mirror. Wolf Lake was her home, and she wouldn't allow a murderer to run free. As the cabin came into view, she noticed the glow of lights. It was comforting, a beacon of safety amid the gathering shadows.

The door door opened to a cozy interior. The smell of fresh bread wafted through the air, mixing with the scent of pine and earth. Raven took a moment to appreciate the comforts of home before grabbing a quick meal. Darren stood at the stove, ladling steaming spoonfuls of tomato soup into two bowls.

"Hey," he said. "I figured you'd be hungry after your morning sleuthing."

"Thanks," she said, slipping off her jacket and draping it over a chair. "I could use some comfort food right about now. But you're the one who should be hungry. I didn't spend all morning playing lumberjack."

They sat at the table and she savored the first spoonful of soup, feeling the warmth spread through her as the flavors danced on her tongue.

He dunked a hunk of bread into his soup. "So, what did you find?"

"Phillip's house. It was so simple, almost sad. It looks like he was trying to turn his life around. I found a journal. He wrote about battling alcoholism and regretting past actions."

"Sounds like he's been through a lot." He took another bite of his bread. "But you shouldn't have entered the house without Thomas's permission and a search warrant."

"I know, I know. You said you traced the SUV's license plate to Eddie Monroe, right? What do you know about him?"

"From what I've heard, he's a class-A prick. Works as a fix-it guy around town, but not someone you'd want to have a beer with."

Raven chewed thoughtfully. "I wonder if Eddie and Phillip were competing for customers. Maybe Eddie had a reason to frame Phillip?"

Darren shrugged. "Could be. People do weird things when money is involved."

Her phone rang. "Hello?"

"Raven, it's Aguilar," said the voice on the other end. "I thought you'd want to know an attorney named Sandra Ford showed up at the station and got Phillip Space released. Thomas isn't too happy about it."

"Already? I just . . ." She swallowed her words, not wanting to admit she'd contacted Ford about Phillip's defense. It stunned her that the attorney had already gotten the suspect out of jail. "I heard from her firm this morning. She wanted information about our side of the investigation. How soon will he be out?"

"Should be in the next hour once we file the paperwork."

"Thank you for telling me. Keep me posted if anything else comes up."

"Will do. Take care, Raven."

Hanging up the phone, Raven turned to Darren. "Sandra Ford got Phillip Space released. He'll be out within the hour."

"Didn't you just talk to her? How's that possible?"

"I'm not sure, but she's obviously even better than advertised. I don't think Thomas is happy with me."

Darren waved the concern away. "Don't worry about Thomas. He'll get over it."

But Thomas wasn't the problem. A killer was still stalking Wolf Lake.

14

He leaned against the bark of an oak tree, his eyes fixed on Raven Hopkins as she emerged from the ranger's cabin. He hadn't expected her to be so persistent in proving Phillip Space's innocence. His lips curled as he watched her stride towards her black Nissan Rogue, her dark braids swaying behind her. It was almost amusing, this tenacity of hers, but she was becoming irritating.

It paid to keep his ears to the sidewalk in the village. Recalling the rumor he'd heard that the sheriff's department would release Phillip later today, he considered her a potential threat to his plans. If she continued down this path, if she dug too deep, she might find something that could lead the sheriff straight to him. That couldn't happen; it would ruin everything.

He knew what he had to do. Distract them all. By releasing Phillip, they were playing right into his hands. He would kill again and ensure it looked like Phillip Space's work.

As she drove away from the ranger's cabin, he slipped into his own car and followed her at a safe distance. When she turned onto the lake road, he continued straight to Phillip Space's house.

Arriving at the residence, he parked in the shadows and approached the garage. With a few swift hammer strikes, he broke the lock and entered the darkened space. The scent of oil and dirt filled his nostrils as he rummaged through the tools scattered about, searching for something that would help him stage the next murder.

"Perfect," he said, a grin spreading across his face as he picked up a wood ax. The weight of it in his hand felt satisfying, promising. He couldn't wait to put it to use.

As he left the garage, his thoughts raced with the thrill of what was to come. Wolf Lake would soon buzz with fear and suspicion, and all eyes would be back on Phillip Space. Exactly where he wanted them. And Raven, with her relentless determination, would be too busy chasing shadows to discover the truth.

Night approached. He cruised along the winding roads in his vehicle, eyes scanning each house as he passed. He needed someone with minimal connections, a person whose absence wouldn't immediately raise an alarm.

Patience. Find the perfect target.

He drove until he reached the outskirts of the village, where the houses were more isolated. His pulse quickened as he spotted a weather-beaten cottage nestled among overgrown shrubs. Snow coated the roof. A lonely fifty-something widow lived there. She had no family in the county and was seldom visited by anyone but the grocery delivery boy and her house cleaner.

She would be his next canvas. His breath fogged the window.

With his target chosen, he retreated to his own home, a modest dwelling hidden away from prying eyes. Flipping through his collection of newspaper clippings and photographs, he studied Raven and Sheriff Shepherd's faces. They were the only two who could catch him, and their persistence drove him over the edge.

It was crucial that he should plan this next murder and leave no room for error. Each detail had to be perfect, ensuring that Phillip Space would once again become the prime suspect. He ran his fingers through his hair as he began sketching out his plan.

Hours slipped by as he immersed himself in his preparation. He could hardly wait for the village to go to sleep.

∼

UNDER THE CLOAK OF NIGHT, he approached the widow's house, his footfalls silent despite the coating of snow and ice encasing the yard. The moon cast a sickly glow over his features as he crept through the shadows, clutching the wood ax in his gloved hand.

The house was nestled among the trees on the outskirts of Wolf Lake. He peered through a window, glimpsing her slumbering form. Death waited just outside her door.

He picked the lock and slipped inside, the wintry air swirling around him. When he edged open the bedroom door, she moaned and turned onto her side, facing away from the gray light following in his wake.

Licking his lips, he stood over her sleeping form. The anticipation of what was about to happen was almost as thrilling as the act itself.

She tugged the blankets over her body and muttered something indecipherable. He raised the ax high enough to scratch the ceiling.

Then he swung.

The wood ax found its mark, the room filling with the sickening crack of bone and flesh. She issued a gurgling scream and lurched up. Gravity dragged her back to the bed. She stopped breathing.

So easy. He surveyed his handiwork.

Blood spattered across the walls. He deposited a dead crow beside the corpse, a calling card that would prove he was the same man who'd murdered Patricia Hudson. Finally, he snipped off a lock of hair, an intimate souvenir to remind him of this night.

He made his way back through the house, leaving no trace of his presence. The night was still young, and he had work to do. Standing beside the home, he hurled the ax as far as his power allowed. It landed in the backyard, the blade buried into the ice and the handle jutting skyward.

He melted into the shadows, leaving behind a trail of blood and death.

∽

A CHILLING WIND whipped snow against the side of Ellen Reynolds' house. The cleaner entered, her keys jingling in one hand while the other clutched an overburdened bucket of cleaning supplies. She hummed to herself as she began wiping down the countertops, wondering why the homeowner hadn't come out to say hello. The woman kept to herself, but she was never one to ignore her.

"Mrs. Reynolds? It's me, Sarah," she called out, expecting the woman to greet her. When there was no response, she scowled with unease.

"Mrs. Reynolds?"

Wiping her hands on her pants, she set down the cleaning supplies and moved toward the bedroom.

The moment she crossed the threshold, her heart lodged in her throat. The sight before her was straight out of a horror movie. Ellen Reynolds lay motionless on the bed, her body contorted like a claw, her blood splattered across the walls.

And there was something in the bed beside her.

Was that... a crow?

"Dear God," Sarah whispered, her hands shaking as she fumbled for her phone. Her fingers trembled as they dialed the sheriff's department.

"Nightshade County Sheriff's Department," came the voice on the other end of the line.

"Th-there's been a murder," Sarah stammered, her eyes flitting away from the lifeless body.

"Stay calm, ma'am," the dispatcher said. "Can you give me your location?"

It took her a moment to remember the address. She couldn't breathe, let alone think.

"Help is on the way," the dispatcher assured her. "Stay on the line until they arrive."

A rustling noise outside the window made her stare into the woods. There, amid the shadows of the trees, she spied movement. A figure watching in the darkness.

"Someone's out there," she whispered into the phone. "In the woods."

"Stay inside," the dispatcher said. "Lock all the doors and windows. We'll be there as soon as possible."

As Sarah hung up the phone, her eyes fell upon Mrs. Reynolds again.

The grotesque display overwhelmed her. She screamed. Screamed until her lungs bled.

When she stumbled out of the bedroom, she fell to her knees, unable to control her limbs.

The killer had seen her face. Would she be next?

15

Thomas and Deputy Aguilar pulled up to the Reynolds' residence as two junior deputies held back the onlookers. The cleaner, a middle-aged woman with tear-streaked cheeks, stood shivering on the front porch. She looked up at them with bloodshot eyes, her voice trembling.

"Th-thank God you're here. I just came to clean, but then I found her. It's horrible."

"Ma'am, you're safe now," he said. "You told my dispatcher the killer was still here?"

"I'm not sure anymore. There was someone . . . something in the woods, but they're gone now."

He snapped a finger and pointed past the tree line. The deputies gave up on controlling the neighbors, who remained along the side of the road, and rushed into the forest to investigate.

"Can you tell me where you found the body?"

"She's in her bedroom," the woman choked out.

They made their way inside the house. The pungent odor of blood hit Thomas's nostrils in the doorway, and he felt a familiar pang of dread. He recognized the similarities to Patricia

Hudson's murder scene all too well. As they entered the bedroom, the grisly sight before them confirmed those fears.

There lay Ellen Reynolds, lifeless and sprawled across the bed. Her eyes stared blankly at the ceiling, mouth agape in a silent scream, while pools of blood splashed the walls, the carpet, the mattress. A dead crow lay beside her.

"Damn it," said Aguilar. "Didn't we just release Phillip Space yesterday afternoon? And now another person is dead."

Thomas rubbed his forehead, feeling the beginnings of a headache. "I know. This seems a little too coincidental, but we can't ignore the connection." As Aguilar snapped photographs, he returned to the cleaner. "Do you know if a man named Phillip Space worked for Ellen Reynolds?"

"Yes," she said, still shaken. "He did yard work for her sometimes. I've seen him here before."

The pieces were falling into place, but Thomas refused to let his emotions cloud his judgment. He couldn't afford any missteps in this investigation.

"Thank you," Thomas said, forcing himself to stay focused. "We'll do everything we can to find who did this and bring them to justice."

As he stepped inside, the phone rang. He glanced at the screen and saw Raven's name. Irritation surged inside him, but he suppressed it; she was a close friend.

"Thomas," she said as soon as he answered the call, "I've been following the news. You don't think Phillip Space did this, do you?"

"Well, we arrested him as a murder suspect, and the second we released him, another body showed up."

"I think you need to consider the possibility of a copycat killer."

"Copycat?" Thomas asked, unable to disguise the skepticism in his tone. "Why do you think that?"

"Because it's not unheard of for killers to emulate others," she replied. "Especially if they're trying to throw off an investigation."

"Raven, we have a strong connection to Phillip Space here."

"Just promise me you'll look into it," she insisted. "I'll gather whatever evidence I can to support this theory. It's either a copycat or someone is framing him."

"Okay. Keep me updated on what you find. Just understand that Phillip Space remains our number one suspect until we verify his whereabouts at the time of the murder."

"I get it. Stay safe, Thomas." With that, the call ended, leaving him to consider Raven's words.

"Was that Raven?" Aguilar asked as she approached.

"Yep," he said, pocketing his phone. "She thinks we're dealing with a copycat killer, or someone is trying to lay blame on Phillip Space."

"Odd," she said, crossing her arms. "I like Raven, but she's been acting strangely lately."

His lead deputy seemed to echo Chelsey's concerns.

"Strange how?"

"Well, I don't know all the details, but it's weird how she involved herself in Phillip Space's release. I'm not sure what to think of that, given the circumstances."

"We need to keep open minds. For now, focus on the evidence at hand and follow any leads we can."

"Agreed, but if Raven turns out to be right about another killer, we'll need to reevaluate everything we thought we knew about this case."

"True. Let's hope the forensic team finds more in the bedroom than they did on Patricia Hudson's porch. They should. The body isn't exposed to the elements this time."

His stomach roiling, he continued to examine the crime scene. The possibility of another killer added a layer of complexity to an already difficult investigation, leaving him with more questions than answers. He'd always trusted Raven, but was she grasping at straws?

The sound of an approaching motor announced the arrival of Claire and her forensic team. Thomas glanced over his shoulder to see them climbing out of a van, armed with bags of equipment. He approached Claire.

"Thomas," she said. "It happened again?"

"Another woman who lived alone," Thomas said, studying her intelligent eyes for any initial reactions. "Ellen Reynolds. Butchered, just like Patricia Hudson. There's also a dead crow beside the body."

"Interesting." She turned towards the house. "I'll take a closer look."

As the forensic team gathered outside, Thomas and Aguilar donned booties, masks, and jumpsuits, preparing to search the house for additional evidence.

"Let's start with the living room," he said to Aguilar, his voice muffled by the mask. She agreed.

It didn't take them long to discern that no struggle had occurred inside. No furniture had been overturned, no lamps lay shattered on the floor. The killer had attacked Ellen in her sleep. With a knife? No. The weapon was sharp, but he hadn't used a knife. Something that would cause blunt-force damage.

After investigating the other rooms, they peered into the bedroom, where the forensic team worked in unison.

"There was no time to put up a fight," she said, her voice hushed to avoid disturbing the team.

He followed the trail of blood spatter, which rocketed from the mattress to the headboard and across the wall behind the bed.

"What are the chances that this is the work of a copycat killer, like Raven suggested?"

"How many killers are there murdering women on the edge of the village? If you ask me, it's unlikely this wasn't the same guy."

"I can't disagree, but we can't rule out the possibility. We need concrete information before we jump to conclusions."

The idea of a copycat killer only added another layer of complexity to an already challenging investigation, leaving him with even more questions than answers. Despite his skepticism, he couldn't deny that perhaps Raven was onto something. Was someone framing Phillip Space? And why? The man didn't come from money or power.

Claire looked back at them. "We need you to step outside. We don't want further contamination of the scene."

"Of course," he said, his gaze lingering on the blood-spattered room one last time before he and Aguilar followed Claire's instructions.

Upon exiting the house, the cold air hit them like a shock.

"We'll search the property while the team works inside," he said.

Beside Aguilar, he stepped gingerly over the snow and ice pack. That was the problem with snowy winters. Once spring approached and the snow pack underwent melting and refreezing, the landscape turned into a skating rink. Silence enveloped them, broken only by the distant cawing of crows.

Always crows.

"Thomas, over there," Aguilar said, pointing at something half-buried in the snow near the edge of the yard.

He approached with a knot of tension in his stomach. As he neared, he saw it—an ax, its blade stained with blood, peeking out of the snow as if it had been left to taunt them.

"This has to be the murder weapon," she said.

"I assumed it was something sharp and heavy."

He studied the surroundings, wondering what could have

caused the killer to drop the ax, leaving it behind in haste. Was it an unexpected interruption or a careless mistake? Doubtful. They hadn't found so much as a fingerprint at the previous murder scene.

"I'll get Claire. We'll need to examine it for prints and see if there's a connection to Phillip Space."

She stepped back from the ax, careful not to disturb the scene. Thomas looked around for tracks, but theirs were the only ones moving through the snow. Another oddity he couldn't explain.

"Something doesn't add up," he said. "While you get Claire, I'll check every inch of the yard."

The bitter cold nipped at his cheeks and nose. As he scoured the snow-covered ground, the question of whether Phillip Space's fingerprints were on the ax made him wonder if he'd set a serial killer free.

16

Raven Hopkins tossed her coat on the chair at Wolf Lake Consulting. The first to arrive, she turned on the lights and set to work, organizing the myriad of documents, photographs, and articles spread across her desk. The scent of yesterday's stale coffee hung in the air.

First Patricia Hudson. Then Ellen Reynolds. She studied the information she had gathered about the two murdered women. Her eyes traced over the crime scene photos, searching for any overlooked details or connections that might support her theory of a copycat killer. The murders appeared disturbingly alike.

Pinned to the wall was a map of the countryside outside the village, marked with red circles where the killer had struck. Was there something deeper at play here?

She grabbed her phone, dialing Darren's number. The forest ranger picked up after two rings. "Hey, it's me," she said.

"You just left. What's up?"

"I don't know what to think of the latest murder. All the background I dug up on Phillip Space tells me he didn't do this, but it doesn't seem like a coincidence that the murder occurred as soon as Thomas released him."

"Tell me everything."

"The sheriff's department believes the killer used an ax on Ellen Reynolds, whereas Patricia Hudson's wound appeared as if it came from a hook. There was no sign of a struggle in either investigation, no forced entry. I think someone is following Phillip Space, maybe even trying to frame him."

"Raven, that's a bold claim. You know how dangerous it can be to defend someone like Space, especially when the evidence points in his direction."

"I know, but I have to follow my instincts on this one. I need you to look into any connections between the victims. Keep an open mind, okay?"

"Yeah, I will. I'll start digging and see what I can find. Be careful, Raven."

"Thanks, Darren."

Whatever was happening in Wolf Lake, she knew she wouldn't rest until she zeroed in on the killer. The ghosts of Patricia Hudson and Ellen Reynolds haunted her thoughts, driving her to seek justice.

As soon as she hung up, the phone buzzed on her desk. She saw Thomas's name flashing. Swiping the screen, she put the phone to her ear. "Thomas, what's up?"

"Raven, Aguilar and I are at the station. I take it you heard about the blood-stained ax in the backyard of Ellen Reynolds' house?"

"I did." Raven's grip tightened on the phone. Had Thomas found Phillip Space's prints on the ax handle?

"It's at the lab for forensic analysis. We need to know if there's any DNA or fingerprints that could link it to Phillip Space or someone else."

"Good call."

"Raven, I realize you don't think Phillip did this."

"I'm not sure what to believe, Thomas, but I have a hard time picturing him as a killer. Keep me updated on the results, all right?"

"Will do," Thomas said before disconnecting the call.

With the prospect of answers looming, Raven couldn't just sit by and wait. She needed to understand Phillip Space's side of the story, to assess him firsthand. Grabbing her keys, she left the office and headed to the countryside.

She pulled up to the small, weathered house. Stepping out of her car, she approached the front porch and knocked on the door. Down the road, a dog barked.

"Phillip Space, this is Raven Hopkins with Wolf Lake Consulting."

She waited, but silence greeted her. Frowning, she knocked again, louder this time.

"Doesn't look like he's home."

Raven spun around to find Lambert leaning against his patrol car, arms crossed. His buzz cut glinted in the silvery light, and a smirk played on his lips.

"Figures," Raven muttered under her breath. She met Lambert's gaze, searching for any hint of mockery. "Any idea where he might be?"

"That's the million-dollar question," Lambert replied, his eyes narrowing. "But you best be careful, Raven. Everything we have points to Phillip Space being a murderer. You shouldn't be here alone."

Raven bristled at the warning, but she refused to let it deter her. "I just want the truth. Nothing more."

"Truth has a way of biting back," Lambert said as Raven climbed back into her SUV. "Next time, call me or Aguilar before you pound on a murder suspect's door."

As she drove away, her thoughts swirled around Phillip Space.

Her vehicle pulled into the sheriff's department parking lot.

She stepped onto the icy blacktop and pulled the collar up on her jacket. Warm weather couldn't come soon enough.

"Morning, Raven," Deputy Aguilar greeted her as she entered the department. Her eyes were glued to a manila folder in her hands, and Raven could see the tension in her jaw.

"Any news on the lab results?" she asked, her voice betraying a hint of urgency.

"Just came in. Thomas is looking them over now."

Raven nodded and made her way to Thomas' office. She found him hunched over his desk, poring over a stack of papers. His face was contorted in concentration. By fighting for Phillip Space, she might have gotten another woman killed. And let Thomas down.

"What did the lab find?" Raven asked, her heart beating faster.

"Space's prints are all over the ax handle," he said, not looking up from the report. "No other prints were found."

Her chest tightened. Was it possible her actions had set a killer free?

"I know it looks bad, but there could be another explanation," she said, gripping the edge of his desk for support.

"Raven." Thomas sighed, his eyes finally meeting hers. "I understand you want to believe Phillip Space is innocent, but you need to consider the facts. You're putting yourself in danger by defending a murderer."

"Wouldn't you do the same if you believed in someone's innocence?"

"Not without considering the consequences. I care about you and don't want to see you get hurt."

"Neither do I, but I can't ignore my instincts."

"But you're willing to ignore evidence?"

Her mouth fell open.

"I'll continue looking into Space's background," he said, "but you need to stay out of it. For your own safety."

For her own safety or because she'd screwed up?

"I'm sorry."

"According to the report, the blood on the ax matches Ellen Reynolds' DNA."

"That seals the deal, doesn't it?"

"Looks that way," Thomas said, his eyes searching her face for any reaction.

"Can I see the report?"

"Sure, here you go," he replied, handing her a printed copy of the lab results. As she scanned the document, her mind grappled with the implications of the evidence.

"Raven," Thomas said. "I know this is difficult for you, but we have to face the facts. Everyone makes mistakes. God knows I've made more than a few. But when we're wrong, we have to admit it and move on."

"Phillip Space's fingerprints are on the ax, and now we have Ellen's blood on it too," added Aguilar, who leaned against the door frame. "There's no denying the evidence."

Raven bit her lip as she contemplated her next words. "Unless this is exactly what the real killer wants us to think."

"Don't do this to yourself," Thomas implored. "You're grasping at straws."

"Am I? Or am I just trying to make sure we catch the right person?"

"We have a mountain of evidence pointing at Space."

As she left the office, she knew she was walking a tightrope between truth and deception. One misstep could send her spiraling into darkness.

Why was she so certain a man she'd never met wasn't a killer?

17

The converted two-bedroom house that served as an office for Wolf Lake Consulting stood before Raven, a testament to Chelsey Byrd's entrepreneurial spirit. She hesitated, knowing she had to face Chelsey with her concerns about Phillip Space, but the thought made her gut churn.

She'd screwed up. And now she had to get herself together.

Raven entered to find Chelsey sitting at her desk, typing away on her computer. Tigger, Chelsey's orange tabby, looked up from his perch on the windowsill, giving Raven a lazy blink. Jack slept in a corner. Raven noticed how quiet Chelsey was today and felt guilty for adding to her friend's stress.

"Hey, Chelsey," Raven said, clearing her throat. "I need to talk to you about something."

Chelsey looked up from her screen. "Sure, what's up?"

"About Phillip Space. I think I made a terrible mistake defending him."

Chelsey's eyes widened, but she remained silent, waiting for Raven to continue.

"I'm afraid I got that poor woman killed," Raven said, pacing the room. "What if Thomas and Aguilar are right? His prints are on the murder weapon."

"There's no turning back the clock, but being wrong is part of this business. Maybe we need to take a step back, give ourselves some time to process everything."

She knew Chelsey was trying to be supportive, but she couldn't shake the feeling of dread that had settled deep within her. Chelsey's phone buzzed, drawing her attention away from the case files. She glanced at the screen and narrowed her eyes in apprehension as she opened an email.

"Raven. You need to see this."

She turned her phone around to show a series of photographs documenting Raven's recent movements: her arrival at Wolf Lake Consulting earlier that day, her conversations with various people, even her more mundane activities like grabbing a coffee. Someone was tracking her every move.

"Who sent this?"

"Anonymous. There's no traceable information, but it's clear someone is watching you."

Raven's anxiety surged. The killer was targeting her. She felt exposed, as if the walls of her haven were crumbling around her.

"Darren needs to see this."

Chelsey was already dialing Darren's number. Within minutes, he arrived at their office without hiding his unease.

"Show me," he said, his tone firm yet gentle.

Chelsey handed him her phone, and Darren studied the photographs. His jaw clenched as determination replaced his initial shock.

"I'll get to the bottom of this. I have a friend who's a digital forensics expert. He might help us trace the source of the email."

As Darren made the call, the door to Wolf Lake Consulting opened, and Scout and LeVar walked in. They exchanged greetings before noticing the tense atmosphere.

"Did something happen?" LeVar asked as he looked from Raven to Chelsey.

"Someone's tracking me," Raven said. "They sent these photos to Chelsey's phone."

Scout's eyes widened behind her glasses, while LeVar's face hardened with resolve. This was a dangerous turn of events.

Scout nodded, her face serious. "I'll do my best to trace the emails," she said, moving towards a computer.

LeVar placed a reassuring hand on Raven's shoulder. "Don't worry. I'll talk to Thomas and smooth things over between you and the sheriff's department. We'll figure this out together."

She managed a weak smile but could not banish the possibility that Phillip Space was the one stalking her. She needed to clear her head and calm her nerves.

Excusing herself, she retreated to the kitchen. Her hands trembled as she reached for the kettle and poured herself some calming tea. The steady stream of hot water provided a small sense of control in the chaos that had become her life.

"Raven?" Chelsey's voice startled her as she entered the kitchen. Seeing the distress on her face, Chelsey hurried to her side, placing a hand on her arm.

"I got Phillip Space released, and now he's following me. This is my doing."

"Hey, it's going to be okay. I trust your instincts. You're one of the best investigators I've ever met. Whatever mistakes you think you made, we'll face them together."

Raven's fingers tightened around the ceramic mug. Another message arrived from Franklin Devereux. The guilt of considering Devereux's offer ate at her.

While Raven scanned the latest offer, Chelsey sorted through a stack of mail on the counter.

"I don't believe it," Chelsey said. "Our energy bill went up by twenty percent over last year." Her expression clouded with worry. "I don't know if we can keep up with these rising costs."

"Can Wolf Lake Consulting pay its bills?"

Chelsey hesitated, her silence speaking volumes. The weight on Raven's shoulders grew heavier, and she stared into her tea as if the swirl of steam could provide answers. A thought crossed her mind, one that might help secure Chelsey's future. What if she told Devereux she wouldn't accept the job unless he hired Chelsey as well? She didn't wish to watch her friend fall on hard times. If Wolf Lake Consulting closed its doors, they would both need new careers.

LeVar appeared in the doorway as Chelsey exited the room. "Raven, can I talk to you for a minute?"

"Anytime." She followed LeVar into the hallway.

"Scout and I haven't found any leads yet, but we will. I'm going over to the sheriff's department to talk to Thomas. What do you want me to tell him? He has to know Phillip Space is stalking you."

"Thomas? You think he's upset with me?"

"Look, don't worry about him or any of the deputies being angry with you. They love and respect you, Raven. We all do."

"Thanks, LeVar. Yes, I suppose you need to tell him the truth. If Phillip Space is following me, maybe that's how the sheriff's department will catch him."

"Keep your head on a swivel. And let me know the second you see him."

She glanced around the office, feeling more alone than ever despite the presence of her colleagues. A dark sensation crawled up her spine, as if someone were watching her.

Movement caught her eye. Across the street, hidden in the shadows, stood a figure whose stare seemed to bore straight into her. Her breath hitched. She threw open the door.

"Who's there?" she called out, her voice barely audible.
The person vanished into the darkness.

18

The sheriff's department was a hive of activity as Thomas hung up the phone, his fingers drumming on the desk. He had just spoken with the District Attorney, who insisted that he arrest Phillip Space once more based on the latest evidence. Arresting Phillip again could incite the public and media, making an already tenuous situation even more volatile. And deep down, Thomas still wasn't entirely convinced of Phillip's guilt.

Yes, the man's fingerprints were on the murder weapon. But Raven's doubt was infectious, and now he wondered if the evidence was a little too convenient.

"Shep Dawg," a familiar voice called out. LeVar entered the room.

"Hey, LeVar. What brings you in today?"

"Look, man," LeVar said, leaning against the edge of Thomas's desk. "I know you're upset with my sister for getting involved in this case. But Raven meant well, you know? She's just trying to help."

Thomas sighed. He knew LeVar was right; he wasn't angry, just frustrated. Her insistence on defending Phillip Space, despite the mounting evidence against him, made the sheriff second-guess every decision he made.

"I'm not upset. But it's my job to protect this county, and your sister is basing her beliefs on hunches."

"She's smart. She might see something we don't. All I'm asking is that you don't hold it against her."

"I never would." He couldn't deny his respect for Raven's intelligence.

"Thanks, man," LeVar said. "But there's a more important reason I'm here. There's something we need to talk about. Pictures of Raven investigating arrived at Wolf Lake Consulting. We don't know who sent them, but it ain't good. Someone is stalking her."

Thomas frowned and leaned back in his chair. "Why would someone photograph her?"

"Could be a warning or someone trying to mess with her head. I'm worried about her safety, dawg. What if the person taking the pictures is the killer?"

The sheriff cared deeply for both LeVar and his sister. "I'd walk to the ends of the earth to defend Raven, but I still think her theories are far-fetched. Why would someone frame Phillip Space?"

"Remember what you told me when I first started working here? You said we should never discount a possibility until we've explored all the facts. Raven's just doing what you taught me to do."

"Point taken. I'll do my best to have someone look over her shoulder, but we're stretched thin. There's only so much I can promise. Just make sure she stays safe and doesn't go off on her own."

"Thanks, Thomas. I appreciate it."

As the door closed behind his deputy, Thomas mulled over the conversation they'd just had. He wanted to give Raven the benefit of the doubt based on their friendship and his respect for her integrity, but he worried that she'd made a grave error in defending Phillip Space.

But who was photographing Raven? And why? Was Phillip playing mind games with her? The questions swirled around in his head.

He stared at the phone on his desk, knowing that he would have to decide soon. The safety of Nightshade County and its people rested on his shoulders, and he couldn't afford to let them down. He had to arrest Phillip Space. The trouble was, he couldn't find the man.

In the kitchen, he poured himself a cup of black coffee. Aguilar's phone rang. The deputy answered it, her expression shifting from curiosity to concern in a matter of seconds.

"Phillip Space's neighbor just called," Aguilar said, hanging up. "He reported a suspicious individual lurking around the property."

Thomas dumped the coffee.

"Let's check it out," he said, grabbing his jacket off the rack in the hallway.

The drive out to Phillip Space's house was quiet. He glanced over at Aguilar, who was frowning as she stared out the passenger window. When they arrived at the property, Phillip Space's neighbor, an older man with a scruffy beard and a worn-out baseball cap, greeted them.

"Thanks for coming out, Sheriff," he said, shaking their hands. "I saw someone outside the house about a half hour ago. I couldn't tell if it was Phillip or not."

"Where was this person?"

"Walking along the side of the house. Before I came out to see if it was Phillip, he disappeared."

"Did you notice anything else?" Thomas asked, scanning the area.

"Well, there was a black woman knocking on the door yesterday. Didn't recognize her, but she seemed pretty determined to get inside."

"Raven," Thomas muttered under his breath, remembering LeVar's concerns about her safety. "We'll look around. Call us if you see anything else out of the ordinary."

"Will do, Sheriff," the man said, nodding.

They spent a half hour checking the property. A hint of tracks moved along the house, but it was difficult to tell how old they were. The snow and ice were so solid that shoes didn't sink into the surface anymore.

A stiff wind blew through the trees, sending a shiver down Thomas's spine as he and Aguilar searched the perimeter of the property.

"Anything?" Aguilar asked.

"Nothing yet."

He sensed they were being watched, but there was no one in sight. As he stepped around a bush, something caught his eye—a lock of hair, the same shade as the ones taken from the murder victims.

"Aguilar." Thomas bent down for a closer look. "Come see this."

Aguilar hurried over, her expression darkening as she saw the hair. "This is just like the others. But why is it outside?"

"Good question." He pulled an evidence bag from his pocket. Carefully, he picked up the lock of hair using a pair of tweezers and placed it inside the bag. "This needs to be sent to Claire for DNA analysis."

"Where the hell is Phillip Space?"

He pulled out his phone and dialed Lambert's number. "Lambert, we need an APB on Phillip Space. We found a lock of hair at his house."

"Copy that, Sheriff," Lambert responded.

As Thomas hung up, he glanced around the property once more. With every new lead, the case seemed to grow more complex and dangerous.

"Let's go see Claire," he said, his eyes never leaving the spot where they'd found the hair. "We need to know if this hair belonged to one of the murder victims."

They walked back to the truck as he wrestled with his thoughts. Aguilar sensed his unease and spoke up.

"Raven seems to get herself into some dangerous situations," she said.

"LeVar's worried about her. Now that we know someone is following her, we need to figure out how we'll monitor her activities while we search for Phillip Space. I just hope she knows what she's getting herself into."

"Maybe it's time we had a serious talk with her."

"But first we need to figure out what's going on here."

As his truck rumbled down the familiar roads of Nightshade County, he worked the recent events over in his mind.

"What have we learned about Patricia Hudson's background?" he asked.

"I couldn't link her to the second victim. Seems like she and Phillip Space attended the same community center for a period. It's not much, but it's a connection we didn't know about before."

"Interesting. Was there any overlap between their time at the center?"

"The records are spotty, but it's something we can look into."

Before Thomas managed to respond, his phone buzzed in the cup holder. Chelsey's name flashed across the screen.

"Hey, Chelsey. What's up?"

"Thomas, did LeVar talk to you about Raven's stalker?"

"She did. I'll do my best to figure out what's going on, but I only have so many hours in a day."

"Some of the pictures were taken outside the office."

Thomas felt a surge of protective anger. "Did the cameras catch who it was?"

"No, but I'll make sure our security cameras cover the whole parking lot from now on."

It scared the hell out of him that Chelsey's proximity to Raven might make her a target.

"We need to figure out who this person is."

It felt like someone was playing them, but with the additional evidence against Phillip, they couldn't afford too many distractions.

"Chelsey just called," Thomas said. "Someone was watching Raven outside their office last night. We need to be on guard."

Aguilar frowned. "What the hell is going on here, Thomas?"

"I wish I knew."

At the county coroner's building, he gave the hair to Claire Brookins while Aguilar paced the hallway, conferring with the DA on the phone.

After she completed her analysis, the medical examiner turned to him. "There's no doubt. The hair belongs to Ellen Reynolds."

"If Phillip Space took her hair as a trophy, why would he leave it outside his house?"

"I can't answer that, but I ran the tests twice to be certain."

The evidence against Phillip Space was mounting, but so were the questions surrounding the case.

19

Raven awoke with a start. The remnants of the nightmare lingered, clouding her thoughts. In the dream, Phillip Space stood over a lifeless body, his laughter piercing through the darkness as he stared at her.

She pushed back the covers and rubbed the sleep from her eyes. Darren's side of the bed was empty; he must have left to meet Chelsey and Thomas at the office. She knew dreams were fickle and unreliable, but the image of Phillip's maniacal grin refused to leave her mind.

The trill of her phone cut through the silence, and she reached for it with a sense of foreboding.

"Raven? It's Darren." His voice was steady and reassuring despite the hour. "I've got some news."

"What is it?"

"Phillip Space and Patricia Hudson both attended the same community center. We confirmed they were members at the same time. I don't think it's a coincidence."

"Are you sure?"

She struggled to suppress the churning in her stomach. Had she been wrong about Phillip all this time?

"Positive. I spoke to a few workers. They remember seeing Phillip there, though they never saw him interact with Patricia."

"Thanks for letting me know," Raven said, her grip tightening around the phone. This information added another layer of complexity to a convoluted case. Did this connection further implicate Phillip?

"Be careful, Raven. I know you want to trust this guy, but the evidence is mounting, and Thomas has an APB out. I love you."

"Love you too."

As she set the phone on the bedside table, her fingers brushed against a framed photo of her with Darren. They looked so happy, their smiles bright as they stood in the glow of a summer sunset.

Were her dreams confirming her true thoughts? The nightmare, the new information—everything pointed toward Phillip Space being involved in something much darker than she'd believed.

As she readied herself for work, she turned on the TV. The news played on the screen. She stood motionless, staring at the images of Phillip Space and Ellen Reynolds as the reporter announced he was wanted for Ellen's murder.

"Phillip Space," the reporter intoned, "a local lawn care worker, has been identified as a person of interest in the brutal killings of Ellen Reynolds and Patricia Hudson. Authorities are urging anyone with information to come forward."

This was her doing. She clutched at her chest, willing herself to breathe, unable to ignore her growing doubts about his innocence any longer.

She called Chelsey on her way out the door. "We need to talk."

"Raven? What's wrong?"

"Phillip Space. Now he's wanted for both murders."

"I know, and I'm sorry, but the sheriff's department has too much on him. There's no doubt."

"Darren told me about the community center. I don't know what to think anymore, Chelsey. My gut is telling me he's innocent, but everything points at him being the killer."

"Maybe there's more to this than we realize. We should look into the community center and see if we can find any connections between Phillip and the victims. We need to be sure. LeVar's on his way here. His professor canceled class this morning, so he can help us with the investigation."

"I'm on my way."

The three of them gathered around the murder board at Wolf Lake Consulting, a map of the town spread out on a desk. LeVar tapped his fingers against the map as he listened to Chelsey and Raven discuss their plan of action.

Chelsey said, "We need to find out everything we can about this community center. If there's a stronger connection between Phillip and the first victim, it might be there."

"Sounds like a plan," LeVar said. "I'm in. We need to catch this guy before he kills again."

The door opened and Scout entered. Raven looked up from the map, her eyes meeting Scout's. The young girl had a laptop clutched under her arm, her straight brown hair framing a serious face.

"Don't you have school today?"

"Just testing," the teen said. "I finished at nine, and now I'm free for the day. I found something interesting."

Scout set the laptop on the table next to the map.

"Watch this," LeVar said. "Scout tracked down the server used by the anonymous email sender. And she found encrypted files."

Raven's jaw dropped.

Chelsey leaned closer, her hair falling over her shoulder as she peered at the screen. "Can you decrypt them?" she asked.

"Working on it," Scout said, adjusting her glasses. "But I need more time. Tracking down the server is huge. I can't tell you who sent the emails yet, but we're heading in the right direction."

"How long before you can?" Raven asked.

"Could be hours. Could be days. But I'm optimistic."

"All right," Chelsey nodded. "Keep us posted, and we'll update you on our end."

"Good luck," Scout said, her eyes fixed on the computer screen as her fingers flew across the keyboard.

The community center was busy when they arrived, its halls filled with laughter and the sound of footsteps echoing off the linoleum floors. They split up and interviewed the visitors, hoping to find someone who could provide information about Phillip Space.

"Excuse me," Raven said, towering over a group of silver-haired women seated in a circle. "Do any of you remember Patricia Hudson?"

One woman looked up, her eyes clouded with age but her memory sharp. "Oh, dear Patricia. She used to volunteer here," she said. "Such a lovely woman."

"Did you ever see her with a man named Phillip Space?"

"Phillip? He volunteered as well and attended a few events, but I can't say much more than that."

Upon talking to several women, Raven came away with the same vague answers. Frustrated, she rejoined LeVar and Chelsey.

"Everyone remembers Phillip and Patricia," Chelsey said, disappointment evident in her face. "But no one remembers them arguing. Nor does anyone recall Ellen Reynolds attending events."

"Let's talk to the center's manager," LeVar suggested. "Maybe they'll know more."

The manager, a middle-aged man with a receding hairline, frowned in thought. "Well, Patricia was a volunteer here for years," he confirmed. "As for Phillip, I remember him helping now and then. He didn't say much, but I gathered he was putting his life back together and making amends. But I don't recall anyone named Ellen Reynolds attending our events."

"Do you have a list of everyone who visited the center?" Chelsey asked.

"Unfortunately, no. But I can give you the names of some long-time staff and volunteers who might remember more."

"Thank you. We appreciate your help."

Back at Wolf Lake Consulting, Raven and Chelsey hunched over their keyboards. The office was quiet, save for the clicking of keys and occasionally of a frustrated tongue. With LeVar by her side, Scout worked in the corner without tearing her eyes from the screen. Once the teenager focused on a challenge, nothing stood in her way.

"Raven, look at this," Chelsey said. "I found an old news article about Phillip. The sheriff's department arrested him six years ago for assaulting a coworker."

"Seriously?" Raven asked, her fingers pausing mid-tap. She rolled her chair over to look at Chelsey's screen. "Why wasn't this in his records?"

"Because they settled out of court. The coworker dropped the charges."

A holler made Raven's head snap around. Scout threw up her hands, her face flushed with excitement.

"Guys! I decrypted those files. You won't believe what I found."

Scout connected her laptop to the large screen in the room, displaying a series of photographs. They showed Raven investigating Phillip's house, the crime scenes of Patricia Hudson and Ellen Reynolds, and even the exterior of Wolf Lake Consulting. Each image was chillingly intimate. Raven shivered, wondering how someone had gotten so close without her knowing.

"Check out the time stamps," Scout said. "These were taken before Phillip's arrest and after his release."

"More proof that Phillip Space is the killer," Chelsey said.

Raven scratched her chin. "What if Phillip isn't our killer but a pawn in someone else's game?"

"Like a setup?"

"The evidence seems a little too convenient. Why would a murderer kill again as soon as the sheriff's department released him? Wouldn't he lie low for a while?"

"I don't know, sis," LeVar said. "Psychopaths don't think like the rest of us."

Scout groaned. They all turned to her.

"What's wrong?" Raven asked.

"I decrypted another file. You'd better look at this."

There, staring back at them, was a photo of Raven taken the day before outside the ranger's cabin. The timestamp left no doubt: The killer had been watching her all along, waiting for the perfect moment to strike.

20

Raven's heart pounded as she stared at the image on the screen. It was unmistakably the ranger's cabin. The anonymous email drew everyone's attention. LeVar came closer to get a better look, his dreadlocks brushing against Raven's arm.

"He's following her," Chelsey said. Thomas, who had just arrived, surveyed the scene with an unreadable expression.

"Raven, you need to be extra careful," Thomas said. "Keep your movements restricted and report anything unusual or suspicious."

She swallowed hard, feeling the weight of the situation. The danger was escalating, and the thought of someone stalking her sent shivers down her spine.

"Let's have a deputy drive past Wolf Lake Consulting at closing time, and also past the ranger's cabin," Thomas suggested, pulling out his phone to make the arrangements. "It's necessary for your safety. And Darren's."

LeVar put a reassuring hand on her shoulder. "We'll figure out who's stalking you. It has to be Phillip Space."

In her mind, the accused murderer seemed the most likely suspect. Why was this happening to her?

"Okay, everyone," Chelsey said, trying to regain control over the situation. "We'll keep an eye out for any more messages and stay vigilant. And if it is Phillip Space, we'll catch him."

Raven forced a smile, appreciating her friends' support. As Thomas made the necessary calls and LeVar continued to offer words of encouragement, she stared at the image of the ranger's cabin, wondering how long that killer had watched her.

Thomas set down the phone. "It's done. The department isn't large enough to watch you every minute of the day, so you'll need to take precautions. Remember, contact me if anything else happens. We'll get through this together."

What he didn't say was that she had caused this mess by bringing in a powerful lawyer to defend the murderer. He didn't need to. She was beating herself up inside for being so reckless.

The team dug into the emails, but there was only one person in the room capable of figuring out who'd sent them.

"Scout," LeVar said, turning to the young computer whiz, "do you think you can decrypt the server's IP address? That would solve the issue in a snap."

Scout squared her shoulders. "I'll do my best. It won't be easy, but I think I can manage it."

"Great," Chelsey said, her eyes returning to Raven. "We need to find this person as soon as possible."

While her friends busied themselves with the task at hand, Raven's thoughts drifted back to Phillip Space. Guilt washed over her as she remembered how she had defended him. Now, with the possibility of him being the killer, she felt foolish for ever having believed in his innocence. Why hadn't she trusted Thomas's judgment? She would confront Phillip Space after the deputies caught him.

"Raven," Chelsey said, noticing her distant expression, "are you okay?"

She looked up, startled by the sudden question. "Yeah, I'm just thinking about what a fool I've been. About how wrong I was to believe in him."

LeVar pulled up a chair. "Hey, don't beat yourself up. We'll find the truth soon enough."

Scout squinted as she worked to decrypt the IP address, her concentration unwavering. "I think I'm getting close," she said after several minutes.

"The sooner we can identify who's behind these emails, the sooner we can put an end to this nightmare."

Raven's phone vibrated on the table, breaking her train of thought. It was Franklin Devereux again. With everyone helping Scout, she slipped out of the room.

Taking a breath, she answered. "Hello?"

"Raven, just checking in," Devereux said. "I trust the attorney I sent did a good job for you."

"Uh, yeah, she did," Raven said, forcing gratitude into her voice while casting a wary glance into the office. They were hard at work. She wished she hadn't accepted Devereux's help. The attorney had gotten Phillip Space released, and now it seemed he was the killer.

"Good to hear," Devereux continued, his tone light but expectant. "I trust you're considering my job offer."

She looked at her friends. Her family. She couldn't abandon them, not when they needed her most. "I appreciate your offer, Mr. Devereux, but I need time to think it over."

"Take all the time you need. Just remember, opportunities like this don't come every day."

"No, they don't," was all she managed to say before ending the call.

Devereux's offer had come with strings attached. Her loyalty to Chelsey and the rest of the team made the prospect of leaving Wolf Lake Consulting unpalatable.

"Who was that?" Chelsey asked, noticing her conflicted expression.

"The attorney who'd defended Phillip Space."

The front door swung open, and Darren hustled into the office.

"Raven," he said, rushing towards her. "I heard about someone taking your picture outside the cabin. What the hell is going on?"

"Calm down," she said, placing a hand on his arm. "We're trying to figure it out."

"Did you find anything?" Chelsey asked.

"I found a shoe print in the mud near where the photo was taken," he said, frustration seeping into his voice. "But that's it. No other clues."

"Did the security cameras catch anything?"

"Only pictures of Raven by her SUV. There are no camera views over that part of the parking lot."

Whoever was stalking her seemed to know where the blind spots were, staying just out of reach.

LeVar paced. "This guy knows what he's doing."

"Look," Darren said, his voice cracking with emotion. "I don't care who this person is or what they want. I won't let them hurt you."

She looked around at her friends and knew she could rely on them, no matter how dire the circumstances. Glancing out the window at the overcast sky, she leaped when the phone rang. Thomas picked it up and put it on speaker.

"Hey, it's Aguilar," the deputy said on the other end. "I checked Phillip Space's house like you asked. It looks abandoned; no sign of him or his vehicle."

"Thanks for the update, Aguilar," Thomas said. "There's a

turnoff half a mile down the road. You can park there without drawing attention."

"Got it."

Thomas ended the call and turned to them. "I'll arrange for more patrols near his house and get Lambert to coordinate with the state police. This guy can't hide for long."

Raven ran her fingers through her braids, her thoughts returning to Patricia Hudson and her connection to the killer. "Chelsey, maybe we should visit Patricia Hudson's family. They might remember something about her relationship with Phillip Space."

"It's worth a shot. LeVar, you and Scout keep working on tracing those emails."

"We're on this like white on rice," LeVar said.

"Lame, LeVar," Scout said without stopping her work.

Raven followed Chelsey out to her Civic.

When they arrived at the Hudson residence, Lambert was already there and waiting. The house loomed before them, its windows dark and uninviting.

"Something's not right," Lambert said as they approached the front porch. "Check out the door."

The front door stood ajar, revealing only darkness beyond. The hairs on the back of Raven's neck stood on end. Lambert removed his service weapon.

The door creaked as he pushed it open. Raven and Chelsey followed him through the entryway.

"Hello?" he called out. "Mrs. Hudson? Deputy Lambert, Nightshade County Sheriff's Department."

There was no answer. Raven exchanged uneasy glances with Chelsey and Lambert.

The family was gone. And time was running out.

21

LeVar's knees bounced under the table, his thoughts consumed by his sister Raven and the danger that encircled her. He glanced over at Scout; her face was a picture of intense concentration as she stared at the computer screen.

"Got it!" she exclaimed.

He pumped a fist in the air when he saw the decrypted server's IP address. They exchanged high-fives, unable to contain their excitement.

"Nice work, Rock the Bells," he said, referring to her online alias. She beamed at him, her glasses reflecting the glow of the computer monitor. In a burst of euphoria, she wrapped her arms around his shoulders, hugging him.

"I can't believe we did it," she said, her voice muffled against his shoulder.

Despite sharing in their triumph, he felt a tinge of unease, acutely aware of the age difference between them. He disentangled himself from the embrace.

"Let me call Thomas," he said, reaching for his phone. He

dialed the sheriff's number and waited for the familiar voice to answer.

"Hey, LeVar. I was just about to check in with you."

"Thomas, we've got some good news. Terrific news, actually. Scout decrypted the server's IP address."

"You're kidding." Thomas sounded both thrilled and surprised. "That could help us pinpoint the general location of our anonymous email sender."

"Hundred percent," LeVar said, though he knew there was more they were overlooking. The digital world was full of smoke and mirrors, and the killer had already proven adept at staying hidden. But this was a start, a solid lead that could bring them one step closer to unmasking the monster behind the murders.

"Send me what she has and keep me updated. We need to follow this lead and see where it takes us."

"Will do, Shep." He looked over at Scout. Her eyes shone with excitement as they delved back into the mystery. "You know, tracking down the exact location through an IP address isn't foolproof."

Scout nodded, her glasses slipping down her nose. "Yeah, I know. It can help determine the town or general area, but not the exact address."

"Right. And the user could be masking his IP using VPNs or similar services." Despite these hurdles, they had a promising lead on their hands. "Cross-reference the decrypted IP address against geolocation databases."

Scout clicked her tongue as she checked the IP address against a list of known VPN servers.

"Nothing," she muttered, shaking her head. "No match on any VPN servers."

"Really? That could suggest they're not using a VPN to mask their location."

"Seems like it. But we still can't be certain."

"True," he said, pulling out his phone. "In the meantime, I'll contact some ISPs to see if they can help us narrow things down."

As he made his calls, he felt a growing sense of urgency. The knowledge that the killer was likely a Wolf Lake resident only heightened his concern for his sister.

"Got something," he said after speaking with several ISPs. "One confirmed the IP address is assigned to a residential user. It's not much, but it narrows our suspect pool down a bit."

"But we still don't have an exact location or identity."

"We're at an impasse here. We need more resources if we're going to find this person before they strike again."

The room fell silent as they weighed their options. LeVar got back to work. He tapped away at the keyboard. Scout mirrored his movements, the two of them working in sync like seasoned partners. They sifted through countless data points. Minutes stretched into an hour, the relentless ticking of the clock counting down to when the killer struck again. Then, just as hope waned, they found it.

"Got him," Scout said as she pointed at the screen. "The IP address is registered on the outskirts of Wolf Lake where the murders have been happening."

Although it didn't give them an exact location, this knowledge brought their investigation into sharper focus. They were no longer chasing shadows; they were on the trail of a killer who thought he could hide from them. He couldn't.

"Okay, so we're closing in on him. We need to share our findings with the team."

"We might be one step closer, but we can't let our guard down. This person is dangerous, and we need to be prepared for anything."

He cleared his throat, deciding it was time for a break.

"Hey, let's take a breather and grab some food," he suggested, hoping it would give them both time to rethink their next move. "We could use a change of scenery."

"Sure. I guess we're not getting anywhere right now."

He forwarded the latest findings to Thomas and Chelsey. As they left their workspace to take a break, his eyes lingered on the screen displaying the IP address. They were missing something crucial.

22

The rustling of branches and the murmur of wind through the trees accompanied Thomas and Aguilar as they made their way through the woods. A local had reported seeing Phillip near this area, and the urgency in their steps reflected their determination to locate him.

"Lambert finally got a hold of Patricia Hudson's family," he said as they pushed through the dense brush. "They were out of town when he called on them."

"But the door was open."

"Yeah. Someone broke inside, but it doesn't seem the intruder stole anything."

"Do you think it was Phillip Space?"

"Could be. If it was, he didn't leave his fingerprints behind."

They were deep in the woods now, the cruiser far behind along a country road.

"Over there," Aguilar said, pointing to a makeshift campsite. The remains of a small fire smoldered and a tattered sleeping bag lay discarded nearby.

"Looks like he left in a hurry."

They approached the site, taking care not to disturb any

potential evidence. Among the scattered belongings, a familiar face caught their attention. A photo of Patricia Hudson.

"Thomas," Aguilar whispered, holding up the picture with a gloved hand. "It's her."

"Phillip was definitely here. We need to find him before it's too late."

She placed the photo in an evidence bag. As they continued to search, Thomas found himself lost in thought. The connection between Phillip and Patricia unsettled him. His instincts told him there was more to this case than met the eye. He shifted his attention back to the task at hand, scanning the ground for more clues.

"Let's keep moving," he said. "We can't afford to waste time.

Together they explored the woods, the shadows around them growing darker and heavier. The silence of the forest seemed to amplify every sound, from the snow beneath their feet to the distant hoot of an owl. Despite their increasing dread, Thomas and Aguilar pressed forward.

He squinted and inspected the area with a meticulous eye. Aguilar stood nearby and studied the treeline, alert for any sign of movement. Her radio crackled.

"Thomas," she said, not wanting to disturb the hushed atmosphere. "We've got news from the sheriff's department."

"Go on."

"A traffic camera caught Phillip Space's vehicle heading into the village. They're sending us the footage now."

Thomas assessed their surroundings. They were a quarter mile into the woods.

"Lambert can go after Phillip. We'll stay here and keep investigating. Lambert," Thomas said into his radio. "Grab a junior deputy. Traffic camera spotted Phillip. I'll send you the details."

"Copy that, Thomas."

Thomas and Aguilar continued their examination of the

campsite. Thomas wondered what had driven Phillip to abandon his home so suddenly. Was he running from the law because he knew everyone believed he was the killer? Had he stolen a photograph of Patricia Hudson as a memento?

"Hey, look at this," Aguilar said. She held up a small piece of fabric, torn and frayed at the edges. "Recognize it?"

"Phillip's shirt," Thomas said, staring at the scrap. "He was wearing it when we released him."

The sun continued its slow descent, bathing everything in a golden light that belied the darkness lurking beneath the surface. Damp earth and decay from melting ice hung in the air.

"Over there," she said, gesturing towards an almost indiscernible trail. Her eyes, honed by years of tracking fugitives, followed a disturbance amid the snow and dead foliage he had missed.

They silently followed the trail. Soon the path opened to reveal a dilapidated shack, its wooden walls stained by time and weather.

"Looks like someone built this place off the grid. It gives me the creeps."

"I wonder how long it has been here," she said, her hand resting on the pistol at her hip.

She edged open the door. Though the shack was uninhabited, signs of recent occupancy were everywhere in the interior—a half-eaten meal lay abandoned on a rickety table. Someone had pinned a map of the county to the wall, two areas marked with precision.

"Look at this," she said, pointing to the markings on the map. "These are the locations where the two murders occurred."

"Someone's been planning. What else is here?"

Aguilar picked up a burner phone lying on a stack of newspapers. She scrolled through the series of cryptic texts displayed on the screen, each message more unnerving than the last.

"Whoever was here was communicating with himself."

"Phillip Space sent himself messages?"

"Seems like it." She bagged the phone. "Or it could be someone else entirely. Whoever it is has lost his mind. Look at this one. *Gut them all and let them burn in hellfire.*"

"And we let this guy walk."

A crooning wind made the walls groan. The dilapidated shack seemed to shiver under the weight of its own secrets.

"Download all the data," he said. "Once we get back to the village, I'll drive it to the county lab for analysis."

"And maybe send a copy of the data to Wolf Lake Consulting as well. They might find something we missed."

"You mean Scout might."

"Well, she is our secret weapon, right?"

Thomas snickered despite the gravity of their findings. "If you'd told me when I lived in Los Angeles that I would move home, serve as county sheriff, and depend on a teenage girl to track murderers, I would have said you were—"

A branch snapped, stopping him. Aguilar removed her gun faster than Thomas could blink. Outside the shack's lone window, night closed in on the forest.

They stepped outside. A gust of wind rustled the branches above. For a long time, they scanned the forest without speaking.

"See anything?" she asked.

"Nothing. The wind could have snapped a branch."

"Perhaps."

While Lambert patrolled the central area where the camera had caught Phillip Space's truck, Thomas crept through the trees with Aguilar by his side. An hour later, it was too dark to see more than a step in front of them, and there was no sign of Phillip Space.

After they returned to the station, he spotted LeVar and

Scout waiting for them in the lobby. They were hunched over a desk as they pored over a laptop screen.

"Hey, Thomas," LeVar said. "We got your message about the shack and the burner phone."

"You're already deciphering the data?"

"Scout's been cataloging those cryptic texts."

"What else?"

"I should be able to link each message to the location from which it was sent," Scout said. "He encrypted the data, but I'm working on it."

"Good work, both of you," Aguilar said. "We need all the help we can get."

"Thomas, are you sure about Phillip not being the sole perp?" LeVar asked.

Thomas sat on the edge of the desk. "Why do you ask? I admit something doesn't feel right."

"Trust your instincts. Your gut feelings have a dependable track record."

"Yeah, but I need more than hunches."

"Tell me about Phillip Space. He didn't graduate college and worked menial jobs, correct?"

"That's right," said Thomas.

"Yet he knows about data encryption?"

Thomas opened his mouth to respond and paused. "It doesn't add up. But all the evidence points to him being the killer."

"It's so perfect, it almost seems like a setup, don't you agree?"

23

Pale light filtered through the blinds at Wolf Lake Consulting, spilling a warm glow across the simple yet cozy office space. Raven and Chelsey prepared sandwiches for everyone, using a variety of deli meats, cheeses, and fresh vegetables. The scent of basil and tomatoes brought an element of comfort to the room.

LeVar was pleased to see his sister working side by side with Chelsey. She'd acted strangely over the last few days, and he knew she blamed herself for Ellen Reynolds' murder.

"Lunchtime, everyone. Take a break," Chelsey said. She handed out sandwiches, urging her team to step away from their workstations and enjoy a moment of respite from the case.

LeVar accepted a sandwich with thanks. He settled down beside Scout, who had been studying her laptop screen before reluctantly tearing herself away to eat. As they bit into their sandwiches, an excited gleam appeared in the girl's eyes.

"Yo, LeVar, have you heard about the latest breakthrough in quantum computing? I read an article last night that said it could revolutionize encryption."

"Man, that sounds overwhelming. But you know I'm all

about learning new things, so go ahead, enlighten me."

Scout's face lit up as she launched into a detailed explanation. "So, instead of using regular bits like our current computers, quantum computers use quantum bits or qubits. These qubits can exist in a state of superposition, meaning they can be both a zero and a one simultaneously."

"Uh-huh, like two things at once, right? Like old school and new school coexisting."

"Exactly. Because of this, quantum computers can process information at an incredible speed and solve complex problems that are currently impossible for our existing technology. And when we apply this to cybersecurity, traditional encryption methods might become obsolete."

"Wow, that's wild." He felt a new respect for Scout—her dedication to staying on the cutting edge of her field inspired him. It served as a reminder of how important constant learning and adaptation was in their line of work.

As they continued to discuss the future of encryption, the others in the room couldn't help but overhear their conversation. Raven stole a glance at Chelsey, both sharing an unspoken acknowledgment. They needed to do their homework if they wanted to keep up with Scout and LeVar.

Scout sketched out invisible diagrams in the air, her words tumbling out with a fervor that was infectious and bewildering at the same time.

"Y'all lost me at quantum," Chelsey admitted, her eyebrows knitting together in confusion. She turned to Raven, who agreed with a nod. "But I guess that's why we got Scout on board, huh?"

"Definitely," Raven said, her eyes lingering on the teenager. "We need someone like her to stay ahead of the game."

The girl's cheeks flushed with a mixture of pride and embarrassment. Her unique skills deepened the bond between them, providing a moment of levity amidst their work.

LeVar leaned back in his chair, taking in the conversation with interest rather than confusion. "Scout, you're seriously impressive. You think I should learn more about this stuff if I wanna join the FBI after college?"

"Absolutely. Technology is constantly evolving, and those who don't grow with it will fall behind."

Raven seemed to consider what Scout had said. LeVar wondered if she was thinking of her own future.

"Hey Raven, you still with us?" he asked.

"Uh, yeah," Raven said, shaking the cobwebs out of her head. "Just thinking about what Scout said. We can all benefit from learning something new, right?"

"That's what makes us such a great team. We're always growing, always adapting."

A knock on the door interrupted the camaraderie. LeVar followed Chelsey down the hallway and found a delivery man on the steps, holding a nondescript package addressed to Wolf Lake Consulting. Warily, Chelsey accepted it and thanked the man.

"Who's it from?" he asked, his thoughts still lingering on quantum computing.

Chelsey shook her head, scanning the plain brown box for its origin. "I don't know. There's no return address."

"Let me open it," he said, extending his hand. His instincts told him to be cautious, that something unexpected might be lurking within.

In the office, she passed the box to him. The others gathered around, curiosity rising at the mysterious arrival.

As he cut through the tape and lifted the flaps, a putrid stench hit him. They recoiled, hands flying to their noses, eyes watering. Inside the box lay a grotesque sight: a dead crow, its glassy eyes staring up at them.

He covered his mouth so he wouldn't get sick. "That's messed up."

"Another calling card from our killer," Chelsey said, anger seeping into her tone. She grabbed her phone and dialed Deputy Lambert, telling him about the gruesome discovery.

LeVar wanted to set the box outside, but the evidence had already been exposed to the elements, and he needed to preserve what remained. Within minutes, Lambert arrived, his face grim. He collected the package and assured them he would have it analyzed right away.

"Thanks, Lambert," Chelsey said. "I don't know how I'll get this smell out of the office."

"I can't help you with that, but everyone needs to be on guard now, not just Raven. If the killer sent this, he's targeting all of you. He must know you're closing in on him."

Lambert took his leave.

Chelsey turned to Raven. "We need to speak with Patricia Hudson's family members. Now that they're home, maybe they can shed light on this situation."

"It's worth a try," Raven said.

LeVar screwed up his face. The dead crow was a message, a taunt. And he couldn't let the killer have the last word.

∿

As they prepared to leave, Raven felt the mission bearing down on her. The crow was a symbol of death, a harbinger of darkness. And a reminder that she'd fought for Phillip Space's freedom.

They pulled up to the house where Patricia Hudson's sister lived. There was a shiny new lock on the door. Chelsey parked her green Honda Civic at the curb, and they stepped into the crisp March air.

"Let's hope her sister can give us some answers," Chelsey said as they approached the front door.

Raven knocked. A moment later, the door swung open, revealing a petite woman with silver hair and kind eyes. She introduced herself as Martha, Patricia's sister.

"Thank you for seeing us, Martha," Chelsey said. "We're trying to find out who killed your sister, and we were wondering if you could help us."

"I'll do anything I can if you find out who took Patricia away from us," Martha said, inviting them inside. They settled in the cozy living room, surrounded by family photographs and the faint scent of cinnamon. Raven noticed the resemblance between Patricia and Martha in their facial features—a strong jawline and high cheekbones.

"Martha," Chelsey began, "did Patricia ever mention anyone she had disagreements with or felt threatened by?"

The woman thought for a moment. "She mentioned Phillip Space a few times. He worked for her. She told me he could be argumentative, and she'd thought about firing him. But she felt bad for him, so she didn't."

"Did Patricia receive any threats before her death?"

"Not that I'm aware of, and Patricia would have told me. The sheriff's department took her personal effects after she died. I'm not sure why."

Raven's eyes lit up as an idea formed in her mind. "Chelsey, maybe we could request her personal effects. There may be clues there that could help us find her killer."

"I'll speak to Thomas." Chelsey turned back to Martha. "Thank you for your help. We're sorry for your loss, but we'll do everything we can to catch the person responsible."

Martha didn't realize Phillip Space had worked at the community center with Patricia, nor did she know who'd broken into her house. After fifteen minutes of questioning, Chelsey wrapped up the interview.

The killer had sent them a message with the dead crow to scare them off. That meant they were closer to solving the case, though Raven wasn't sure how. Regardless, she would see the investigation through, no matter how dark the path became.

With Chelsey at her side, she stepped out of the house. The air seemed colder than before. She glanced at her phone just as it buzzed with an incoming message.

Raven, I need your answer about the job offer this week.

Franklin Devereux. How could she make a critical life decision when she found it impossible to think straight?

"Who's that?" Chelsey asked, peering over Raven's shoulder.

"Uh, nobody important." As Raven hid her phone from view, Chelsey gave her a curious glance. "We should head back to the office."

Chelsey unlocked the car and motioned for Raven to climb in. As the engine hummed to life, Raven's phone buzzed again. Damn Franklin Devereux.

But when she checked the message, she found it had come from her bank. Her checking account balance was running dangerously low.

"Everything okay?" Chelsey asked, concern lacing her voice as she navigated through the streets.

"Wrong number."

Though she was loyal to Wolf Lake Consulting, she couldn't afford to stay in her current position any longer. What if she missed a payment on her SUV and the bank repossessed her sole means of transportation?

She had no choice but to accept a higher-paying job, yet the decision was still difficult. But catching Phillip Space was her priority. Franklin Devereux and her bills would have to wait until she closed the case and brought the killer to justice.

24

Inside the medical examiner's office, Thomas considered the unsettling sight of a dead crow inside its packaging, which Claire had set on the stainless-steel table. The lights hurt his eyes.

"Thanks for coming in on your day off, Claire," he said.

The killer's audacity and the cruel symbolism behind sending such a macabre message made him rock on his heels.

"Anytime, Thomas," she said. She scanned the evidence before them, her green eyes unblinking. "Let's see what we can find."

With a snap, she slipped on a pair of latex gloves and began the forensic analysis. She started by examining the packaging, noting the type of material used and any identifying marks.

"Any chance we'll find something useful?"

"We'll be looking for fingerprints, hair, fibers, or traces of DNA. Anything that might help us identify the sender."

He leaned against the wall, his arms crossed over his chest. It seemed like such a long shot. She moved on to the dead crow. Her practiced hands examined its feathers and body, and she documented every observation with the same attention to detail she had given the packaging.

"I'd rather not ask, but how did he kill the crow?"

"Based on the bruising beneath the feathers, I'd say he stoned it to knock it down, then he snapped its neck. I'll know more once I've finished my initial examination."

They were dealing with a calculating and ruthless killer. He felt a mix of fascination and disgust. Claire's painstaking professionalism did not waver. She paused.

"Find something?"

"Maybe," she said, picking up a strand of hair with a pair of tweezers. "We should run a DNA test."

"Could it be the killer's?"

"Hard to say. It could be anyone's hair, really. From the packaging facility to the delivery person. But it's a lead worth pursuing."

He stared at the hair strand, knowing that it might be the only tangible link to the person who had sent this message to Wolf Lake Consulting.

She placed the hair strand into an evidence bag before labeling it. "I'll test this now, but I can't make any guarantees."

Claire offered him a small, reassuring smile before turning back to the examination table.

As he continued to observe her work, he distanced himself from the emotional implications of the task at hand. Yes, the madman was targeting his friends, but he focused instead on the clues that could move the investigation forward. Each new discovery, however minor, brought them one step closer to unmasking the person behind the murders.

They awaited the results of the DNA test. The air was thick with tension, punctuated only by the humming of equipment and the occasional rustle of paper. His eyes shifted from the dead crow on the examination table to the young medical examiner, who busied herself with reviewing the pathology report.

"Broken neck," she muttered as she studied the document. "That's what killed it."

"Any idea how long ago?"

"Based on the state of rigor mortis, I'd say it happened within the last forty-eight hours. This helps us determine when the package was sent."

Thomas mentally cataloged the information. He noticed the subtle crease between Claire's eyebrows as she studied the report.

"Any other—" he began, but was interrupted by the buzzing of his phone. It was LeVar; he quickly answered.

"Thomas, Scout decrypted more data from that burner phone you found in the shack. You need to see this."

"Thanks for letting me know. Aguilar and I will follow up with you after I finish working with Claire."

"Find anything on the packaging?"

"We think so. Still processing the data."

"Keep me posted," LeVar said before ending the call.

"Another lead?" she asked, her curiosity piqued.

"From the burner phone. It could be big. We sent the data to the lab for decryption, but Scout beat them to the punch."

"How much would I have to pay you to let me borrow Scout for a few months?"

"A king's ransom. But just say the word, and I'm sure she'll jump at the opportunity."

He walked from one wall to the next, his hands buried in his pockets as Claire deciphered the results. Each step was a silent plea for good news, an unspoken prayer that this lead would get them closer to solving the case.

"So the DNA test results say we're dealing with a middle-aged male." She glanced at the monitor. "Unfortunately, it doesn't match any profiles in our database."

Thomas wasn't surprised. What were the odds the killer was in the system?

She took samples from its claws and beak, her movements precise and efficient. As she worked, she explained her reasoning. "If we find any residue on the bird, it might give us an idea of where it was before it was killed. Studying its diet could also provide some insight into its origin."

"Interesting. I hadn't thought of that."

"I'll send these samples off for analysis."

"Keep me updated on the results," he said.

His phone hummed as he removed the keys from his pocket. Reading the screen, he noticed a message from Raven. He tapped the text and skimmed through the information she had gathered from Patricia Hudson's sister.

"Interesting," he murmured, looking up at Claire. "Raven and Chelsey spoke to Patricia Hudson's sister. It seems the argument she'd had with Phillip Space frightened her."

"That's disturbing. Definitely worth looking into."

He typed a response, wanting to forgive Raven for getting Phillip Space released, but there was no time for personal feelings. Before he left, Claire stopped him.

"Thomas, wait."

He turned to find her holding a pair of tweezers and a magnifying glass as she leaned over the crow.

"Anything new?"

"An unfamiliar substance under the crow's claws. We'll need to run further tests to identify it, but it could be another valuable clue."

"What kind of substance?"

"It might be soil from a patch of land where the snow

melted. With the varying terrain and soil types around Wolf Lake, knowing where it died could be crucial."

"Excellent work, Claire." He looked at the crow one last time, knowing its lifeless body might hold the key to the secrets behind the murders. "Call me as soon as you identify the location."

Claire nodded, already turning her attention back to the task.

As he exited the medical examiner's office, Thomas sensed the killer in the shadows, taunting him with cryptic messages and gruesome tokens.

"Hey, Aguilar," he said into his phone after a quick dial. "I'm heading over to Phillip Space's last known location again. Maybe there's something we missed. Meet me there in twenty minutes."

"Got it, Thomas. See you there," Aguilar said.

He climbed into his pickup, started the engine, and pulled away from the curb. His phone buzzed as he settled into the seat, and he answered without looking, assuming it would be Aguilar with more information on their next steps. Instead, it was Scout's voice that greeted him, excited and breathless.

"Thomas, I narrowed down the internet activity in the village using the timestamp from the emails. It's a breakthrough that might lead us to the anonymous sender." If they could pinpoint the origin of those emails, it might put them closer to the killer than ever before. "I'll keep working and notify you if I find anything else."

"You're an invaluable asset, Scout. Keep up the great work."

He pictured her cheeks coloring at that remark. As he drove to meet Aguilar, his thoughts swirled with possibilities and connections. The hair, the substance under the crow's claws, the narrowed list of internet activity—each piece of the puzzle was significant in its own right.

Now it was up to him and his team to unmask a murderer.

25

Animals scattered from the path as Thomas and Aguilar trekked through the woods, armed with new insights from the crow and Scout's internet activity tracking. The wind nipped at them, and the half-frozen, half-melted snow made the going treacherous.

"This way," he said, his breath fogging in front of him. "Scout found internet activity near here."

Aguilar scanned the area for any sign of Phillip Space. "What would we do without her?"

"Hopefully, we won't have to find out," Thomas muttered, picturing the girl hunched over her computer, working tirelessly to help them solve the case. The teenager was considering an early graduation. If she chose a faraway school instead of Kane Grove, the sheriff's department would lose a tremendous asset.

A half mile from the shack and campsite, they noticed more details that had evaded them before: a trail of footprints, a cigarette butt, and a makeshift fire pit. They stopped to examine the scene, collecting evidence and snapping pictures.

"Look at these footprints," Aguilar pointed out, crouching

down beside them. "They're fresh. He was here in the last twenty-four hours."

Thomas nodded, shooting photos with his phone. "And this cigarette butt? Phillip Space is a smoker, isn't he?"

"He is." She placed the butt in an evidence bag for forensic analysis. "I've seen him take smoke breaks while working on lawns."

"Let's hope there's DNA."

As they moved closer to the shack, Thomas's thoughts drifted back to the crow and its unsettling message. Had Phillip sent it? And why? The answers eluded him, slipping away like shadows in the fading light.

"Hey, Thomas. Check this out."

She gestured towards stones arranged around the charred remains of a small fire that made up a crude pit. Thomas kneeled as he examined it, wondering what secrets it might hold.

"He had to stay warm."

"Could be where he cooked his meals as well."

"After we search the area, we'll take the evidence back to the lab. The sooner we put this all together, the closer we'll be to finding where he's hiding."

Together Thomas and Aguilar gathered the remaining evidence. As they made their way back through the woods, the brush rustled. They removed their weapons in unison.

When a rabbit scampered across the trail, they slipped the service weapons back into their holsters, giving each other a relieved look. A short walk later, the shack loomed before them like a specter, its decaying exterior camouflaged among the bare trees that surrounded it.

"Ready?" she asked.

"Let's do it," Thomas replied, reaching for the door. It creaked open, revealing the dilapidated interior.

As they stepped inside, the air grew colder still, as if the shack were a tomb preserving secrets long forgotten. They split up to search the room.

"Come look at this."

He joined her in the far corner, where a patch of half-frozen soil had been disturbed. Intrigued, they dug through the icy earth, their fingers growing numb. The task was arduous, and Thomas wished he'd brought a spade. Ten minutes later, they unearthed a weathered chest.

"What in the hell?"

Thomas brushed the dirt from the lid. He pried it open, revealing its contents: newspaper clippings about the murders.

"Someone's been keeping a close eye on the case. And I think we both know who that someone is."

"Looks like it," Thomas said.

But another object caught his attention—a worn diary nestled among the clippings. He picked it up, flipping through pages filled with erratic handwriting.

"Listen to this," he said, reading aloud. "'Patricia Hudson—she thinks she can control me, manipulate me. But I'll show her. I'll make her pay for how she treated me.'"

Aguilar looked up, her eyes wide. "This has to be Phillip's diary. It confirms his fixation on Patricia."

"Seems that way." He skimmed more entries filled with ramblings and plans for revenge. The chilling words painted a vivid picture of a man consumed by hatred and teetering on the edge of madness. "They can all burn in hell."

"What a psycho. We need to take this back to the station. This might be the final nail in his coffin."

He nodded with a heavy heart, knowing they were closer than ever to understanding Phillip Space's deranged mind. But as they packed up their evidence and left the shack, he knew darker revelations awaited them.

Thomas squinted as he scanned the surrounding woods. He felt a vibration in his pocket and pulled out his phone, seeing Scout's name flash on the screen. "Hey, what have you got for us?"

"Tracked the activity on that burner phone," Scout said. "LeVar called around, and the only place in the village that sells that make and model is a convenience store down the road from Wolf Lake Consulting. Trouble is, management wipes out the surveillance footage every seven days."

"And I suppose the activity dates back further than seven days."

"At least a month."

"Ugh," Thomas muttered under his breath. He glanced at Aguilar, who paused in her examination of the woods to question him with her dark eyes. "The burner phone came from town, but no footage. Someone's covering their tracks well."

"Too well," Aguilar said.

"Keep up the good work, Scout."

"Thank you, Thomas," the teen said, the pride evident in her voice before she ended the call.

The drive back to the station took them from the dense woods to the vibrant streets of Wolf Lake. As they walked into the office, Lambert looked up from his desk, his head cocked to one side, expectant.

"Found something," Thomas said, dropping the bag of clippings and the diary on Lambert's desk. The lanky deputy leaned in for a closer look.

"Newspaper clippings about the murders," Aguilar explained, her tone grave. "And a diary we believe belongs to Phillip Space."

"Diary?" Lambert raised an eyebrow. "What does it say?"

"Mostly ramblings about Patricia Hudson. A desire for

revenge," Thomas said, running a hand through his sandy hair. "Phillip's fixation on her is clearer than ever."

Aguilar propped herself on the edge of Lambert's desk. "Scout found a lead on that phone, too. Burner phone from a convenience store in town, but the store's surveillance footage doesn't go back to when it was purchased."

"Smart," Lambert mused, his eyes narrowing as he considered the information. "Makes it harder for us to pin anything on whoever bought it. Still, I'll check with the manager and ask if she remembers who bought it. I doubt they sell that many prepaid phones. Let's keep at it. The more we uncover, the better our chances of finding this sick bastard."

Thomas nodded. "And this time, we won't allow him to walk."

It was time to connect the dots and bring an end to this nightmare.

As the day grew late, Thomas paced the cramped office, his brows knit together in anticipation. The forensics report was due at any second. Aguilar sat across from him, drumming her fingers on the table as she shared his impatience.

"I wonder why it's taking so long," he said.

"Be patient. Claire promised to call as soon as she had something."

At last, the desk phone rang loud enough to make him jump. Seeing the medical examiner's number on the screen, he put her on speakerphone.

"Hey, Claire. What have you got for us?"

"Forensics came back inconclusive on the hair strand and the cigarette butt," she said, her words heavy with defeat. "They came from the same person, but we couldn't find a match in any databases. And to make matters worse, there was no DNA on the box, the diary, or the newspaper clippings."

"How is that possible?"

"He must have worn gloves the entire time."

It was another dead end, leaving them without the proof they needed to lock away Phillip Space forever.

"What kind of lunatic wears gloves to write in his diary?"

"Ready for the good news?"

"We could use some."

"So, I analyzed the substance I found under the crow's claws. It's a specific type of soil found only in certain parts of the village."

"Can you be more specific?" Thomas asked, increasing the volume on the speaker.

"Actually, yes," Claire replied, excitement creeping into her voice. "This soil has a unique composition and is found near large bodies of water, like Wolf Lake. It's also prevalent between the shoreline and the village outskirts where Phillip Space lives."

"Can this help us narrow down the killer's location?" Aguilar asked.

"Potentially," Claire conceded. "It's not a guarantee, but it provides a starting point for your next search."

He shared a glance with his deputy. A lead, however tenuous, was better than nothing.

"Thanks, Claire," he said. "We'll check it out."

They would comb every inch of Wolf Lake's outskirts until they found their monster.

26

Little was left of the day beyond the windows. Inside Wolf Lake Consulting, Raven and Chelsey stood in a sea of cardboard boxes filled with Patricia Hudson's personal effects. A sad curiosity pervaded the room.

"Where should we start?" asked Raven.

"We'll take it one box at a time."

Tigger, the orange tabby, claimed a spot atop a cabinet while Jack chewed a bone on his dog bed. As they sifted through Patricia's belongings, memories of the woman seemed to permeate the air. Her life, now reduced to a collection of objects and trinkets.

"Look at this." Raven lifted a tarnished silver locket. "It's beautiful."

"She had good taste. But we need to find something more . . . substantial. Something that can help us understand why Phillip Space wanted to kill her."

Raven continued rummaging through the box. Amidst the clutter, her eyes fell upon a worn-out journal. Its leather-bound exterior marked by age and use, the journal was a silent witness to the many thoughts and emotions Patricia had experienced throughout her later years.

"Chelsey, look at this," she said, passing the journal to her partner. "I think we might have found something important."

Careful not to smudge the inside, Chelsey opened the book; its pages were filled with neat cursive handwriting. As they read, Patricia's voice seemed to echo within their minds, carrying with it a world of secrets and fears.

"Raven," Chelsey whispered, her fingers tracing the faded ink. "We might be onto something here."

"Keep going."

As they continued their search, the sun dipped beneath the horizon, bathing the room in a soft amber glow. Piece by piece, they unraveled the mystery that had consumed Patricia Hudson's life.

Shadows danced on the walls as Chelsey turned the brittle pages. The room had grown darker, but neither woman wanted to break their focus by turning on another light. Raven sat on the edge of her chair, her hands entwined in her lap.

"Listen to this. The next entry is about Phillip Space."

Raven edged closer, her chest tightening as she prepared to hear more about the man she had once defended.

"April 15th," Chelsey read. "Phillip charged me for landscaping work he didn't complete. Was it an honest mistake, or is he trying to cheat me out of my money? I confronted him, and his response was unsettling. He became abusive."

"Keep reading."

"May 2nd. Phillip's behavior hasn't improved. Today, he came to my house unannounced, demanding payment for services he claimed to have rendered. I refused, and his anger flared. The way he glared at me made me want to phone the sheriff. And say what? I wonder if he's hiding something."

"Patricia was afraid of him." A knot formed in her stomach at the knowledge that her defense of Phillip might have been the gravest mistake she'd ever made.

"June 12th. I can't get over this feeling that something terrible will happen if I don't distance myself from Phillip. But how can I fire him after the way he acted when I confronted him about the unfinished work? My sister warned me not to hire Phillip, but I took pity on him because he's had a rough life and wants to better himself. We all make mistakes."

"God, Chelsey. What have I done?"

"Raven, you couldn't have known," Chelsey reassured her. "We're going to find the truth, and we'll do right by Patricia."

The glow of a single lamp illuminated the leather-bound journal.

"July 7th," Chelsey said. "I confronted Phillip today about the unjust charges on my latest bill. He became furious and started yelling at me. His face turned red, and he clenched his fists," Chelsey continued. "I thought that he was going to hit me, but then he stormed out of the house. I've never seen him so aggressive before. Call me foolish, but I paid him. What if he seeks revenge? I live alone."

"Patricia must have been terrified." She could almost hear Patricia's trembling voice as Chelsey recounted the terrifying encounter.

"Here's something interesting. She writes, 'I considered firing Phillip after this incident, but I couldn't bring myself to do it. Despite his anger, I know he's had a horrible life. It's difficult for him, and I can't help but feel he's trying.'"

"Compassion didn't cost Patricia her life. I did."

"No, you didn't."

"What else did she write?"

"She ends the entry with this: 'My fear of Phillip grows each day. I need to let him go without putting myself in danger. But how?'"

They shared a glance. Raven sighed and rubbed her temples, trying to stave off a tension headache.

"Patricia must have felt trapped. Stuck between her fear of Phillip and her reluctance to make his life worse."

"Sometimes compassion can be a double-edged sword," Chelsey said, her voice laced with sadness.

"We owe it to her to make sure no one else suffers at Phillip's hands."

"Amen."

Chelsey closed the journal with a soft thud. The sound echoed through the room, reverberating off the walls like a promise.

Raven's fingers grazed the edges of an old photograph hidden beneath a stack of personal effects. As she pulled it out and studied the captured moment, she glanced up from the journal that had consumed her attention.

"Look at what you found," Chelsey said.

The photograph depicted Patricia and Phillip working together in her yard, the sun casting warm rays upon their faces as they tended to the plants. They both seemed at ease, sharing a connection through their task.

"Phillip looks so different here," Chelsey said. "Almost friendly."

Raven tilted her head, studying the image. Her eyes narrowed as she tried to reconcile the man in the photograph with the one described in Patricia's journal. The contrast was unsettling, like staring at two completely different people.

"Appearances can be deceiving," Raven said, returning to the journal. She flipped through the pages, Patricia's penned fears echoing in her mind. Each word weighed on her like a stone.

"Maybe there's more to this story than we realize. What if there's some truth to Phillip's side of the story?"

"You mean he was making amends and putting his life back together?"

"Right."

"Perhaps. But Patricia's fear was real. And right now, everything points to Phillip being the killer."

"I can't pretend I'm not responsible for Phillip being free. If Thomas is angry with me, I understand."

"Thomas isn't angry with you. He loves you; we all do."

"I made a huge mistake."

"Where did you find that attorney, anyway?" Chelsey asked, her brow furrowing in curiosity.

Raven hesitated. She couldn't tell Chelsey about Franklin Devereux's offer. "Oh, I, uh, found her through a mutual connection."

"Interesting," Chelsey mused, her eyes lingering on Raven before returning to the photograph.

Raven let out a quiet breath, grateful Chelsey had dropped the subject.

"What if there's more to this? What if Phillip isn't the only suspect we should look at?"

"You still think someone else could be involved?"

"Maybe. My gut tells me not to dismiss other angles. We have to find Phillip first."

"But how do we find him? He's been off the grid since Thomas released him."

Raven frowned, drumming her fingers on the table. "We'll have to start by talking to the people who knew him best—his bar buddies, neighbors, anyone who might have seen him in the days leading up to the murders."

"We'll try, but the sheriff's department looked all day without results."

Raven had always trusted her instincts, and they had never led her astray. Until now, it seemed. The evidence against Phillip was mounting, and she couldn't deny the connection between him and Patricia. But something deep within her urged caution.

Outside, night fell upon Wolf Lake.

27

Thomas Shepherd's hair blew across his face as he stared down at the map spread over the hood of his Ford F-150. Aguilar stood beside him, concentrating on the locations around the lake. The wind picked up around them, blowing snow off the trees near the water.

"Here we are," Thomas said, using a finger to trace a line between Phillip's shack and Patricia's house. "We know the soil Claire found under the crow's claws was unique to this area, so our killer must hunt close by."

"True." Aguilar shielded her eyes from the light reflecting off the lake. "But we need to narrow it down. There's too much area to cover in one day."

"Let's use the location of Phillip's shack and Patricia's house as two points of our triangle. Then we can find areas where our target soil exists."

They continued studying the map, pinpointing areas where the killer stalked based on the evidence they had. As Thomas studied the invisible triangles, he recognized the urgency of their mission. If they didn't find the killer soon, how long before he struck again?

"Darren," Thomas called out, looking up to see him approaching. The forest ranger for Wolf Lake Park was an important resource in their search. Not only did he have extensive knowledge of the area, but his experience as a police officer in Syracuse made him an asset to their investigation.

"Thomas, Aguilar," Darren said, tipping his hat. "What do you need from me?"

"Your expertise." Thomas gestured to the map. "We're trying to figure out where our killer caught the crow, based on the soil we found under the claws, the location of Phillip Space's shack, and Patricia's house. Any ideas?"

"Let me look," Darren said, leaning over the map. His midnight-blue Chevrolet Silverado 4x4 was parked nearby, its engine still ticking as it cooled.

Thomas watched as Darren scanned the map.

"Here." Darren pointed to a spot on the map. "There's a dense wooded area between Phillip's shack and Patricia's house that could fit the bill. The soil there is similar to what Claire found."

"Perfect. That cuts down on the area, so we'll start our search there. Are you game?"

"Count me in. I know this park like the back of my hand, and every pair of eyes helps."

"Awesome," Thomas said, grateful for the assistance.

As they gathered their gear and prepared to venture into the forestland around Wolf Lake, Thomas believed they were on the brink of a significant breakthrough. Phillip Space couldn't hide forever.

∽

AFTER THE SEARCH CONCLUDED, Thomas and Aguilar drove back to the station and summarized their findings to Lambert. Darren had returned to his cabin to adjust the security cameras covering the parking lot.

The sheriff spread the map out and showed Lambert everywhere they'd looked. They were deep in discussion when the door opened, revealing Raven and Chelsey hurrying toward their desks.

"We found a ton of information in the journal," Raven said. She held up the leather-bound book.

"There are several entries about Phillip Space," Chelsey explained, stepping forward to join her partner. "We think they might help."

Thomas took the journal from Raven's outstretched hand, flipping through pages that were filled with elegant, loopy handwriting. As he read, his eyes widened at each new revelation.

"Here's an interesting passage," he said. "'Phillip has been acting strangely lately. I can't quite put my finger on it, but something about him unnerves me. I've even started locking my doors at night, just in case he comes back to argue about the payment.'" He looked up at the others, his expression grave. "'I don't want to believe he could be capable of anything sinister, but there's a darkness in him I can't ignore.'"

"Keep reading."

He obliged, continuing to read the entries detailing Patricia's growing unease around Phillip. With every word, the room seemed to grow colder.

As Thomas closed the journal, he looked up at Raven. She'd fought for Phillip's release, but Thomas still respected her opinion. She had put aside their differences to seek justice for Patricia, and in that moment he saw her as the ally he'd always known her to be.

"Thank you for finding these passages. We're doing everything we can to locate Phillip and get answers."

Raven set her hands on her hips. "That's all I want. Justice for

Patricia and Ellen."

"Then let's work together," Thomas suggested, extending a hand. "For Patricia and Ellen."

Night had descended over Wolf Lake, and the moon cast a silvery glow on the sidewalks outside their windows.

"Based on the soil found under the crow's claws, we believe our search needs to expand around Wolf Lake. We didn't find where he's been hiding the last few days, but we will."

∼

THEY STARTED the new day at the break of dawn and met at the edge of the lake, ready to begin their search. The members split into pairs: Thomas and Aguilar, Chelsey and LeVar, and Raven and Darren. They moved through the woods, checking off each area they'd cleared.

Phillip was out there somewhere, a predator in his element. The thought sent a shiver down Thomas's spine. He pushed himself harder, determined to bring this nightmare to an end.

"Thomas, over here," Aguilar said, drawing his attention.

He hurried over to where his deputy stood, crouched by a patch of disturbed soil. The ground was soft and damp where yesterday's sunlight had melted a patch of snow. The unique soil they had been searching for was unmistakable.

"Good find. Mark this spot and inform the others."

Hours of challenging hikes led them through the woods and over ridges. The task was daunting, but the hope of finding Patricia's killer fueled their resolve.

In the late afternoon, as the sun dipped below the treeline, Thomas caught his breath. His thoughts turned to Raven, and he wondered if she had found anything significant. He wondered how much guilt she harbored for defending a serial killer. No one should have to carry that burden.

The phone buzzed with a call from Lambert.

"Thomas," Lambert said, urgency in his tone. "You're not going to believe this. I just arrested Phillip outside the ranger's cabin. I spotted him while patrolling."

"Was he looking for Raven?" Thomas asked, his heart racing with anticipation.

"Could be."

As the deputy relayed the news, Thomas shook his head in disbelief while Aguilar stared, waiting.

"Good work, Lambert. We'll be there as soon as we can." Thomas ended the call and turned to Aguilar. "Lambert's got Phillip. He found him near the ranger's cabin."

Aguilar grimaced. "All this time we were searching, and he returned to the cabin?"

"Here's the plan. Meet up with Chelsey, Darren, and LeVar. Keep searching around the lake. I want to make sure we don't miss anything. I'll head back to the station and begin the interrogation."

"I hope he confesses and finally brings this investigation to an end. Hey, you didn't mention Raven."

"That's because she needs to come with me."

"Whatever for?"

"Phillip Space refuses to talk to anyone but her. I need to drive her to the station."

Aguilar hesitated before nodding. "All right. Let's round up the troops."

They found the others on the far side of the ridge. Raven appeared shocked when Thomas explained why he needed her.

As he led her back to his truck, he wondered what Phillip wanted with her. Did the killer think she would defend him again? The mystery swirled around him as he drove Raven back to the station. It was as if the shadows whispered secrets, daring him to uncover what lay hidden beneath.

28

The truck's engine hummed as it cruised down the winding road, cutting through the dense forest that surrounded Wolf Lake. Raven stared out the window, her thoughts consumed by the upcoming interrogation of Phillip Space. The implications of their conversation preoccupied her. What did he want?

Thomas glanced across the cab, sensing her unease. "Raven, you've got this," he said. "You have a way with people, and I'll be there the entire time."

"But he . . . gutted those women, and I fought for his freedom. Ellen Reynolds is dead because—"

"I'm stopping you right there. You secured legal defense for Phillip Space, and the attorney convinced *me* to let him go. This isn't on you."

Her heart pounded. The phone buzzed in her pocket, and she pulled it out to see Darren's name on the screen.

"Hey," she answered, trying to sound more confident than she felt.

"Raven, I heard about the interview with Phillip. Do you want me there for support?"

She stopped, tempted by the offer, but shook her head. "I appreciate it, Darren, but I need to face my fears. Besides, Thomas will be in the room."

"Don't go anywhere near Phillip Space. Sit across the table from him and let him say what he wants to say, but the second you feel uncomfortable, get the hell out of there."

"I will."

"Call me when you're done."

His tone was filled with worry, and she could imagine him pacing around the search site.

"Love you," she whispered, ending the call and slipping the phone into her pocket.

As the pickup continued its journey toward the station, Raven knew her interactions with Phillip would shape the course of the investigation. She couldn't let fear control her actions.

The station's hallway echoed with the sound of footsteps as Raven and Thomas made their way to the interrogation room. The scent of burned coffee filled the air, mingling with the aroma of disinfectant. As they approached the door, she took a breath and steeled herself for what lay beyond.

"Remember," Thomas said, "I'll be with you during the interview."

Raven nodded, grateful for his reassurance even as her stomach contents congealed into a brick. Inside the room, Phillip Space sat with his hands cuffed to the table in front of him. Deputy Lambert stood sentinel with a junior deputy. The killer's face was pale, eyes darting around the room. The man looked like a cornered animal, making Raven more cautious than ever. A cornered animal would lash out.

Thomas nodded to the deputies, and they exited the room, leaving the two of them alone with a serial killer. She looked to

Thomas for direction, and he gestured for her to take a seat and begin.

"As you requested," Thomas said, "I brought Raven with me."

"I want to talk to her alone," Phillip said.

"No can do. If you want to speak with her, you'll do so with me present. Otherwise, I'll take you back to the cell, and we can wait for your attorney."

"I don't have an attorney."

"If you can't procure Sandra Ford, you'll receive a public defender."

The killer gave an indifferent shrug.

"Hello, Phillip," Raven said, forcing a warmth into her voice that she did not feel. "I'm Raven Hopkins, but I guess you know me already. And I take it you know Sheriff Thomas Shepherd."

"Yes, I do."

Raven took a seat across from Phillip, and Thomas positioned himself beside her, his gaze never leaving the accused man. She studied the killer's face, searching for any hint of the truth behind his stare. "We're here to talk about Patricia Hudson and Ellen Reynolds."

Phillip's breath hitched, his eyes filling with anguish. "I didn't . . . I didn't kill them."

"Take it slow, Phillip. Tell us about your relationship with Patricia. You knew her, correct?"

He hesitated, swallowing hard before speaking. "I worked for her. Did lawn care, you know? But we had our disagreements." He paused, his gaze flicking to Thomas as if seeking reassurance.

"Go on," Thomas encouraged, his own expression unreadable.

"Patricia, she wasn't happy with my work lately. We argued about it. It was my fault. I swore I'd performed the work she hired me for, but I was mistaken. By the time I tried to apologize, she scolded me and told me never to return."

"That must have angered you," Raven said.

"Somewhat. But I swear, I didn't hurt her."

He seemed genuinely distraught, but perhaps he finally felt the guilt over killing two women.

"Phillip, we're trying to understand what happened. Patricia's writings said you've led a difficult life. Can you tell us more about your personal troubles?"

The man's face crumpled as he fought back tears. "Everything just kept piling up. I was drowning."

"Drowning?"

"Debt. I started drinking to hide from my life. That made things worse, and I couldn't hold a job. Not until Patricia hired me to work on her property. She said so many nice things about me, and that led to others hiring me. She's the last person I would hurt."

He choked on the words.

"Take a breath, Phillip."

He struggled to regain his composure. She couldn't help but feel a pang of empathy for the broken man, and she chided herself. He was a cold-blooded killer.

Phillip clenched his fists, eyes darting around the room as if searching for an escape. "I don't want to say anything else with him here," he said, glaring at Thomas.

"Sorry, but I can't leave the interview," Thomas said.

The accused murderer's eyes flitted back and forth from her to Thomas, finally settling on a spot on the floor. She leaned forward in her chair, trying to catch his eye.

"Why did you want to speak with me?" she asked.

He lifted his head, his expression a mix of fear and gratitude. "You're the only one who believes I'm innocent."

Except she didn't. But Phillip saw her as his last hope. She exhaled, willing herself to remain composed.

"All right, let's talk about what happened. We need to go through everything step by step."

Phillip grunted and continued to avoid direct eye contact. His body language remained tense, as if bracing for an unseen attack.

"Tell us about your relationship with Patricia in the weeks leading up to her death."

"Like I said before, we had our disagreements. I scared her by yelling. She wouldn't speak to me anymore."

"We need more information. The evidence places you at the scene. Help us understand why you lost control."

"I didn't hurt Patricia, and I barely know Ellen Reynolds. Why would I kill them?"

"Explain why your fingerprints are on the murder weapon," said Thomas.

"What murder weapon?"

"The ax. It belongs to you, right?"

He shook his head in confusion. "I own an ax, yes. It's in my shed."

"No, it was behind Ellen Reynolds' house."

"Then another person put it there. Maybe they just want to pin the murders on someone, and I'm an easy target."

Thomas quirked an eyebrow. "Phillip, do you ever experience blackouts or forget how you got somewhere?"

"What? No."

Raven studied the arrested man. "Phillip, I want to help you, but I need you to be completely honest with us. Can you do that?"

"I have been honest."

"Tell me about the last time you saw Patricia Hudson."

Phillip closed his eyes before answering. "That was our fight," he confessed. "She was angry because I hadn't finished the landscaping work around her yard."

"Go on." She noted the dark circles under his eyes and the way his hands trembled in his lap.

"Things got heated. I yelled, but I never laid a hand on her. I swear."

As a private investigator, she had learned to read people well, but Phillip was difficult to decipher.

"Why didn't you finish the work Patricia had hired you to do?"

He hesitated, as if ashamed to admit his reasons. "I've been dealing with personal stuff."

"You've been drinking again, haven't you?"

Phillip seemed unable to answer.

"Have you sought help for your drinking?"

"I tried," Phillip replied, his voice thick with emotion. "But it's hard to make ends meet when the debt keeps piling up."

Raven understood all too well the suffocating pressure of financial instability. She glanced over at Thomas, who remained silent but attentive.

"Phillip, I want to believe you, but we need more than just your word to clear your name."

"Why did you run after we released you?" Thomas asked.

"Because everyone had made up their minds that I was a killer," he said. "I just wanted to get away."

"So you went to the shack in the woods?"

The killer's forehead scrunched. "What shack?"

"Come on, Phillip. We found the lockbox."

"There's an old shack in the forest about a mile from my house. Nobody has used it in years. I pass it sometimes during hunting season, but it's not mine. Look, I didn't kill anyone."

"Then what were you doing outside the ranger's cabin?"

He turned to Raven. "Looking for you."

She sat back. "Why me?"

"Because I knew everyone thought I was guilty for the second murder. I thought maybe you'd see I'm innocent and help me like before."

Phillip broke into sobs and became inconsolable. She thought about her mother's struggles, and a tear crawled down her cheek. They tried to calm him down, but he was beyond help.

"That's enough for now." Thomas looked at her. "Raven, I think you should take a break. This is getting too emotional for both of you."

She hesitated, torn between her desire to find the truth and the need to protect herself from becoming emotionally invested. "You're right. I'll take a break."

Thomas gave her a wink as she rose from the chair. As she left the room, Phillip's sobs echoed down the hall. The sound haunted her, making her heart ache with sympathy and doubt. Was she doing the right thing? Could she trust this man who seemed so desperate for her to believe in his innocence?

She wandered through the station, sensing that the deputies watched her. Her mind replayed the details of the interview.

As she decompressed, Lambert entered the room to guard Phillip as Thomas joined her. She leaned against the chilly wall, which rattled from the ancient heating system. The sheriff stood beside her.

"Is something else bothering you?" he asked.

Raven didn't wish to reveal her private struggles. "No, it's just this case. I know this sounds like lunacy, but he doesn't believe he killed anyone."

He drew up his shoulders. "Are you taking his side again?"

"No. It's possible he murdered those women in a drunken rage and doesn't remember."

"We know Phillip has a violent streak. What about the picture? That might be worth questioning him about."

Raven's thoughts shifted to the photograph of Phillip engaged in a brawl outside a bar. She recalled the anger on his face, so different from the broken man she had just spoken with.

Thomas retrieved the photo, and they returned to the interview room where the killer was waiting. Thomas slid a photograph across the table, depicting Phillip in a fierce brawl outside a local bar.

Phillip lowered his eyes to the picture, his face contorted with surprise. "Where'd you get this?"

"It's evidence," Raven said, her tone impassive. "Care to explain?"

"Explain what? I was defending myself. Who took this picture anyway? They didn't get the entire story."

"A man named Eddie Monroe took the picture."

Phillip's face twisted with disgust at the mention of the name. "Eddie Monroe? He's been out to ruin me for years. You can't trust anything he says."

Thomas folded his arms, looking unimpressed. "That may be true, but the picture doesn't lie. What were you fighting about?"

"It doesn't matter what started it. Eddie hated me, and he wanted to ruin my name. He must have been waiting for an opportunity like this."

Raven's eyes narrowed as she studied the killer. Something about his reaction told her there was more to the story. "Why did Eddie hate you so much? What happened between you two?"

He looked away, his jaw clenched. "We had a falling out years ago. Personal matters. Eddie never let it go."

She sensed he was holding back. "Phillip, if you want us to help you, you need to be honest. What really happened between you and Eddie?"

His shoulders sagged, and he looked down at the table,

defeated. "Fine," he whispered. "It was just stupid school stuff. We got into a fight, and I hurt him. Broke his nose, actually. He never got over it, even though it was a million years ago."

Thomas and Raven exchanged a glance. They sensed they were on the brink of uncovering a hidden truth, one that could change the course of their investigation.

"Please, Raven. I didn't do it. You have to believe me. Get me that attorney."

His desperate pleas tugged at Raven's heart.

29

Raven peered into the woodstove's crackling fire and tossed another log into the blaze, her thoughts consumed by the interview with Phillip Space. She couldn't decide if Phillip was guilty or innocent, and that fact alone shook the confidence in her own judgment.

"Hey," Darren said, coming up behind her. He sat down beside her on the floor, placing a comforting hand on her knee. "You okay?"

She twisted her braids around her fingers. "I don't know, Darren. I can't get over this feeling that I'm missing something."

"What makes you so unsure?"

"Maybe it's Phillip's demeanor or the way he opened up about his problems. I can't tell if he's guilty or innocent," she said, her eyes searching his for reassurance.

"You know, when I was a police officer, there were plenty of times when I'd been wrong about a suspect. It's not an exact science, Raven."

"Like when? You never make mistakes."

"Yeah, right. Once, we had a string of robberies and all the evidence pointed to this guy who lived in the neighborhood.

Turned out he was just a compulsive hoarder, and the real thief was his neighbor." Darren paused, considering another example. "Another time, I thought a woman was innocent because she had a solid alibi, but she'd been lying to cover for her boyfriend, who happened to be our prime suspect."

"Those examples don't exactly instill confidence," she said, almost able to laugh. "They make me more uneasy about the uncertainties of investigative work."

"You're doing your best. Nobody has all the answers, and sometimes you have to trust your instincts."

"Right now, my instincts are a mess," she admitted, rubbing her eyes. "I don't know what to believe anymore."

"Give it time. The truth has a way of revealing itself when you least expect it."

As she stared into the fire, the conflicting images of Phillip haunted her, and she wondered if she'd ever be able to discern the truth. Her thoughts remained tangled in webs of doubt. She crawled into bed, pulling the thick quilt up to her chin, seeking solace in its warmth. The chilly March night seeped through the slits in the cabin walls, but the fire still crackled in the hearth.

"Need any help with the firewood?" Raven called out as Darren pulled on his boots and jacket.

"Got it covered. You get some rest. We'll talk about the investigation after you've gotten a good night's rest."

Left alone in the room, she reached for her phone on the bedside table. A message lit the screen, reminding her of her checking account balance, which shrank daily. She bit her lip, wondering how long they could keep living like this.

Franklin Devereux's job offer dangled in her mind like ripe fruit, tempting her with financial security. It was hard not to consider it, especially with bills piling up and the future uncertain. Was she willing to risk the peace she'd found working with Chelsey and her friends?

Darren returned, arms laden with chopped firewood. He stacked them by the fireplace before shedding his jacket and boots. She listened to his movements, still tossing and turning under the quilt. When he finally crawled into bed beside her, she cursed herself for not appreciating the life they had built together.

"Darren, do you ever think about what our lives would be like if we hadn't chosen this path?"

He turned to face her. "What do you mean?"

"Living in this cabin, the simplicity of it all. Do you ever wonder if we're missing out on something?"

He paused, considering her question. "I think about it sometimes. But then I remember the life we've built together, and I wouldn't trade it for anything."

His certainty warmed her heart, but her thoughts kept circling back to the job offer. Was she becoming greedy, wanting both love and money?

"Do you think there's any chance Eddie Monroe might have set up Phillip somehow?"

"Why would he do that?" Darren murmured, his voice heavy with exhaustion.

"Maybe to steal Phillip's business, or . . . I don't know." She hesitated, feeling foolish for voicing her concerns. "It's just strange, isn't it, that he captured that photo of Phillip fighting outside the bar? Right place, right time? Or is there more to it?"

"Maybe." Darren yawned. "But right now, you have nothing that points to Eddie being involved. Besides, people capture conflict on their phones all the time. Doesn't mean they're killers."

As he drifted off to sleep, the warmth of his body pressed against hers, she stared into the darkness. The question did not cease. And with each passing moment, the answer seemed to slip further from her grasp.

Sleep refused to come. She remembered Thomas's words as he'd collected Patricia Hudson's belongings—photographs, letters, and other mementos that might hold vital clues. She'd hoped to find something that would dissociate Phillip from the murders, but the journal made her more certain that he could kill if provoked. Yet the way he'd reacted when they'd shown him the photograph of the fight threw another wrench into the works.

Could Eddie Monroe be the murderer, framing Phillip to throw them off? The guy sure was brazen; he'd asked her for money to see the picture.

Exhausted by her racing thoughts, Raven succumbed to a restless sleep. In the depths of her dreams, she sat across from Franklin Devereux, his eyes boring into her as he slid an employment contract over the desk. Hesitantly, she signed her name, feeling as if she had just sold her soul.

"Raven, you won't regret this."

Devereux smirked, and the scene shifted.

Now she stood in a dimly lit room, the atmosphere heavy with despair. Chelsey, her face gaunt and eyes hollow, huddled in a corner, a needle clutched in a trembling hand. The sight of her friend in such a state tore at Raven's heart, a painful flashback to her own mother's struggles with addiction.

"Chelsey, no!" Raven cried out, rushing to her side. "Please, don't do this."

"Too late. You chose your path, and now I have to choose mine."

"Chelsey, please."

Chelsey injected the heroin, her body shuddering as the drug took hold. And as her eyes rolled back in her head, Raven screamed.

Jolting awake, her heart pounding, she untangled herself from the sweat-soaked sheets. She gasped for air, wiping away the tears that dampened her cheeks. Blinking, she glanced at the digital clock on the bedside table. The red numbers read 4:00 a.m. Darren slumbered beside her, unaware of her turmoil.

Careful not to wake him, she slipped out of bed and tiptoed across the wooden floor towards the knotted pine cabin kitchen. Retrieving the laptop from a drawer, she opened it and reviewed the investigation notes, desperate to distract herself from the vivid nightmare.

It was just a dream. Nothing more.

She scrolled through the documents and images they had collected. As she studied the evidence, her mind spun, searching for any piece of information that could lead them closer to solving this case and putting her restless conscience at ease.

Darren would tell her not to obsess, but she couldn't help herself. Frustration mounted as she sifted through the autopsy reports.

Her eyes lingered on a photo of Phillip; his expression was unreadable. The question of his guilt or innocence tugged her in opposite directions, and the suspicion surrounding Eddie Monroe added another layer of complexity. Despite the early hour, she forced herself to press on.

She had to solve this for Chelsey and Thomas. And if Phillip Space was innocent, she would prove it.

30

The door clicked shut behind Raven as she left Wolf Lake Consulting. Her footsteps faded into the distance. LeVar slumped down in his chair, his eyes lingering on the space where Raven had been only moments before. The room felt colder, somehow empty without her presence.

"Y'all noticed it too, huh?" LeVar asked, breaking the silence. "Raven's been acting . . . different lately."

Scout adjusted her glasses. "I thought it was just me," she said, looking over at Chelsey. "But she seems off. Like she's not really here, you know?"

Chelsey sat on the edge of her desk, her arms folded. "Yeah, I've seen it too. It's like something's eating away at her. I hope it wasn't what I told her about the taxes and energy bill."

"What about the taxes and energy bill?" LeVar asked.

"Uh . . . nothing. Don't worry about it. We were talking about Raven, right?"

LeVar rubbed his chin. "Her focus ain't what it used to be. And she's still hung up on Phillip Space being innocent. Plus, she's evasive. That's not like her at all."

"It's like she's constantly distracted. I mean, have you seen her eyes lately? They look so tired."

As they spoke, images of his sister's recent behavior flashed through his mind—her once-vibrant smile strained, her eyes distant and unfocused.

"Something's definitely going on with her," Scout said. "We need to figure out what it is. We can't afford to have her off her game right now."

Their shared concern lent a dense quiet to the room. They all knew Raven's wellbeing was crucial, not only to the success of their investigations, but to the fabric of their tight-knit group.

"We need to keep an eye on her, make sure she's okay. And if that doesn't work, a little intervention never hurt."

Chelsey cringed. "Be careful. She's not the soft and cuddly type."

"I can handle my sister."

Chelsey's fingers curled around the edge of the table as she rolled a shiver out of her body. "She's been distant lately, even in our personal moments. I keep thinking she'll come around, but she never does."

The sound of the office door opening interrupted their conversation, and Darren stepped inside. He held an inquisitive expression that seemed to take in everything at once, and his timing, as always, was impeccable. As Chelsey, LeVar, and Scout exchanged glances, Darren closed the door behind him and crossed the room to join them.

"Am I interrupting something?" he asked, his eyes flicking from one to the other.

"Actually, we were just discussing Raven," Chelsey said, filling Darren in on their observations and concerns. He listened, his hands stuffed in his pockets, his expression unreadable.

When Chelsey finished, Darren nodded. "I see," he said, his

voice low and measured. "She's acting fine at home, but I trust your judgment. If you say something's wrong, then I'll talk to her."

"Thanks, Darren," LeVar said. "We're just worried about her, is all."

"Any idea what's bothering her?" Scout asked.

Darren hesitated for a moment before shaking his head. "I couldn't tell you. But whatever it is, I'm sure we can help her through it."

The silence in the room became deafening as LeVar studied Darren's face, searching for any sign of hidden knowledge. He considered the forest ranger a close friend, someone who would never hold out on him. But Darren had a guarded look on his face that made LeVar wonder.

"You sure you haven't noticed her acting weird? All secretive and such?"

The ranger's eyes turned away as his jaw tightened. "We all have our secret challenges. She deserves her privacy too."

"Of course, we respect that," Chelsey said, her hand resting on LeVar's arm. "But if she's struggling with something, we want to help."

Darren sighed, his shoulders slumping. It was clear he knew more than he was letting on, but he kept his secrets locked behind a steely gaze. His silence spoke volumes, adding to the sense of unease that already permeated the room. Was something going on with Ma? Were Raven's financial troubles worse than they knew?

"Look, we're not asking you to betray her trust," LeVar said. "Just give us a clue, something to work with."

Before Darren could respond, his eyes caught sight of a photo pinned to the bulletin board across the room. As if seizing the opportunity to divert the conversation, he walked over and plucked it from the cluttered array of case files and witness statements. "This photo," he said, holding up the image of Phillip Space engaged in a heated altercation with an unidentified man. "It might be worth looking into."

"We've already determined Phillip has a belligerent streak. Doesn't prove he's a murderer, but the facts keep adding up."

"The question is, who's the guy?"

"Apparently, an enemy."

"If this guy has reason to set up Phillip, he could be the killer."

The others exchanged glances, their interest piqued by this new angle. The animosity depicted in the photo provided a tangible lead worthy of exploration, a thread that might unravel the mystery they had been grappling with. Why hadn't they thought of the other man in the photo?

"Fair point," Chelsey said. "We should find out who he is."

LeVar studied the picture as he considered Darren's suggestion. He couldn't deny the potential significance. He had a difficult time believing Phillip Space was the victim of some elaborate setup, but he knew better than to question Darren's instincts.

"All right," LeVar said, unable to mask his interest. "Let's focus on this guy. We need to find out who he is and what his connection to Phillip might be."

Darren's shoulders tensed as he placed the photograph back on the board. It was clear he knew more about his girlfriend's situation than he was letting on, but he kept his secrets locked behind a stoic expression. His eyes often strayed to Raven's empty desk, as if this knowledge were a burden.

"We should talk to the bartender at the bar where the fight took place," Chelsey said. "We need to find out who this guy is and what led to the altercation."

Scout hopped out of her seat, rearing to go though she was underage. "We can ask other patrons, See if anyone else witnessed the fight or knows anything about the man in the picture."

LeVar sensed the restless energy in the room, the desire to learn if his sister's doubts about the investigation were valid. He knew they would need to address her situation eventually, but for now their focus had to remain on the task at hand.

"No sense letting the grass grow under our feet," he said, pushing himself up from the table. "We'll interview the bartender and any witnesses we can find. I have a hard time buying this person murdered two women just to make Phillip Space the fall guy, but I listen when my sister raises concerns."

31

Inside The Broken Yolk, the familiar aroma of donuts and coffee filled the air. Raven had spent countless mornings here, the cafe acting as a sanctuary in times of trouble. Today she needed this respite more than ever.

"Morning, Raven," Ruth, the cafe's owner, greeted her with a smile as she wiped down the counter, her apron dusted with flour. "The usual?"

"Actually, I'll just have a strong coffee and a croissant today, please."

"One strong coffee and an extra-sweet croissant, it is. Oh, your mother is here."

"She is?"

Raven glanced over to where Ma stood, chatting animatedly with a worker as she set a batch of her famous cinnamon rolls on the counter. Ma and Naomi Mourning always baked treats and dropped them off for Ruth.

She made her way to a quiet corner at the back of the room, taking a table tucked away from the regular morning crowd. Her fingers tapped on the table, drumming out an anxious rhythm. She watched her mother, who was now exchanging goodbyes with Ruth, the two women sharing a hug before parting ways.

"Here you go, sweetheart." Ma approached the table, carrying a steaming cup of coffee and a flaky croissant. She set them down, her dark eyes softening with concern. "You look like you could use this."

"Thanks," she said, reaching for the coffee and taking a sip, letting the bitter liquid scald her tongue before swallowing. "I really need this."

"Problems?"

Her gaze lingered on the rich brown liquid in her cup, the steam rising and dissipating like the ghosts of lost opportunities. She debated whether to burden her mother with her worries.

"Things have been rough lately. Money's tight, and I'm not sure if I can keep the SUV. Then there's my job at Wolf Lake Consulting."

"Your job? But you love working with Chelsey and LeVar. There can't be trouble at the office. You know you can always talk to me, right? No matter what it is, I'm here for you."

Raven swallowed the lump in her throat. "I know, Ma. Thank you."

She glanced out the window, watching the raindrops trace their way down the glass. It would be so easy to confide in her mother, to let her in on the storm brewing inside her. But she didn't want to be a bother.

"Really, I'm okay. Just tired and a little overwhelmed."

"I know when something's wrong. You don't have to hide it from me."

She felt her resolve crumbling, her facade cracking under the weight of her mother's love and concern. She sighed, the fight draining from her. "I'm not sure what to do."

"Tell me about it," Ma said, her thumb stroking the back of Raven's hand.

"Ma, I've been struggling with my finances lately, and I'm not sure about my job."

"Is that so?"

She nodded, looking down at her coffee cup as she traced its rim with her finger. "I might lose the SUV if things don't improve, and things aren't going so well with Wolf Lake Consulting's profits. It's just been really tight. But please keep that between us."

"I remember when your father left us and how difficult it was to make ends meet. But you know what got us through? Our resilience and determination."

"Resilience, huh?" Raven managed a small, half-hearted laugh. "Resilience won't pay the bills. Sometimes I feel like I'm running on empty."

"Raven, you're stronger than you give yourself credit for. You're an excellent private investigator and have made a difference in people's lives. You work with your best friend and your brother, and they both love you. What more could you ask for?"

"Sometimes I second-guess myself."

"Self-doubt is normal, dear. But remember, you're the one who solved the Brandt case, and you helped that lost girl find her way home last year. You have a gift, my love."

Raven absorbed her mother's words, allowing their truth to seep in like a healing balm. "You're right, of course. I shouldn't let setbacks define me."

"You need to keep moving forward, no matter what life throws your way."

"There's something else I need to tell you." Raven took a sip of her coffee, gathering her thoughts. "I got a job offer from Franklin Devereux."

"Devereux?" Ma raised an eyebrow. "Isn't he that wealthy businessman who owns half of Center Street in Harmon?"

"That's him. He offered me a position in his company's security department. Actually, he wants me to lead his team. The salary is more than what I'm making now. A lot more."

"Well, that sounds like a tempting opportunity. But have you considered how this will affect your relationship with Chelsey?"

Raven's gaze dropped to her half-eaten croissant, her appetite vanishing. "I haven't been able to tell her yet. I mean, Chelsey and I are close, but I can't help thinking that maybe it's time for a change, you know? Something to get me out of this rut."

"Money is important, but there's more to life than just a paycheck. You've built a good thing at Wolf Lake Consulting, and you've helped so many people."

"Chelsey has been like family to me. But I'm drowning. This job offer could be my lifeline."

"Sometimes we must make tough choices," Ma conceded. "Don't let money be the sole factor in your decision. Think about what you truly want, and how this choice will affect the people you care about."

Images of Chelsey from her nightmare swirled in her head. It was just a dream, but didn't all dreams grow from a seed of truth? There was more to consider than just a salary increase.

"I'll think about it, I promise."

"Just remember, whatever you decide, I'll support you. Take some time to think about it. Consider all the factors, not just the financial ones. Sometimes the most difficult decisions are the ones that need to be made, but you need to make them for the right reasons. Maybe you could talk to Chelsey about your struggles."

Raven's fingers tightened around the cup. "No," she said, shaking her head. "I can't let her know I'm thinking of quitting. She's counting on me."

"Sharing our burdens helps to lighten the load. And I think Chelsey might understand more than you give her credit for."

"No, I need to handle this on my own."

"Stubborn as a mule. Always have been."

"No arguments. But Chelsey has enough on her plate with the new taxes and higher energy rates."

"Which means she knows what you're going through."

Ma was right, but Raven couldn't bring herself to risk her friendship with Chelsey.

"Thanks, Ma. I'll think it over."

"You know, Buck and I will help you," Ma offered, her voice filled with compassion.

She shook her head. "No, Ma, I can't accept that. I need to do this on my own. I'm an adult."

"Okay, if that's what you want. Remember, you're stronger than you think," Ma said, placing some money on the table and rising from her seat.

"I can't take your money."

"Fool, that ain't for you. That's a tip for the server."

The moment of levity made Raven laugh at herself.

"Take care, baby girl," Ma said, giving her daughter one last look before walking away.

Left alone at the table, she peered into her coffee as if she could read in it the answer to the questions plaguing her: Should she stay at Wolf Lake Consulting, risking further financial instability? Or should she accept Devereux's offer—one that would solve her money issues forever?

"Can I get you anything else?" the server asked, pulling Raven's attention back to the present.

"Another coffee, please."

She needed an excuse not to return to work and face the people she planned to betray.

"Coming right up."

As the girl disappeared, Raven sought calm amidst the chaos of her worries. Devereux was waiting for her decision, and Chelsey's business might not survive the year.

For once, Raven needed to think of herself.

32

The bar stank of stale beer and shattered dreams. The team—Darren, Chelsey, LeVar, and Scout—shuffled in, their eyes adjusting to the darkness. They spotted a middle-aged man wiping down glasses with a damp cloth behind the bar. His name was Mike, and he was known for his straightforward demeanor.

"Darren. Long time no see," Mike called out, recognizing him from the state park. His gaze fell upon Scout, and his eyebrows shot up in surprise. "And you brought a young one to my bar? What can I get you? A Shirley Temple?"

"Mike, she'll only be in the bar for a minute," Darren said with a snicker, "and we're not here to drink. Scout's helping us with something important."

"All right, all right," Mike said, laughing. "Just making sure you know the rules."

"Don't forget, I was a cop before I started policing wildlife." He gave Mike a wry smile, setting his forearms on the bar. "Remember the last time you tried to pull a fast one on me, Mike? Ended up with my pants drenched in beer."

Mike let out a hearty laugh, pointing at Darren accusingly.

"That wasn't on me. It was that rickety stool's fault. You've always had a knack for picking the worst seats."

LeVar and Chelsey exchanged amused glances while Scout looked from one man to the other, clearly entertained by their banter.

"Oh, speaking of seats," Darren said with a teasing glint in his eyes, "Do you still have that lopsided chair in the corner? The one you always 'reserved' for customers you didn't like?"

Mike pretended to look offended. "Darren, I'm hurt. I'd never do such a thing." He winked at Scout. "Only for this one here when he needed . . . shall we say, a humbling experience?"

Scout couldn't help but giggle, and even Chelsey and LeVar joined in. The atmosphere lightened. For a moment, it was just two friends catching up, reminiscing about the good old days.

Darren gave Mike a mock salute. "Always good to be back, Mike. Just keep that chair away from me this time."

Mike chuckled. "No promises."

"Listen, we're here on business. This is Chelsey Byrd. She heads up Wolf Lake Consulting. And LeVar is a deputy with the sheriff's department."

Chelsey stepped forward. She held up a photo, showing it to Mike. "We need your help to identify this man. He was fighting with Phillip Space, and we think it might be connected to a case we're working on."

Mike squinted at the photo, studying the men captured in the grainy image. Recognition flashed in his eyes, and he let out a low whistle. "That's Jackson Anders. I had to ban him from this place. Started too much trouble; couldn't handle his temper."

"Jackson Anders, huh? What can you tell us about him?"

"Jack's always been a hothead. Got into fights over the smallest things. He seemed to have it out for anyone who was doing better than him."

"Like Phillip?"

"Yes, like Phillip. Jackson saw him as a symbol of everything he couldn't have—someone who'd come from nothing and become a business owner, respected by the community."

LeVar sat on a stool. "Sounds like someone we need to look into."

"Jack had a problem with people who were successful or well-liked," Mike said, wiping a glass with a white cloth. "He'd find any reason to pick a fight with them. Just couldn't stand seeing others do better than him."

"Did he ever target anyone besides Phillip?" Chelsey asked.

Mike paused, considering the question. "I remember one fella, a doctor from out of town. Good guy. Didn't deserve the trouble Jack gave him. But Jack saw him as another example of someone doing better than him. Ended up getting into a brawl right here in the bar. I had to call the sheriff's department to break it up."

LeVar drummed his fingers on the counter, lost in thought. "So it seems like Jack has a history of going after people he perceives as threats to his own sense of self-worth."

"Sounds about right," Mike said, placing the now-clean glass on the shelf behind him. "And Phillip was just unfortunate enough to get caught in Jack's crosshairs. That's my guess."

Darren sat beside LeVar. "Do you think he could have taken things further this time? Maybe even murder?"

"Whoa, now. You're the former cop, not me."

"Humor us."

"Hard to say. But if there's one thing I know about Jack, it's that he's unpredictable. Can go from calm to a raging storm in the blink of an eye."

"Did you see the fight?"

"I didn't, but I heard about it. Maggie was tending bar that night."

"Ah, your second in charge."

"More like first. You should come back when she's on. Maggie's out of town for the day, but she'll be on shift tomorrow night."

"Mike, what else can you tell us about Jackson's past?" Chelsey asked. "Anything that could help us understand his actions better?"

Mike yawned and rubbed a knot out of his shoulder. "Well, I don't know the entire story, but I've heard some things over the years. He has a history of violence, that's for sure. Been in more than one scrap, usually ending with someone in the hospital. And it's not just bar fights. I've seen him get into it with cops too."

"Confrontations with authority figures?" LeVar interjected, his expression grim.

"Yup. He's always been a bit of a loose cannon. I remember one time, he got pulled over for speeding, and instead of calming down and taking the ticket, he tried to fight the officer. Ended up with a broken nose and a night in jail for that stunt."

Scout frowned. "So he's unstable?"

"Seems like it. One day he's all friendly and laughing, the next he's on the warpath. Heard he struggled with drugs. That might have something to do with it."

"Sounds like a toxic mix of envy, insecurity, and a need for validation," Chelsey mused, her hands clasped. "The sort of person who might go to extreme lengths to ruin someone's life."

"It fits," Darren said, nodding at her assessment. "Someone who matches the profile of a potential killer."

"Wait," Mike said, his eyes wide. "You think Jackson Anders could be . . . ?"

"Let's not jump to conclusions," said LeVar, holding up a hand. "We don't have enough evidence to say for sure, but it's worth looking into. Either way, we need to monitor him. If he's involved in the attacks, we can't afford to let him slip through our fingers."

Chelsey squinted in contemplation. "Raven seems convinced someone set up Phillip Space for the murders. We'll gather what information we can, and if it points to Jackson Anders being our guy, we'll take it from there."

Uncovering the truth was not only crucial for Phillip Space's innocence but also for the safety of their community.

As they climbed into their respective vehicles, Darren couldn't escape the uneasy feeling that had settled in the pit of his stomach. The drive to the sheriff's department was a quiet one, each of them lost in thought about the implications of their discovery.

"Phillip could be innocent," LeVar said as they neared their destination. "But if we're right about Jackson, he's still out there, and who knows how many more people could be in danger."

"We can't let anyone else become a victim. Thomas will know what to do," Darren said. "We've uncovered solid evidence, and that will make a difference."

"Let's hope it's enough."

As they pulled into the parking lot of the sheriff's department, Darren took a moment to collect himself. The importance of their discovery and the consequences for both Phillip and the community played in his mind.

Was Raven right about the arrested man's innocence?

33

Thomas and Aguilar, their breath visible in the cold air, stood at the edge of the property, taking in the sight of Jackson Anders' dilapidated house. The melting ice on the walkway glistened in the light. The windows were devoid of life and held an aura of abandonment and neglect.

"Looks like no one's been here for a while," Thomas said.

"Feels like we're walking up to a haunted house," said Aguilar, her eyes assessing the yard and the shadows cast by the skeletal trees. "But we've gotta check it out."

They approached the house, aware of Jackson's volatile nature and the violence he was capable of. The front door creaked open on its own, hanging ajar, a disturbing sign that amplified their apprehension. Thomas glanced at Aguilar, the unspoken question hanging between them. Could this mean Jackson was in danger?

"Better safe than sorry." Thomas's hand rested on the butt of his gun. "We go in without a warrant, but we say it was because we thought he was in trouble."

"I can buy that. After you."

Thomas announced their presence and called out to Jackson, but no reply came. As they crossed the threshold, he replayed the image of the suspect fighting Phillip Space in his mind, trying to make sense of their connection. The jealousy, the rage, the troubled past. It all seemed to fit, but perhaps too well.

"Stay alert," Thomas said as they stepped into the dark, musty interior of the house. The air felt thick with hatred.

They were trespassing in the home of a dangerous man, searching for evidence that might connect him to multiple murders. And as they moved deeper into the darkness of the abandoned sanctuary, Thomas worried they were walking a fine line between pursuing justice and provoking a monster.

The wan light filtering through the grimy windows weaved disfigured shapes on the furniture and scattered belongings. He wrinkled his nose at the acrid smell of stale food as they ventured further inside.

"Looks like Jackson left in a hurry," Aguilar said, stepping carefully over a broken picture frame. "Or someone turned this place upside down."

"Either way, we need to find evidence linking him to the murders."

As he moved from room to room, his thoughts considered potential scenarios. What if Jackson was hiding inside, watching them? What if he'd already fled, leaving behind a trail of dead bodies?

A sudden crash from the adjacent room jolted Thomas, his heart pounding.

"Everything okay?" he called out.

"Sorry," Aguilar answered sheepishly. "Knocked over a stack of dishes."

He allowed himself a grin before returning to the task. The house seemed to be an endless maze of clutter and decay, each corner revealing more disarray than the last. But in the chaos,

Thomas spotted something that stood out—an empty bottle lying near a pile of discarded clothing. Picking it up, he saw the label: medication prescribed for schizophrenia.

"Hey, Aguilar. Found something interesting here."

"What is it?" She emerged from the kitchen. "Jackson's meds?"

"Looks like it. This might explain his erratic behavior."

"It doesn't prove he's our killer. If anything, it suggests he was doing what he could to gain control of his emotions."

"True. But it's a piece of the puzzle. You didn't break any dishes, did you?"

"Nope. Just knocked them over. The kitchen is such a mess, he'll never know the difference."

Was Jackson Anders their man, or were they chasing ghosts? He crossed the unkempt living room. Surveying the disorganized mess, his eyes landed on a pile of newspapers. The headlines quickened his pulse.

"Aguilar, check this out."

"Newspapers?"

"Look." Thomas held up a paper, revealing articles about the murders. Someone had underlined notes about the victims and how they died. He flipped through the others, finding the same pattern in each edition. "He's been following the murders."

"Or planning them. This is unsettling."

"Still think Phillip Space is our man?"

"Not so much anymore."

He scanned the highlighted words, as if trying to decode some hidden message. Was this damning evidence against Jackson, or just the ramblings of a disturbed mind?

"Thomas, we need to check the rest of the house, but this is damning evidence. I don't want to jump to conclusions, but we need to let the team know what we found."

"Right." He glanced around the living room once more,

taking in every detail. "Make sure everything stays exactly as we found it. We don't want to give Jackson any reason to believe we're onto him."

Together they began the careful process of securing the house and preserving the evidence for further investigation. After checking the bedrooms, Thomas radioed dispatch that they'd finished searching. As they exited Jackson's home, a sense of dread enveloped the sheriff. Would they be able to find Jackson before he claimed another victim?

"Thomas," Aguilar said. "We'll find him."

"I should have listened to Raven."

"You did, and we let Phillip Space go. Then another person died."

"Now what? I can't let him go again until we're sure, but every second that passes, I worry I'm holding an innocent man in a cell."

They climbed back into their vehicle. The sun was setting on another day in Nightshade County. And for Thomas Shepherd, the weight of that darkness was growing heavier.

The sheriff's office was a somber place when Thomas and Aguilar returned. They gathered their team around the worn wooden table at the center of the office, each face illuminated by the buzzing lights.

"Jackson Anders," Thomas said, laying out the incriminating newspapers on the table before them. "He collected articles on the murders and underlined passages. I'm starting to think he's our guy."

LeVar picked up a newspaper and studied the highlighted articles. "If he isn't guilty, why would he save these newspapers?"

"His house was a mess, like he'd been living in chaos," Aguilar added. "And we found medication prescribed for schizophrenia."

Lambert scratched behind his ear. "This is serious. He could be anywhere, and if he's not taking his meds . . ."

"Exactly," Thomas said. "We need to find him. It's possible he's losing touch with reality. We'll launch a manhunt." Each person wore a steely expression. They were ready for the challenge. "Here's the plan. We're down a junior deputy and need extra help. LeVar, grab Darren at Wolf Lake Consulting. I want you two to head over to Jackson's workplace. See if anyone there has any leads on where he might be."

"Got it, Shep," LeVar said. He headed for the door.

"Lambert, call Chelsey and Scout. I want you to comb through local surveillance footage. Look for any sightings of Jackson. If he's been anywhere near the crime scenes, we need to know."

Lambert picked up the phone. "On the case, boss man."

"Good. Aguilar, you and I will work here. We need to delve deeper into Jackson's criminal records. There might be something in his past that can tell us where he is."

As his team dispersed, each member focused on their respective tasks, he felt a swell of pride at their unity. They were all committed to catching a killer. Even if Jackson Anders were innocent, he was a danger to himself and others without his medication.

Aguilar sifted through the criminal records, each new discovery painting a darker picture of the man they hunted.

34

It was dark by the time Raven returned to the cabin. Her mind was a whirlwind of thoughts and doubts. Darren had spent the afternoon helping the sheriff's department investigate the murders. She got the distinct impression the others hadn't wanted her to help.

She entered the home. Darren sat by the woodstove, his hands rubbing together in front of the dancing flames. The scent of burning pine filled the air, and the warmth of the crackling fire made her feel at home.

"Hey," she said, closing the door behind her.

He looked up as she entered. There was no hiding the turmoil in her eyes or the tension in her shoulders. She sensed something significant had transpired during her time away. Without a word, he gestured for her to join him on the couch.

She settled next to him. Their bodies found solace in each other. She took a deep breath, gathering the courage to share her conflict. He remained patient, his dark eyes fixed on her.

"You look like you have something to tell me," he said.

"Devereux raised the salary offer. I'm struggling, Darren. I don't want to lose the SUV, and I don't know if I can handle destroying my relationship with Chelsey."

"Tell me more."

With a mixture of vulnerability and desperation, she opened up about everything—the free-falling account balance, her loyalty to Wolf Lake Consulting, and her fears of damaging the bonds she'd formed.

"Money isn't everything," he said. "You need to follow your heart and decide what matters most to you."

She stared into the fire, watching as the embers floated like sprites. She knew she needed to dig deep within herself and search for what truly mattered to her.

He listened with empathy as she confessed her fears. His hand reached out to take hers. The warmth of his touch provided silent assurance.

"Raven, I won't let you lose your SUV. I'll help you make the payments and take care of the repairs."

She scoffed, shaking her head. "No, Darren. I can't let you do that. It's not your responsibility to pay my bills. We're not married."

"Should it matter? At least let me help you in some other way. You don't have to face this alone."

She looked into his eyes, seeing the sincerity behind his offer.

"It's not just about the money. I'm torn between staying at Wolf Lake Consulting and taking Devereux's offer. I do meaningful work with Chelsey and the team, but the financial security is hard to turn away from."

"Is it worth leaving behind something you value?"

"Maybe not. But I worry about how my decision might affect the future of Wolf Lake Consulting. Chelsey's struggling. I didn't want to tell you, but the increased village costs are taking a bite out of her profits."

"Have you talked to her about it?"

"Briefly. Chelsey runs the show, but I feel like we built that place together, you know? If it dies, a part of me will die with it."

"Raven, relationships are built on trust and open communication. Chelsey is your friend, and friends help each other through difficult times."

She nodded as she contemplated her options. Her fingers tightened around his, seeking strength and reassurance.

"All right. I'll talk to Chelsey. I owe her an honest conversation about my struggles. Hopefully she'll come clean about hers as well."

"I think you'll find that the more open you are with her, the stronger your bond will become."

"You're probably right."

The fire provided a welcome respite from the chill of doubt and uncertainty.

"Ya know, when I left the Syracuse PD to become a ranger, I took a huge pay cut. But I love it here. The fresh air, the peace. It was the best decision I ever made." He paused, allowing her to absorb his words. "Sometimes we need to listen to our gut, even if it means going against what seems like the sensible choice. Money is important, but it can't guide our principles."

"No, it can't."

"Ask yourself what truly matters to you. Life is full of uncertainties, and it's in those moments of doubt that you need to trust yourself the most."

His words resonated, stirring long-buried memories and emotions. She thought back to the day she'd first joined Wolf Lake Consulting, the excitement of being part of something meaningful, and the friendships she had forged since. Clarity emerged from the haze of confusion and illuminated a path she hadn't considered.

"It's about who I am, what I value, and the people I care about."

"You got it," Darren said, the corners of his eyes crinkling with affection. "Take your time, weigh your options, and be true to yourself. No matter what you decide, I'll back you up."

"I can't let Wolf Lake Consulting go under. No matter what I choose, that place holds too many memories. Considering my own struggles, I'm not one to talk, but I feel like Chelsey makes questionable decisions in her business."

"Like what?"

"For starters, she doesn't have a vision for the future. It's all about profit for the current month. That's why she's never prepared when Murphy's Law comes calling."

"What would you do if you were running the show?"

"Quite a few things. I'd focus on return on investment instead of profit. It's shortsighted to take on dozens of low-paying clients when one high-profile investigation pays just as much and takes a fraction of the time."

He nodded in agreement, his hand coming to rest on hers. "Why haven't you told her any of this?"

Raven shrugged. "I guess because I didn't think it was my place."

"You work there, and you're her friend. She'll listen. Speaking of challenges," Darren said, shifting in his seat, "I wanted to fill you in on what we learned about Jackson Anders, the guy who got into a fight with Phillip Space."

"That's his name?"

"Turns out, Jackson has a history of mental illness and an unstable past. Mike at the bar suggested Jackson has been in his share of brawls. And Jackson hates Phillip."

Raven's eyes widened as she absorbed the information. "So you're saying it's possible that Jackson might be the one who killed Patricia and Ellen, not Phillip?"

"That's what I'm saying. It's just a theory, but considering his troubled background and animosity toward Phillip, it's worth looking into."

The revelation sank in. If Jackson was the killer, then an innocent man was suffering under false accusations.

"Then we owe it to Phillip and the victims to find the real killer."

"We'll do everything we can to sort this out."

They sat in silence a little longer, their shared resolve encompassing them. Since this case had begun, she'd believed Phillip was a troubled man trying to get his life together, not a killer. Now she had to prove it.

But could she keep Wolf Lake Consulting afloat?

35

Morning rose over the frost-covered landscape, painting a serene picture. Raven lay in bed, staring at the ceiling, her dark braids splayed out over the pillow like tangled vines. Her heart galloped in her chest, the weight of the decision she had to make bearing down on her with the force of a thousand waterfalls. She knew she couldn't keep running, and her conscience told her what she needed to do, but the thought of the conversation she must have with Chelsey filled her with apprehension.

Groaning, she reached for her phone on the nightstand and dialed Chelsey's number. As the phone rang, she grounded herself in the present moment, embracing the uncertainty that lay ahead.

"Raven, you're up early." Chelsey sounded harried.

"I need to talk to you about something important. Can we get together before work?"

"Can it wait? I'm at the office, and there's water all over the floor. I don't know what happened, but I'm trying to find a plumber who won't cost an arm and a leg."

Now wasn't the time to drop the bombshell of Devereux's job

offer. She forced a smile into her voice. "I'll come right over and help you figure it out."

"Thanks, Raven. You're a lifesaver."

"See you soon."

She set the phone on the nightstand, the conversation she'd intended to have still at the front of her mind. But for now, Chelsey needed her, and that was what mattered most.

Raven threw off the covers while Darren lay snoring. Without showering, she dressed and made her way to her Rogue, praying it wouldn't give her trouble this morning. Her thoughts turned to her mother's boyfriend, Buck. Perhaps Buck could help with their plumbing situation; it wouldn't be the first time he'd come to her aid.

The door to Wolf Lake Consulting opened, revealing the chaos within. She sidestepped over the threshold, taking in the waterlogged floor and Chelsey's frazzled appearance. Papers floated like lost ships on the sea of water, and Tigger, Chelsey's orange tabby, perched on a shelf, his eyes wide with alarm.

"Chelsey, what happened?" She felt an unexpected sense of calm wash over her; she knew helping her friend through this crisis was the right thing to do.

"Pipe burst," Chelsey said, wringing out a rag over a bucket. "I tried shutting off the water, but I'm not sure which is the main; it just keeps coming. Every plumber I call tells me there's an extra charge for working this early."

Raven surveyed the damage. "Don't worry, I've got an idea. Buck is good with plumbing. Maybe he can help us out."

"Your mom's boyfriend? You think he'd be able to fix this?"

"It's worth a try. He might not charge us as much as a professional plumber, which could help with our financial situation. What do you think?"

Chelsey glanced around her once-pristine workspace. "Yeah, let's call him. We don't have any other options."

She pulled out her phone and dialed Buck's number as Chelsey continued to salvage what she could from the flooded office.

"Hey, Buck. It's Raven. We've got a bit of a situation here at Wolf Lake Consulting. A pipe burst, and we were wondering if you might help us out."

"Sure thing," he said. "I was just throwing salt on the walkway, hopefully for the last time this spring. Give me ten minutes, okay?"

"Thanks a million. We'll be here."

Her muscles strained as she helped Chelsey lift the heavy filing cabinet, water dripping from its edges. They moved it to a dry corner of the room, their clothes soaked and sticking to their skin. Her braids had come loose; damp strands clung to her face.

"Remind me to invest in waterproof storage," Chelsey mumbled, wiping sweat from her brow with the back of her hand.

"Ha, will do." She glanced around the office. Tigger perched on a windowsill, watching the chaos with wide, curious eyes. "Hey, at least Tigger seems to be enjoying the show."

Chelsey let out a short laugh. "He has a twisted sense of humor."

"There's one silver lining in all of this."

"What's that?"

"You didn't bring Jack to the office this morning."

Chelsey palmed her forehead. "Oh, that would be an epic circus. All I need is Jack splashing around like he's playing in mud puddles."

Their laughter mingled, echoing through the disarrayed workspace. It was a strange sound considering the crisis, but it felt genuine. It was moments like these that made Raven realize she was right where she was supposed to be.

By the time they pushed the desks against the wall, the door opened and Buck stepped inside, a toolbox in hand and a reassuring smile on his face. His presence seemed to fill the room, offering a warm, comforting energy that both women needed.

"Looks like quite the mess you've got here," he said, surveying the scene. He chuckled, shook his head and found the source of the problem. The water was pouring from under the sink. "You're lucky though. It's just a burst connection. Shouldn't take me more than an hour to fix."

"That's all?"

"Not a big deal. But you should have shut off the main. No worries. I'll show you where it is."

"Thank you so much for coming, Buck."

"Happy to help," he said, setting down his toolbox and getting to work.

Raven wiped her hands on her damp jeans and resumed moving vulnerable equipment away from the water's path. She stole glances at Chelsey, who was racing to tackle the mess. Despite their exhaustion, there was a sense of camaraderie between them that grew stronger.

The rhythmic sound of Buck's wrench echoed through the room, accompanied by a low hum as he worked to repair the pipe. Raven, her heart pounding with uncertainty, seized the moment to address her own concerns.

"I know we discussed this before, but I've been struggling with my finances. My checking balance is down to nothing, and I'm not sure what to do about getting my Rogue fixed."

Chelsey paused in her efforts to salvage the paperwork. "I had no idea things were that bad. If I'm being honest, Wolf Lake Consulting is struggling just as bad. I didn't even have the funds for a plumber."

Was the business in even worse shape than she'd feared?

"Is there anything I can do?"

"Just having you by my side is enough."

Guilt tightened its hands around Raven's throat. As they sifted through the sodden paperwork, Raven took the lead, organizing the documents into neat piles and devising a plan to restore order to their workspace.

A short while later, Buck wiped his hands on a rag, surveying his handiwork with a satisfied nod. "There you go, ladies. Good as new," he announced, closing his toolbox. Raven and Chelsey exchanged relieved glances, grateful for the man's expertise. "Actually better than new."

"Thank you so much, Buck," said Chelsey, fumbling for her wallet. "How much do I owe you?"

"Ah, don't worry about it," he said, waving off her attempt to pay him. "You two are family. It's no trouble at all."

"Are you sure?" Raven asked, touched by his generosity. "We don't want to take advantage of your kindness."

"Positive. Just promise me one thing: Swear you'll monitor those pipes, and make sure you don't put any rice down the drain. Even with a garbage disposal, rice forms clogs, and clogs cause the pressure to build until bursts occur."

"Thanks for telling me," Chelsey said. "I'll be more careful in the future. And thank you for coming out. I won't forget this."

"Anytime." With a wave and a wink, Buck left, leaving Raven and Chelsey alone to put the office back together.

"Guess we've got our work cut out for us," Chelsey muttered, tucking a strand of damp hair behind her ear.

"Nothing we can't handle," Raven said, rolling up her sleeves. "We've faced worse."

Mid-morning light streamed through the windows as they finished. They set the desks in their respective locations.

"Another positive."

"What's that?"

"All this mopping. The floors are gleaming."

Raven laughed. "You're right. They look like new."

"But I have to get control over this situation. Let's brainstorm a new budget and see where we can cut costs."

Raven nodded, assessing all aspects of Wolf Lake Consulting's finances. She recalled the ideas she'd told Darren about. "We could start by increasing our rates. We've been charging the same prices since we started, and our experience and expertise have grown by leaps and bounds. It would also help to focus on high-paying clients and take a step back from the stuff that ties up our time."

"True. But I'm worried that raising our prices might drive away clients."

"Maybe we can offer a discount for referrals or repeat customers. That way we can keep our loyal clients while attracting new ones with our increased rates."

"I like that idea."

They bounced ideas off one another and refined their financial plan. As they worked, Raven couldn't help but feel the weight of Devereux's job offer pressing down on her.

And it was only a matter of time before she lost her SUV.

36

Raven's hands ached as she wrung out the damp cloth and wiped down the surfaces of the office. The stink of mildew still lingered in the air, a reminder of the plumbing incident that wouldn't dissipate soon. As she worked, her thoughts drifted back to the conversation she'd had with Chelsey.

The door opened as she tossed the cloth into a bucket. She glanced down the hallway to see Thomas and Aguilar enter. They had been grappling with their own challenges, including the pursuit of Jackson Anders.

"Thomas, Aguilar. It's all right to enter now. I'm just cleaning up the last of this water damage."

"I wish you had called me," Thomas said as he stepped into the room. "I would have helped."

Aguilar followed closely, nodding in agreement.

"Any updates?"

She knew Jackson Anders had become the prime suspect in the series of grisly murders that had rocked their small community.

"Nothing worth mentioning yet," Aguilar said. "He hasn't been home in days, and nobody in the village has seen him."

As they spoke, Raven finished cleaning the last of the wet surfaces and tossed another dirty cloth into a trash bin.

"Let me know if there's anything I can do to help," she offered, trying to hide her growing unease. Did Thomas and Aguilar blame her for the Phillip Space situation?

"Will do," Thomas said. "And thanks again for cleaning up this mess. Chelsey and I owe you."

"It was the least I could do. So you think Jackson Anders is the killer? Where do you think he's hiding?"

"We've checked everywhere we could think of—his known haunts, friends, family. It's like he vanished."

Aguilar nodded in agreement. "It's frustrating. We don't have any proof he killed those women, but he's off his meds and on the run. The longer he's in the wind, the more dangerous he becomes."

Raven glanced down at her hands, realizing they were trembling. "Did you find anything at his house?"

Thomas hesitated before speaking, as if he didn't want to bring Raven back into the investigation. "We found medication for schizophrenia, newspaper clippings related to the murders, and the state of his home . . . it wasn't good."

"Clearly, he's unstable," Aguilar said. "Like I said, we can't prove he's a killer, but those newspaper clippings look bad for him."

Raven conjured images of Jackson's unkempt home, dark and foreboding, entrapping its owner in a twisted web of delusion and obsession. Plus, he'd attacked Phillip Space, suggesting he had a motive to set up Phillip for the murders.

"Chelsey should know about this," Raven said.

As if summoned by her words, Chelsey appeared in the doorway, a bandana pulling back her sweaty hair. Her sleeves were rolled up to her elbows, hands chapped from scrubbing the kitchen.

"Know about what?" she asked, her gaze darting from Raven to the officers.

"Jackson's mental state. They found evidence at his house that he's suffering from schizophrenia."

"Thomas told me last night. The question is, where is he?"

"I don't like that someone is taking pictures of you," Thomas said, turning his attention to Raven. "Stay vigilant."

"Jackson's unpredictable," Aguilar added. "We can't underestimate him, though his motivations are unclear. He could be acting out of jealousy, paranoia, or both. If he can't find Phillip, he might target someone else."

"Someone like us?" Chelsey asked.

"Desperate people can be dangerous," Aguilar conceded, sipping her tea. "Whoever is taking those pictures knows your team is investigating the case. We have to consider all possibilities."

"Then what should we do?" Raven asked.

"Stay in groups and take necessary precautions," Thomas said. "It's better to be safe than sorry. We're working with neighboring police departments and the state police to track Jackson down. He can't stay on the run forever."

"Watch your surroundings," Aguilar said. "And don't hesitate to call us if anything seems off."

"Let's not let it paralyze us," Chelsey said, as if reading Raven's thoughts. "We have work to do, and we can't let fear stop us from catching him. Besides, if he's following us, that will make it easier to find him."

Chelsey was right. They had a business to run, clients to help, and a murder investigation to solve. They couldn't afford to let anxiety stop them.

"Thank you for the warning," Chelsey said. "Please keep us updated. But for now, we have to finish cleaning."

"There are outfits in the village that specialize in cleaning up after floods," Thomas said.

"I'm aware, but that's not in the budget right now."

"Have you called insurance?"

"Why bother? They'll only raise my rates. We saved the equipment, and that's all that matters."

Thomas looked at Raven and she shrugged.

"Well then," Thomas said, his eyes lingering on her face before he turned to leave with Aguilar. "We'd better get back at it. Talk to you later."

"Scout needs to know about this," Raven said. She seemed worried as she glanced out the window. "She's young and vulnerable, and if Jackson's as dangerous as we fear—"

"Agreed," Chelsey said. "Plus, she walks to the office from school by herself. I'll call Naomi and fill her in. We should all keep a low profile for the time being. Then we'll figure out our next steps and how to keep ourselves safe."

"It pays to be cautious."

The road ahead was uncertain, but they would navigate it together. And that knowledge made the shadows seem just a little less daunting.

Chelsey dialed Naomi's number. When the call connected, she wasted no time in relaying the information they'd just learned from Thomas and Aguilar.

"God, that's terrifying," Naomi said over the speaker. "But thank you for telling me. I'll make sure Scout knows. If I can't get away from work, I'll send someone to pick her up from school."

"Please do," Raven said. "There's no reason to believe he'll target Scout or LeVar, but we should take precautions."

"Absolutely. Keep me updated if you hear anything else."

"We will," Chelsey said.

Throughout the morning, they tackled client calls and sifted through case files with renewed focus. Despite the darkness hovering over them, they found strength in each other. If only Raven could snap her fingers and solve Wolf Lake Consulting's issues.

Then what? Even if a genie granted a wish and she saved the business, would she turn down Franklin Devereux? She had her own obligations to think about.

During their lunch break, they sat around the small table in the office's kitchen, discussing ways to make themselves less predictable targets for Jackson.

"Maybe we can change our routines," Chelsey said. "Drive different routes, take turns picking up supplies, that sort of thing."

"Smart. We could also look into upgrading the security system."

Chelsey's jaw tightened. It was obvious a security upgrade wasn't in the budget.

Afternoon crept toward dusk. Inside, Raven checked that all the windows were securely locked while Chelsey secured the doors.

"All right, everything's secure," Raven said. "Remember, let's check in with each other later tonight."

"You bet." Chelsey fidgeted with her car keys. "I'll call you once I'm home and settled."

"Same here."

Their bond had strengthened in the face of danger. They stepped out into the fading daylight, the office door shutting behind them.

"Goodnight, Raven. Stay safe."

"You too."

As Raven drove away from the office, the day's events caught up to her. She was exhausted, yet her mind wandered to

Chelsey, imagining her friend's business crumbling while she earned a six-figure salary with Devereux. And there was still Jackson Anders to worry about.

At a red light, Raven glanced at the rearview mirror, half expecting to see a sinister figure following. But the road was empty. She exhaled, trying to keep her rampant thoughts under control.

Back at the cabin, she didn't relax until Darren returned from rehabilitating the trails for spring hikers. The phone call from Chelsey came right on time, and they reassured each other they were safe for the night.

As she lay in bed, listening to the hushed sounds of the night, she knew an innocent man was in jail.

And a killer was following her.

37

Raven awoke to the glimmer of dawn seeping through the curtains of the knotted pine cabin. Her body felt heavy from yesterday's cleanup. She glanced at the digital clock on the nightstand: 6:36 a.m. With a moan, she slipped out of bed, and her bare feet touched the cold wooden floor.

Donning a thick sweater and a pair of boots, she stepped outside into the brisk morning air, her breath visible as it mingled with the chill. It didn't take long for the March cold to jolt her awake. The world around her was still, the trees like silent sentinels guarding the secrets of the forest. She fumbled for her phone in the pocket of her sweater. An unopened message from Darren awaited her. She wasn't surprised he was already working; the spring camping and hiking season would begin as soon as the weather shifted, and that could happen any day now.

Hey, Raven. I'm clearing the brush off the trails again. We need to talk about Jackson Anders. Can we meet at the cabin later?

A muscle in Raven's jaw pulsed at the mention of Jackson's name. The suspect hated Phillip Space and wanted to make his enemy suffer. What lengths would he go to? Murder? Her thumbs hovered over the screen as she typed her response quickly.

If I don't see you at the office, we'll talk over dinner.

Slipping her phone into her pocket, she opted to clear her head with a run. Inside, she changed into her running clothes and headed into the growing light. The rhythmic footfalls against the ice and packed earth resonated like a metronome, steadying her thoughts as she navigated the winding trail. Each inhalation burned her lungs until her body adjusted.

Down the trails she ran. With every turn, she marveled at how much work Darren had completed in the last week.

But a part of her wondered if Jackson Anders was in the forest. Was he the psycho taking pictures of her?

Instead of draining her energy, the five-mile run left her invigorated and ready to face the day's challenges. When she returned to the cabin, she stripped off her sweat-soaked clothes and stepped into the steaming shower, letting the hot water wash away the lingering chill. The heat penetrated her soul and provided a temporary reprieve from her worries.

Afterwards, she wrapped herself in a towel and padded to the kitchen. The aroma of freshly brewed coffee filled the air. As Raven sat at the kitchen table and picked at her breakfast, the phone rang with a call from Chelsey.

"Hey, Chelsey. I should be there within the hour. What's up?"

"We've got a problem. A key client just canceled their contract with us because of the rate increase. They're not happy."

"Wait, what? You already raised the prices?"

"Well, yeah. That's what we talked about yesterday, right?"

"Sure, but we need to take things one step at a time. How many clients did you alert?"

"All of them."

"All of them?" Raven wiped a hand across her mouth. "Okay, don't do anything else until I get there."

"Did I screw up?"

"Don't worry about it. We'll find other clients, and the ones that accept the new rates will become our most valued. Let's just talk about things before we move forward."

"I hope you're right. I'm just worried about what this means for the business."

"Trust me, we'll make it work. Focus on the clients we still have, and I'll do what I can from my end."

"Thanks, Raven. I appreciate it." Chelsey's gratitude was palpable, even over the phone. "Talk to you in a few."

Raven ended the call, her eyes fixed on her cold breakfast, her appetite gone. After she dressed, she returned to the table. Before she could toss the remains in the garbage, someone worked a key into the door. She whipped around and found Darren entering the cabin. The frosty morning had turned his cheeks and nose pink.

"I thought you were clearing the trails."

"I was," he said, removing his jacket.

"Admit it. You couldn't wait to see me."

"Something like that." He set two steaming mugs of tea before them. "Raven, I've been thinking a lot about Jackson Anders. These photographs worry me. With the investigation closing in on him, I fear he might lash out at us. Or at you."

She tightened her fingers around the mug. The warmth seeped into her palm. "I know. He's been on my mind. But Chelsey and I discussed this yesterday, and we can't let fear control us."

Her gaze flicked to the trees outside the cabin. Was Jackson in the shadows?

"But we need to be cautious. We're not only dealing with a potential serial killer, but one who knows you're on the case."

She allowed herself to melt into his comforting presence. But then she straightened and lifted her chin.

"If he shows his face, I'll take him down."

"Maybe I should drive you to work in the mornings," he suggested, watching for her reaction. "Just until we have a better handle on Jackson's movements."

Raven shook her head. "I appreciate the offer, but I don't need protection. I can take care of myself."

He sighed. "What if we find someone to watch the cabin when no one is here? Someone who knows the area and can keep an eye out for Jackson?"

"Like who?"

"Your mom's boyfriend, Buck. He knows the woods like the back of his hand. Maybe he could drive by the cabin when we're away, just to make sure everything's all right."

Raven considered the suggestion, weighing the potential benefits against the risks. "It couldn't hurt to ask. But we need to be careful about involving others. We don't want to put anyone else in danger."

"Buck spends the entire year waiting for hunting season. He won't shy away from Jackson Anders."

"If you think it's a good idea, I'll talk to him. And I promise to watch my back while I'm driving to and from the office, okay?"

"Please do. I worry about you, Raven."

She touched his cheek and planted a kiss on his lips. "I appreciate the concern, but I'm armed and dangerous."

"No arguments there."

"If you're expecting the woodland creatures to clean the park for you, you might have a long wait on your hands." She tilted her head at the window. "It's spring, remember?"

"Mother Nature doesn't think so."

"The calendar says it is. Before you know it, there will be dozens of hikers in the state park."

"You're trying to get rid of me, aren't you?"

She jingled her keys. "I really have to go."

"Okay. Just remember to keep an eye out for Jackson."

"I promise."

They kissed again, and he walked her to her vehicle before disappearing into the woods. As she climbed into her SUV, the fugitive consumed her thoughts.

"Stay safe," she whispered, more to herself than anyone else.

At the office, she found Chelsey pinning a map of Jackson Anders sightings to the wall. Raven wasted no time picking up the phone and dialing Buck's number.

"Hey, Buck," Raven said when he answered. "Listen, I need to talk to you about something important. I need another favor."

"Sure thing. You don't have another burst pipe, do you?"

"Nothing like that."

"What's going on?"

"Jackson Anders—Ma might have told you about him. Darren and I think he's dangerous. We're looking out for him, but we could use some help. Could you maybe drive past the cabin once or twice a day when we're not there? Just make sure everything looks normal?"

"No problem. You know I'd do anything to help you guys."

"Thanks, Buck. That's twice you've saved my life in the last twenty-four hours."

"Anytime."

She ended the call.

"Everything all right?" Chelsey asked.

"Darren and I talked earlier. He's worried about Jackson targeting us at the cabin, so I'm hiring Buck to look around. We're just taking some precautions, that's all."

"Understandable. Thomas and I have LeVar checking on the A-frame while we're away."

Raven slid into her chair. "Any more clients click the delete button?"

"No."

"That's an encouraging sign. Perhaps your memo will work in our favor after all."

"I hope so. Gosh, I screwed up as usual." Chelsey pushed the hair off her forehead. "I just wish I had the money to bring in someone like Naomi to run operations like she does for Shepherd Systems."

"You mean an account manager?"

"More like a strategy advisor and account manager. Someone to keep me from falling on my face."

"You built a great company," Raven said. "We'll find a way to push through this rough patch. Anyway, I have a few ideas in my head."

"I'm open to suggestions."

"We'll talk about them when we have time. Now I have to determine if Phillip Space is innocent. I can't face another day with him locked behind bars."

38

While Chelsey continued the investigation from Wolf Lake Consulting, Raven arrived at the sheriff's department. Thomas had seemed reluctant to allow her to speak to Phillip Space again, but he'd relented. His own search for Jackson Anders had led him in circles, and he was open to her opinions again. Her mind spun with thoughts of the violent confrontation between Phillip and Jackson, their faces marred by bruises and cuts.

The sterile scent of the holding cell filled the air as they approached. In the silence, their footsteps sounded loud as they echoed against the concrete walls. Phillip Space sat on the cold bench, his eyes fixed on the bars that separated them. The lights flickered, drawing a stark contrast between the shadows in the cell and the brightness of the hallway.

"Mr. Space," Thomas said, adjusting his posture in the uncomfortable chair opposite the suspect. Raven stood beside him. "Let's talk about your fight with Jackson Anders. Start at the beginning. Tell me everything that happened."

Phillip shrugged. "I don't know why he picked a fight. I was in the bar, just minding my own business, and he came at me."

Thomas gave her a doubtful glance.

"It's the truth," Phillip said.

She studied Phillip's face, searching for any signs of deception. In her time as a private investigator, she had seen countless criminals, but Phillip Space didn't strike her as the typical sociopath. Still, looks could be deceiving.

"People don't pick fights without reason," Thomas said.

"Maybe he didn't need one. He's not the type to think straight."

Thomas clenched his jaw and turned to Raven, inviting her to take the lead.

She pulled a chair from the wall and placed it beside Thomas, sitting forward with her elbows on her knees. Though she had a talent for spotting lies and deception, the man before her remained calm and composed, his eyes locked on hers.

"Phillip," she said, "we believe there was more to your altercation with Jackson than you're letting on. Can you think of anything that might have set him off?"

"Look, I already told you. I don't know what got into him. Maybe it's his condition." He paused as if carefully choosing his next words. "I'm sorry for what he's gone through, but you know how unstable he can be."

She glanced at Thomas, who gave her a nod to continue. Turning back to Phillip, she studied him, trying to locate the violent streak the sheriff's department suspected he possessed. So far, he seemed to be a master at keeping his emotions in check.

"Jackson's mental health is certainly a factor to consider, but we cannot ignore the possibility that something else—perhaps a disagreement between the two of you—might have triggered his outburst."

"Nothing happened between us. One second, I was signaling the server for another beer. The next, Phillip was in my face, saying he was gonna beat the hell out of me. Ask him what the fight was about. You're barking up the wrong tree."

"Fine. Let's talk about your past," Thomas said. "We have reports of a few incidents involving you and violence or aggression. Can you explain those?"

"I've had my share of misunderstandings, sure, but I'm no monster. People judge me without giving me a fair chance. It's difficult being the outsider."

"Can you give us an example?"

"Take what happened back in Treman Mills. A store owner accused me of stealing. I didn't take anything, but he wouldn't listen. He got all up in my face, yelling and threatening me, saying he knew I was a drunk and a waste of space."

"Did you fight him?" Raven asked.

"Only to defend myself. But that didn't matter to the police. They believed the store owner over me, just because I was down on my luck."

Was it possible this man had been wrongly accused time and time again?

"Has there ever been a situation where you were the aggressor?" Thomas pressed.

"Never. I don't start trouble, but I won't back down if someone comes at me."

Raven considered her own past and that of her family. How many times had people prejudged her? Even now that she was an accomplished private investigator, some people couldn't look past her Harmon roots. Then there was LeVar. To many, he would always be a gangster, no matter how long he worked as a sheriff's deputy.

She watched the way Phillip's fingers idly traced the cold metal bars that separated them. Despite his calm exterior, she couldn't help but wonder what churned beneath the surface. She shifted gears, hoping to move the questioning forward.

"Phillip," she said, "let's talk about your relationship with Patricia Hudson."

"What about it?"

"You admitted to a disagreement with Patricia."

"Everyone has disagreements from time to time. Listen, I overreacted. I admitted I did. But I was in a bad place, and I swore I'd finished working in her yard. I was wrong. My regret is I didn't see the truth sooner and tell her I was sorry."

As the arrested man spoke, she noticed the slight tremor in his hands and wondered whether the disagreement held more significance than he let on. Had Patricia been special to him?

"Was there anything else that might have caused a strain in your relationship with Patricia?"

"Nothing that comes to mind," he said.

If they were going to find justice for Patricia and Ellen, they needed to piece together the puzzle, and Phillip Space remained a vital piece.

"And you swear you don't know why Jackson attacked you?"

"I swear."

"Did he know Patricia?"

"Doubt it. Then again, it's a small village, so how can I say?"

"When we speak to Jackson, will he say you started the altercation?"

"Probably, but Jackson doesn't remember things so well when he's having . . . issues. You'll find this hard to accept, but I feel bad for the guy. I didn't want to fight him, didn't want to hurt him, but he gave me no choice."

He wrapped his fingers around the bars. For the first time, a helpless look came over his face.

"You helped me once," he said, looking straight at her. "Please. You have to believe me. I don't know how my ax ended up in that woman's yard, but I swear I never touched her. Someone is making me look like a murderer, but I'm not."

"The evidence says you are. Who would set you up?"

"I don't know."

"Think, Phillip. Would Jackson Anders do this? Was his grudge strong enough that he'd want to see you arrested?"

"It's possible."

"And no one else wants to ruin you?"

"Why would they? Who the hell am I in this community?"

The conversation had reached an impasse.

"I think we're done here for now," Thomas said.

Phillip stood. The blood drained from his face.

"What? You're gonna leave me in here?"

"I'll be back to speak with you again. But next time, I need you to be more forthcoming."

"I was, I swear. Ms. Hopkins, please. Don't go."

She turned her back. If she looked at him a moment longer, she would break down.

Yet she didn't buy his story about the fight. Something must have precipitated the altercation. As unstable as Jackson Anders was when he forgot to take his medication, he wouldn't attack an innocent man, would he? Was Jackson so far gone that he'd become a murderer?

A thorn of truth burrowed under Raven's skin. Since Phillip Space's lockup, there hadn't been another murder.

39

Raven turned her SUV into the parking lot outside Wolf Lake Consulting. The interview with Phillip Space still resonated in her head. As much as she wanted to believe in his innocence and place the blame on Jackson Anders, she agreed with Thomas. They couldn't release the murder suspect. Too much evidence pointed toward him being the killer.

She switched off the engine. More than anything, she wanted Chelsey's insight, her ability to discern truth from lies. Stepping out of her car, she approached the office and unlocked the door. As she stepped inside, she noticed a note taped to the wall. It was from Chelsey.

Back in half an hour. - C.

The scent of humidity and coffee greeted her as she entered. Tigger stretched lazily on a shelf before leaping down to follow her into the main working area. With a quick scratch behind Tigger's ears, she settled into her chair and sifted through the investigation files.

Each fact, every detail, seemed to dance before her eyes, taunting her with their inconclusiveness.

"Hey Tigger. What do you think? Is Phillip a cold-hearted murderer, or just the fall guy for someone with a grudge?" The cat blinked up at her, offering no insight.

Raven turned back to her work. Time seemed to slow, each tick of the clock echoing through the small office as she scoured the files.

The door to Wolf Lake Consulting opened with a sudden burst of wind.

"Chelsey?"

No answer.

She shot out of her seat just in time to see Franklin Devereux enter the office. His six-foot-four frame seemed to fill the room as he scanned the space, eyes landing on Raven. He gave her a thin smile, his gaze never leaving her face.

"Hello, Raven. I hope I'm not interrupting anything important."

She had been so focused on her work that she hadn't heard his SUV pull up outside.

"Mr. Devereux, hi," she stammered, clearing her throat. "No, I was just going over some case files."

"Good, good." He stepped further into the office, his polished leather shoes clicking against the hardwood floor. "The murder investigations?"

Something in her throat clicked when she swallowed. "As a matter of fact, yes."

"Always on the job. That's why I find you so interesting."

"Can I help you, sir?"

He pulled out a chair and sat across from her desk. She shot a look at the clock. What if Chelsey returned and found Devereux in the office? How would she explain his presence?

"I wanted to talk to you about our conversations. Have you given any thought to the job offer? I gave you a deadline, yes?"

A bead of sweat formed at the base of her neck. Chelsey might walk in at any moment.

"I've been thinking about it, but as you can see, I've also been a little distracted."

"It's a once-in-a-lifetime opportunity, one that I think you would be wise to consider."

"I know," she said, fidgeting with the edge of a file folder. "But it's complicated."

"Is it?" He raised an eyebrow, crossing his arms over his chest. "I don't see how. This is a chance for you to lead your own team and make a difference in people's lives. And let's not forget the benefits package. Does Wolf Lake Consulting offer life and health insurance?"

Another check mark against her current job.

"I just need to think about it some more."

"The clock is ticking. Don't take too long. I'd hate to fill the job with another applicant. Six figures, remember?"

Her fingers drummed on the desk as she weighed the offer against her loyalty to Chelsey and Wolf Lake Consulting. The room became smaller, trapping her between the past and an uncertain future.

"Will you let your allegiance to a struggling private investigation firm hold you back? There's another world out there. One with sufficient room for growth."

She clenched her jaw, searching for words that wouldn't betray her uncertainty. "I appreciate the offer, Mr. Devereux, but Chelsey has been there for me since day one."

"I'm willing to give you more time, but I need a response within forty-eight hours. After that, I'll have to move on to other candidates. Think about it, Raven. You've done so much already, but with me, your potential is limitless."

"Isn't there some other way?" she asked, desperation creeping into her voice. "Can't I work for both you and Chelsey?"

He shook his head, a hint of pity in his eyes. "It's an all-or-nothing deal. You know as well as I do that you can't serve two masters."

He walked towards the door. "I'll give you the forty-eight hours, but not a moment more. When that time is up, I expect your answer—one way or another."

The deadline landed like a sucker punch. A mountain of case files lay scattered across the desk and blurred together into an indistinguishable mess of ink and paper. She struggled to focus on anything but the ticking clock.

"Forty-eight hours. I'll give you an answer by then."

"Excellent." Devereux straightened. "Just remember, this is a one-time offer. Don't let it slip away because of misplaced loyalty."

Raven bit the inside of her cheek, the metallic tang of blood filling her mouth. "You make it sound so simple."

"Because it is," he insisted, his eyes locked on hers. "Sometimes we have to make tough choices to get what we want. And if you truly want this, you won't let anything stand in your way."

As he left the office, his ultimatum hung in the air like the blade of a guillotine. Raven tried to lose herself in the files once more, but her thoughts were a whirlwind of pros and cons, loyalty and ambition.

With each passing second, the pendulum swung closer to the edge, threatening to sever the ties that bound her to Wolf Lake Consulting. And to Chelsey.

She paced in the hallway and stared blankly at the door. She imagined leaving this world behind for a new life, a new career, but the thought of abandoning Chelsey, her friend and mentor, made her sick.

The door swung open. She jumped and covered her chest, but it was Chelsey returning. Straightening her braids, she tried to appear relaxed. It wasn't working.

"Raven, are you all right?"

"Uh, yeah. I'm fine." She forced a smile onto her lips. "Just lost in thought, you know?"

"Lost in thought about Phillip Space and Jackson Anders?" Chelsey asked, stepping into the hallway, her eyes searching Raven's face for any hidden emotions.

"Yes, that's it. Did you find anything interesting when you were out?"

Chelsey led the way into the office and took a seat at her desk.

"Nothing new. There's still no sign of Jackson Anders, and it's been awfully quiet since Lambert arrested Phillip Space."

"But if Phillip is the killer, who's following me and taking my picture?"

"I wish I knew. But we can't ignore the evidence. His fingerprints are all over the murder weapon, and he admitted the ax belongs to him."

Raven sneaked a look at the security camera, fearing she would see Franklin Devereux returning.

"Are you sure you're all right?" Chelsey asked.

"As good as I'll ever be. Come on. Let's figure out where Jackson Anders is hiding."

40

Raven arranged the clutter on her desk into neat piles.

"All right," Chelsey said. "Let's go over what we have so far. You and Thomas spoke with Phillip Space today, right? What did he have to say about Jackson Anders?"

"Phillip insisted he's innocent. He mentioned that Jackson started the altercation, but he doesn't know why."

"Interesting. And Thomas said no one has seen Jackson since the last murder. It sounds like he's guilty and on the run."

"His motives are still unclear, but him stopping his medication could play a part in this. He's a danger to himself and others. But Chelsey, none of this matters if our firm can't keep its doors open. We need to figure out a way to pay the bills."

"I've been thinking about ways to cut costs and attract more clients." She spread a handful of papers across the table, detailing her plan. "I believe we can lower our costs with a more efficient heating system, and we should build a social media presence."

Raven skimmed the documents, impressed by Chelsey's thoroughness. It was a solid plan, one that would benefit the company. There were holes, but nothing a little ingenuity couldn't overcome. Yet, as she read through the proposal, she knew she was betraying her friend. Here was Chelsey, working to improve their business while she considered leaving for another job.

"This is a terrific start. You've put a lot of thought into this."

"I just wish I had someone with more business experience to help me run the private investigation firm. I'm in over my head, and a business strategist would free me up to concentrate on investigations like this one."

"Give me a day to toss a few ideas around. For one thing, email marketing is far more effective than social media. So is content marketing."

"What is content marketing?"

"Like blog posts and YouTube videos. Evergreen stuff. Back to Jackson Anders. He's not hanging out in the bars and hasn't returned to his house. On the other hand, Phillip Space's fingerprints are on the murder weapon, not Jackson's."

She rose from her chair and assessed the map of Nightshade County pinned to the office wall. Chelsey had marked various locations as possible hideouts for Jackson, but none of her theories were bearing fruit.

"These spots represent his known haunts. I'm starting to think he fled the county."

"Maybe we need to look at it from another angle. His buddies say they haven't seen him, not that he has many friends. Who could he stay with if he wanted to disappear?"

The ring of the phone stopped Raven short. She snatched the receiver.

"Raven?"

"Hi, Thomas," she said, recognizing the sheriff's voice on the other end.

"We got a break in the case. A huge break. This morning, a

witness saw Jackson leaving an apartment complex in the village center. She thinks he's dating someone who lives there."

"Are you sure it was him?"

"Positive. The description matches, and the witness recognized him from the news."

"Thanks for letting us know. Give us a few minutes. We'll meet you at the station." She turned to Chelsey. "That was Thomas. A witness spotted Jackson Anders leaving an apartment complex in the village."

"Finally, some progress. Which apartments?"

"Brockway."

"That's only two blocks from here."

"Right."

As she prepared to delve deeper into the new lead, her phone buzzed with an incoming text message from Darren.

"Excuse me for a minute, Chelsey," she said, stepping away from her desk to answer the message. "I need to update Darren on the situation."

"No problem. I'll gather my belongings."

Raven returned the message and told Darren about the new lead. She felt a strange mixture of excitement and dread knowing that they were closing in on a murder suspect. After setting the phone aside, she threw her bag strap over her shoulder.

"Everything okay?" Chelsey asked.

"Darren just wanted an update. He's worried about our safety."

"Tell him not to worry. We're just helping Thomas's team, not taking down Jackson on our own."

Before they left, her phone rang again. She answered without checking the screen, risking that the caller might be Devereux.

"Raven, it's Buck," the caller said. "Just drove by the cabin like you asked. I wasn't there for ten minutes when I saw an unfamiliar vehicle driving real slow past the state park. It was an SUV."

"Did you get a plate number?"

"Sorry. The driver took off after he spotted me watching. I tried to pursue, but—"

"No, no. Don't put yourself at risk."

"Hey, if someone bothers Serena Hopkins' daughter, I'm gonna step in."

"And I love you for that, Buck, but I care about your safety. If the driver returns, get the plate number."

As they walked to Chelsey's car, she instructed Buck to stay back and give Jackson Anders room. The call ended.

Chelsey looked across the seat. "Buck spotted Jackson Anders?"

"He spotted *someone*. All he said was the person appeared to be canvassing the cabin as he passed the state park. Jackson Anders drives an SUV, right?"

"That's correct. Should we have Thomas send a deputy to the state park?"

"No need. Darren's heading back to the cabin to check it out. Let's give him some time to investigate first. We can follow up with Thomas on the apartment complex lead in the meantime."

"Have faith, Raven. We're getting closer." Chelsey turned out of the parking lot. "Hey, I have an idea. Why don't I join you and Darren at the state park tonight? I can take one of the empty cabins. We can stake out the park together, just in case Jackson or whoever was driving that SUV comes back."

"Thanks for the offer, but Darren and I can handle it. Besides, you and Thomas should stay together. No sense in placing yourself in harm's way."

"Are you sure? I could bring Tigger and Jack, and we could

make a night of it. Order some pizza, watch a movie, maybe even catch this guy."

"Really Chelsey, it's fine. Darren has experience as a police officer, and I know how to defend myself. We'll be okay."

Chelsey eyed Raven. "Okay, if you're sure. But if you change your mind, just call me. Anytime, day or night."

"Thanks, my friend. I promise we'll be extra vigilant."

"Now let's get back to work and figure out where Jackson is hiding."

41

With Aguilar in the passenger's seat, Thomas pulled his truck beside an aging brick apartment complex just as the sun began its descent. A quick check of the area showed a few people on the sidewalk, rushing to escape the chill. But no sign of Jackson Anders.

"You ready?" Aguilar asked. She opened the door and stepped out.

Thomas followed suit. "The woman we're looking for is Elaine Norwood. Our witness spotted Jackson Anders leaving her apartment."

A vehicle backfired, and he flinched, remembering the bullet that had almost taken his life in Los Angeles. His fingers brushed against the scar on his back, a reminder of how close he'd come to losing everything.

They climbed the stairs and approached the door of the apartment, marked with the number seven in chipped paint. Thomas, feeling the weight of his badge, knocked three times.

"Who is it?" asked a voice from behind the door.

"Sheriff Shepherd and Deputy Aguilar with the Nightshade

County Sheriff's Department. We'd like to ask you a few questions."

The door opened after a pause, revealing a woman with dark hair and eyes that held a wary expression. She seemed to know why they were there.

"Are you alone, ma'am?" Thomas asked.

"Yes," she said, stepping aside to allow them into her modest dwelling. "Please, come in."

"Thank you," Aguilar said as they crossed the threshold. Her eyes flashed from one corner of the apartment to the other, scoping out potential threats.

Muted colors adorned the walls and simple furnishings spoke of a quiet life. He glanced at Elaine, who stood by the door, wringing her hands.

"Ms. Norwood, we're here to ask about Jackson Anders. We received a report about him leaving your apartment. Where is he now?"

"Why do you want to know about Jackson? Is he in trouble?" Elaine's eyes darted from one officer to the other in concern and disbelief.

"He's a person of interest in an ongoing investigation," Aguilar said. "When did you last see him?"

"Last night," she replied without hesitation. "He came over for dinner, like he usually does on Fridays. But I haven't seen him since."

Thomas chose his words carefully. "We believe Jackson might know something about the murder cases we're investigating."

The color drained from her face. She shook her head as if trying to reject the notion. "No, no, that can't be true. You must be mistaken."

"Jackson hasn't been home in days, and we're worried he's off his medication. Has he acted strangely in the past week?"

"Jackson has schizophrenia, but that doesn't mean he's capable of murder. He's misunderstood, that's all."

"How was he last night?"

"Fine. He even helped me make the paella. Everyone thinks he's dangerous because he hears voices, but I've known him for several months, and the last thing he'd ever do is kill someone."

Thomas glanced at Aguilar, who was watching Elaine with a mixture of pity and skepticism. They had seen this kind of loyalty before; it wasn't uncommon for people to defend those they cared about, ignoring warning signs and evidence to the contrary. But there was something in her words, in her insistence that Jackson was misunderstood, that resonated with him.

"Elaine," he said, "we're not here to condemn Jackson. We need to find out the truth. If he is innocent, we will do everything in our power to clear his name. But we need your help. If he didn't hurt anyone, why is he on the run?"

"Because..."

"Yes?"

"Jackson saw the news, all right? He figured out you want to arrest him for those murders. No one will give him the benefit of the doubt, so he's lying low."

"But he came to your apartment?"

She shifted her feet. "He loves me. If you find Jackson, just talk to him. Please, give him a chance to explain himself."

"Where is he staying?"

"I don't know. It's the truth, okay?"

Was her defense of Jackson more than blind loyalty? It seemed like a plea for understanding. He considered his own experiences and the way people had judged him since his childhood—the isolation, the judgment, the constant battle to prove himself.

"Elaine," Aguilar began, "we understand you care about Jackson. However, we need to find him and make sure he's not a danger to himself or anyone else. Can you promise us that if he contacts you, you'll let us know?"

Elaine bit her lip, uncertainty clouding her eyes. She glanced at Thomas as if searching for reassurance that their intentions were honorable.

"I'll tell him you want to talk."

"That's all we ask," Thomas said. He felt compelled to offer some comfort, some indication that he understood what it meant to be judged based on a condition. "You know, I've experienced my share of misunderstandings. Our challenges don't define who we are."

"The sheriff makes an important point," Aguilar said. "We're not here to make assumptions or condemn anyone without evidence."

Elaine offered them a weak smile. They exchanged goodbyes.

In the truck, Thomas couldn't stop himself from ruminating on Elaine's words and the parallels between Jackson's struggles and his own.

"She cares for him," Aguilar said. "But love can blind you to the truth."

42

As the vehicle prowled through the murky darkness, his eyes fell upon the village apartment. The sight of Sheriff Thomas Shepherd's pickup parked outside made a grin creep across his lips. The engine slowed to a crawl, allowing him to savor the scene before him. There was an undeniable poetic beauty in the way he had orchestrated events.

Perfect. Just as he'd planned.

The satisfaction that washed over him was akin to a wave crashing upon the shore, relentless and powerful. He considered the web of manipulation he had spun, each thread crafted to lead the authorities on a wild goose chase. At the forefront of their investigation stood Jackson Anders and Phillip Space, two expendable members of society.

Fools. Jackson and Phillip never stood a chance.

His eyes lingered on the sheriff's truck as its headlights swept across the buildings. A thrill of excitement rushed through his body.

With one last look at the apartment building, he eased his foot onto the accelerator, allowing the vehicle to pull away from the scene. The engine's roar was the only sound as he drove into the coming night.

The glow of the dashboard lent a wan pallor to his face. Up ahead, the sheriff's truck pulled away from the apartment complex.

He recalled the warm blood on his hands, the thrill as life drained from their eyes. His fingers twitched on the steering wheel, craving that feeling again. Looking at the mirror, he watched the apartment shrink into the distance. Soon he would leave another calling card. Another crow. He held power over life and death.

The thought of his next victim made the blood rush into his head. He imagined her struggle, her cries, the sweet silence when it was over. That whore from Wolf Lake Consulting had been asking too many questions. He would pay her cabin a visit tonight.

As he drove, the streetlights glinted off his empty eyes. He thought of Jackson, the unstable man with schizophrenia. It had been child's play to manipulate him, to let the poor fool take the fall. People were so quick to blame those who were different.

The sheriff couldn't decide whether Phillip or Jackson was the killer. Good. Let Thomas Shepherd chase his tail.

Ahead, the road stretched dark and empty. Somewhere out there, his next victim waited. He pictured her fear when she realized the truth, imagined her desperate cries for mercy. The thoughts excited him. That private investigator had gotten too close to the truth.

He would silence her tonight.

43

The sudden intrusion of the engine's rumble broke the stillness in the surrounding woods, causing birds to fly from their perches with a flurry of wings. The chill nipped at LeVar's cheeks as he exited his black Chrysler Limited and crossed the lot at Wolf Lake State Park.

"Hey, man," Darren said, dragging a pile of brush behind him.

"Yo, ranger bro. How's life in the great outdoors?"

"Can't complain, except for this Jackson Anders fellow driving past the park. Come on; it's cold outside."

Darren led the way into the modest but cozy living space. The scents of wood smoke and fresh pine filled the air. A pot of soup heated on the stove.

He glanced around, taking in the simplicity of the cabin's furnishings: a well-worn sofa, a small dining table, and a small television that seemed out of place in the rustic decor. "I see you're still embracing that back-to-nature vibe. You sure you don't miss policing the city?"

"City life isn't for me, my friend," Darren said with a shrug, pouring them mugs of coffee. "This is where I belong. It's peaceful, you know? Plus, it's nice working out of my backyard."

He nodded, understanding the perspective even if he didn't share it completely. As a convert from city life, he appreciated the beauty and tranquility of the forest, but sometimes he missed the energy and excitement of urban life. Still, if Darren was happy here, that was all that mattered.

"Can't argue with that." He sipped his coffee. The warmth spread through him, banishing the cold from his bones. "I guess you and Raven have everything you need here."

"More than enough." Darren raised his mug in a toast. "To the simple life."

"To the simple life."

They clinked their mugs together and settled into companionable conversation as the woods around the cabin slowly reclaimed their stillness.

The more Darren spoke, the more his expression grew somber. He set the mug on the table.

"LeVar, I've been meaning to talk to you about Raven."

"What about my sister? I know she's going through some stuff, but she won't open up to me. Chelsey is worried sick. What's going on?"

"Financial troubles." Darren rubbed his stubbled chin. "She's working herself ragged trying to make ends meet, but she won't accept help. It's frustrating."

"Man, I tried talking to her too, but you know how stubborn she can be. She wants to handle it all by herself."

"Too stubborn for her own good." Darren's eyes drifted to the window, as if Raven might appear among the trees. "I just don't want her to get overwhelmed."

"Neither do I." LeVar took another sip of his coffee before wiping his mouth. "Maybe we can come up with a plan or something, help her out without her realizing it."

"I thought about it, but if she figures it out, she'll put me in a headlock."

Before LeVar could laugh, a crash brought both men to their hands and knees.

"What the hell was that?"

They jumped to their feet.

"Someone just broke my window," Darren shouted, rushing to the source of the noise.

LeVar moved behind him, reaching for the radio on his belt. Peering through the jagged remains of the shattered window, he caught sight of a figure sprinting into the dense forest. The hairs on his neck stood on end. He could feel it deep in his gut: This was the killer they were hunting.

"LeVar, that's him. It has to be Jackson Anders."

Without hesitation, Darren vaulted through the broken window, glass crumbling beneath his boots as he gave chase. LeVar followed. Ahead, a silhouette darted between the trees, always just beyond sight.

"Wait up. He might have a gun."

Branches whipped at his face and snagged his dreadlocks as he pushed himself to run faster.

"Stay on him!" Darren shouted back, his tone a mix of determination and fury. He leaped over a fallen log, eyes locked on the fleeing figure ahead of them.

The forest ranger was faster than LeVar had believed. Darren's legs pumped as he raced to catch the intruder.

Radioing the report to dispatch, LeVar struggled to keep his footing in the melting snow. The chase continued for what felt like an eternity, and the temperature dropped with every passing minute. After what felt like miles, the figure vanished, slipping between the trees like a phantom.

Darren skidded to a halt, panting. "I lost him. What in the hell? He was right here."

"I don't know." The cold was seeping into LeVar's bones, and he realized neither of them were wearing jackets. "We should head back. It's getting colder."

"No. He has to be close."

"He's gone, Darren. It will be dark soon. If we keep running, we'll get lost. Anyhow, the sheriff's department will catch him when he exits the forest."

"Doubtful. This guy is a ghost." The ranger hugged his body and shivered. "But you're right. No sense in freezing to death."

As they retraced their steps through the woods, LeVar adjusted the radio frequency to contact the sheriff. "Thomas, you there?"

The sheriff replied a second later. "LeVar, I got word from dispatch. What's happening out there?"

"Someone attacked the cabin. Broke the window and took off like a bat out of hell. We chased the guy as long as we could but lost 'em in the woods."

"Jackson Anders?"

"That's what Darren thinks, but I didn't see a face."

"All right. I'll join Lambert and the others. We need to sweep the woods ASAP. Are you armed?"

"Gun's back at the house," LeVar said.

"What about Darren?"

"Nope."

"Okay. If you see Jackson Anders, don't engage him. Stay safe, both of you. That's an order."

LeVar glanced at Darren, who nodded in frustration. Together they returned to the cabin, determined to reach the grounds before night fell.

Not long before they lost daylight, LeVar and Darren entered the violated sanctuary of the ranger's cabin. A biting draft sliced through the room. He peered through the jagged empty frame where the window once was, the forest beyond eerily silent.

"Let's get this window secured," Darren said. He crossed to a storage closet, rummaging for tools and supplies.

"Got it." LeVar rubbed his arms in a futile attempt to warm himself. The heat from the woodstove fled through the opening. Darren returned with a handful of nails, a hammer, and a sheet of wood.

"Hand me that tarp over there, will you?" Darren nodded toward a folded blue sheet in the corner.

As they worked, nailing the wood and tarp over the broken window, the cabin's temperature rose.

"This fix will keep the cold outside where it belongs, but it's no good. You lost your view of the forest. If Jackson returns—"

"Nothing I can do about it until tomorrow morning. I'll grab a new pane first thing. Until then, this will have to suffice."

"Use extra blankets. Despite our work, you'll feel a draft tonight."

"I don't think Raven and I will get much sleep tonight."

The once tranquil cabin was now a battleground, and they were soldiers on the front lines.

As the last light of day faded into the encroaching night, the two men settled into an uneasy silence and listened for danger.

Their eyes never strayed far from the window. The tarp billowed like the belly of an insatiable beast.

44

Back at Wolf Lake Consulting, Raven sat at her desk and read the clock on the wall. The ticking seconds served as a constant reminder of Devereux's ultimatum, and she could feel the pressure mounting. Across the room, Chelsey hunched over a stack of papers, her brow furrowed in concentration as she organized the financial aspects of their company. She seemed unaware of Raven's restlessness.

It was time. She had to tell Chelsey the truth about the job offer.

"Chelsey," Raven said, biting her lip.

"Hmm?" Chelsey replied, not lifting her eyes from the papers.

Maybe this wasn't the right moment to share her worries.

"Nothing."

Her phone buzzed with an incoming call. It was Darren. "Hey, babe."

"I was hanging out with LeVar at the cabin, and someone shattered the window. We're fixing it now, but I'm pretty sure Jackson Anders did this."

Raven's body tensed. In the background, she heard the ongoing repairs.

"It's supposed to go down to twenty-five degrees tonight. What are we going to do?"

"Don't worry about that. LeVar and I covered the opening, and I'll replace the pane tomorrow."

"Are you sure it was Jackson?"

"I didn't see his face, but I noticed fresh tire tracks in the parking lot. They could be from that SUV Buck mentioned."

"I'll come home and help."

"No, we're on the job. Stay and finish your work. I'll have the cabin warm for you."

"Keep me in the loop."

They ended the call. She turned to Chelsey, who had paused and looked up from her work. "Darren found tire tracks near the cabin. They might be connected to that SUV Buck spotted. And someone broke a window. Darren thinks it was Jackson."

Chelsey set the papers aside and considered the implications. "That's not good. He could be hiding in the woods near the cabin. That would explain why no one can find him."

"Thanks for planting that seed in my head."

"Sorry."

"No, you're right. If he knows he's a suspect, he might be desperate."

The two of them sat in uneasy silence. They knew all too well that a dangerous man like Jackson Anders could pose a significant threat to anyone involved in the investigation. Outside, the wind rustled through the trees and tossed rain against the windows.

"If Jackson is in the woods, can we track him down?"

"It's possible. The woods outside the campgrounds stretch for miles, and the ice makes it harder to track prints. Still, if we put enough people on the job, we should be able to locate where he's hiding."

Before Raven could finish her thought, Chelsey yawned and stretched. "We've been at this for hours. My body is telling me to go home, but there's still work to do. We could use a break."

"I suppose we could," she said, chewing on a pen.

"Is everything all right? You seem distracted."

Raven hesitated, torn between her loyalty to Chelsey and the life-changing job offer.

"Chelsey, remember when I told you about my finances?"

"Sure I do."

"Well, I didn't tell you everything. Things are . . . getting worse. I received a warning about the balance on my checking account, and I'm not sure I can pay to repair the Rogue."

"Why didn't you tell me you were struggling so much? Do you need a loan? I'm happy to help."

"I can't accept money from you."

"Yes, you can."

"Listen, there's something else." She tugged at her braids. "Do you know who Franklin Devereux is?"

"Yeah, everyone does."

"He kinda offered me a job."

The color drained from Chelsey's face. "To work on his security team?"

"Not quite. He wants me to oversee the entire team. There's a secure, six-figure salary and benefits. And now he wants my decision."

Chelsey's mouth opened as she took in the revelation, her eyes searching Raven's face.

"So you'd be the boss. And you're thinking about it?"

Raven swallowed hard, looking away. "I don't know. It's under consideration."

The heavy silence that followed threatened to suffocate

them. Chelsey was too stunned to speak. This was Raven's worst fear. The last thing she wanted was to upset her friend.

The ringing desk phone offered a reprieve. Chelsey checked the ID before answering and placed the call on speakerphone. "Thomas, where are you?"

"Hey Chelsey," Thomas said, his words tumbling over one another. "Lambert and two deputies are scouring the forest for Jackson Anders. Aguilar and I just left and are headed to Elaine's place. She called and said Jackson phoned her and sounded disturbing."

"What do you mean by disturbing?"

"Like he might hurt himself. Or someone else."

"Can I help?"

"Elaine's insisting he's innocent, but we can't rule out the possibility she's defending him and not telling us the entire truth. We need to find him, and we need to do it soon."

"I'll join you in the search. Give me five minutes to meet you at the apartment. Keep me posted if you find anything else."

"Will do. See you in a few."

Chelsey placed the phone on the receiver and wound a strand of hair around her finger. "I need to leave. Thomas needs my help to find Jackson Anders."

"You mean he needs *our* help?"

"Go home, Raven. It's more important that you think about Franklin Devereux's offer."

"Come on, now. Don't be that way."

"Be what way? You need to look out for yourself. I can handle the search."

Raven knew she'd hurt Chelsey. "My priority is working with you to catch a killer. For goodness' sake, he attacked our cabin."

"Then grab your belongings. Thomas needs me."

Snatching her keys, phone, and firearm, Raven rose from her desk. She knew she had to say something, to make things right with Chelsey before they continued with the investigation.

"I'm sorry I didn't tell you about the job offer sooner. I should have been honest from the start."

Chelsey struggled to compose herself. "Thank you for telling me now, at least. To be honest, I don't blame you. You deserve higher pay, and I can't give you the job security Devereux offered."

Raven chewed the inside of her cheek, torn between her conflicting desires. "Our friendship, this firm we've built together . . . that means more to me than any salary."

"Do what's best for you. I won't stand in your way if you accept the offer."

"I'm so sorry."

"Sorry for what? For taking an amazing offer? If I were you, I'd snatch it up before he changes his mind. Anyway, you do what's best for you, and I'll support you no matter what. But right now, I have to focus on helping the sheriff's department."

Raven followed Chelsey out the door and into the storm. She noted Chelsey was saying *I* have to help Thomas, or *I* have to find the killer. Already, Raven wasn't part of the team. They lowered their heads and rushed to the Honda Civic, the urgency of their task propelling them forward.

In the car, Chelsey gripped the steering wheel. Raven stared out the window, watching the buildings blur past as rain pelted the windshield. Tiny ice pellets ricocheted off the hood and signaled that the temperature was dropping in a hurry.

She looked over at Chelsey, but her friend didn't return the glance. Was Raven selfish for considering the offer? Would accepting it mean betraying Chelsey and everything they had worked so hard to build? Chelsey had always been there for her.

Their friendship might not survive if she walked away from Wolf Lake Consulting.

45

The din of conversation inside the crowded bar enveloped Thomas as he stepped through the door. Chatter hummed through the establishment like a smoky haze.

Aguilar, Chelsey, and Raven were at his side. Darren's friend Mike wasn't working tonight, but maybe someone had witnessed the brawl between Phillip Space and Jackson Anders or could tell them where Jackson was hiding.

They had spent two hours canvassing Elaine's apartment, but there was no sign of Jackson. Now his eyes swept over the sea of unfamiliar faces until it landed on a shock of fiery red hair behind the bar.

He weaved his way through the crowd, the others close behind. Chelsey was keeping her distance from Raven. He didn't know what had happened between the two of them, but solving their issues wasn't his priority.

The bartender looked up at their approach, a radiant smile spreading across her freckled face.

"Margaret O'Reilly?" Thomas asked.

"Call me Maggie."

Her Irish lilt was warm and lively. Thomas explained their purpose for being there, detailing the fight between Phillip Space and Jackson Anders. Her smile faded, her keen green eyes growing thoughtful.

"Aye, I remember that fight," she said with a nod. "An ugly business, it was."

"Can you tell us what happened?"

Her gaze grew distant as she recalled the details. "That Jackson fellow seemed in high spirits at first, laughing with another man at the bar. But then his mood soured quicker than milk left out overnight. He stormed through the place and found that the other fellow. Phillip, was it? Next thing I knew, they headed outside. The whole thing happened so fast."

Thomas exchanged a look with Raven.

"This other man Jackson was sitting at the bar with," Raven said. "Is it possible he said something to Jackson that set him off?"

The bartender thought for a second. "I suppose that could have happened."

"Do you know who the other man was?"

Maggie paused, dredging up the memory. "Ah yes. Eddie something. Monroe, I believe. He's a regular. Friendly type, always quick with a joke."

Eddie Monroe.

The name hit Thomas like a thunderclap. Raven's eyes locked on his and narrowed. Eddie was the man who'd told Raven about Phillip Space spying on Patricia Hudson. Had he caused the fight between Phillip and Jackson? Worse yet, had he set them up for the murders?

After the interview concluded, Thomas thanked Maggie for her time. He stepped out into the night air with the others. The sounds of the bar faded behind them as they walked to their vehicles, questions hanging in the silence.

Thomas stopped beside his pickup and looked at the team members.

"Eddie Monroe," he said. "That's the name of the informant, the one who tipped Raven off about Phillip Space."

Raven nodded, arms folded across her chest. "Yeah, and now we find out he was at the bar talking to Jackson right before the fight happened."

"You think this Eddie guy is involved somehow?" Aguilar asked.

"It's mighty suspicious. He points the finger at Phillip, then gets Jackson riled up to go after him. Seems he wanted to pit them against each other."

Chelsey scuffed the gravel with the toe of her sneaker. "But why would he do that? What's his motive?"

They stood in contemplation. A chilling breeze rustled through the trees, carrying the scent of flurries.

Thomas rubbed his chin. "We already made a mistake by jumping to conclusions, and I don't want another mistake. But I think we better have another chat with Phillip and see what his relationship is with this Eddie character."

Raven agreed. "And we need to find Jackson. He's not taking his medication and might be a danger to his girlfriend."

"I'll call the station and have them pull everything they can find on Eddie Monroe. His address, rap sheet, known associates, the works." He glanced around at the others. "We'll stake out Elaine's place again in case Jackson turns up. And first thing tomorrow, we'll pay Mr. Monroe a visit."

As they climbed into their vehicles, Thomas felt the thrill of the hunt stirring in his blood. The pieces were coming together, and soon they'd have their killer.

He slid behind the wheel of his truck, cranking the engine. Before pulling onto the road, he glanced over at Raven, whose window was lowered. Chelsey stared straight ahead, avoiding her partner.

"You good with staking out Elaine's place tonight?" he called to her.

Raven gave him a thumbs up. "You know me. I'm always up for a good stakeout."

Thomas grinned. "All right then. Let's roll."

They drove away from the bar and into the night. Clouds blanketed the moon and deepened the shadows between the trees. Up ahead, the road spooled into a black abyss.

Monroe had seemed like a harmless busybody. Now it appeared he might be at the center of the murders. What was his connection to the victims? And why pit Jackson and Phillip against each other?

He shook his head, flexing his fingers on the steering wheel. They were missing something, some vital piece. He hoped Phillip or Jackson could fill in the gaps.

Looking into the mirror, he saw the bright gleam of Chelsey's headlights behind him. He felt reassured, knowing she'd have his back tonight. They drove through the gathering storm, heading into the unknown. The hunt was on.

A short while later, he pulled into the station parking lot and hopped out beside Aguilar, the others close behind. Killing the engine, he turned up the collar on his jacket and hustled to the entrance. Inside, the station hummed with activity. Two deputies typed reports and answered calls, phones jangling. The sharp tang of coffee permeated the space.

Thomas waved to Lambert. "I need you to run a full background check on Eddie Monroe. Cross reference it with info on our murder victims. Look for any connection."

"You got it, boss man."

"Let me know the minute you find something." Thomas clapped him on the shoulder.

He headed for his office, unzipping his jacket. It had been a long day, and the night stretched before him. He rubbed his eyes as he settled at his desk, and his thoughts turned to the stakeout. He trusted Chelsey and Raven to keep watch over Elaine's place. If Jackson appeared, they'd be ready.

Leaning back, he closed his eyes, picturing the victims' bodies and the dead crows laid beside them. All that blood.

Soon he'd interview Phillip about Eddie Monroe. For now, he allowed himself a moment of stillness and decompression as the investigation hurtled forward. The killer was free outside Wolf Lake. And Thomas would find him.

46

Raven's attention shifted between the mirror and Chelsey, who sat in the driver's seat. Parked down the street from Elaine's apartment, they waited for Jackson Anders to emerge. She knew the admission that she was leaving Wolf Lake Consulting had hurt her friend. It seemed every choice was the wrong one.

"Any sign of him?" Raven asked.

"Nothing yet."

Static burst through the radio, and Thomas's voice came through. "Lambert just filled me in on Eddie Monroe. Turns out he was a foster child, moved around a lot. No arrest record."

"Does that connect him to the murders somehow?" Chelsey asked.

"Maybe. LeVar and Scout found an old newspaper article about a fire in the town where Eddie lived as a teenager. The headline read 'Tragic Fire Claims Lives of Foster Parents.' Eddie was supposedly at a friend's house when it happened."

"Faulty gas line," Raven said, reading LeVar's text. "So, what's the significance?"

"Could be nothing. But it's a strange coincidence, don't you think? Death seems to follow this guy around."

"Definitely worth looking into."

"There's more. Apparently, there was an addendum to the original case file. A firefighter's report states that someone tampered with the gas line. It wasn't an accident."

"Are you saying Eddie could've caused the fire?" Chelsey asked, sitting forward.

"Can't say for sure. But it's worth noting that a week after the incident, Eddie moved to another foster family and town. Almost as if someone was trying to distance him from the tragedy."

"Did they ever question him or treat him as a suspect?"

"Negative. The case was closed quickly, as the judge felt sympathy for the boy. The whole thing was eventually forgotten. His alibi that he was at a friend's house seemed solid, but who knows?"

If Eddie was involved in that fire, what else could he be hiding?

Chelsey drummed her fingers on the steering wheel. "So what do we do with this information?"

"For now, consider him a suspect. Until we talk to Jackson Anders, we can't verify what happened in the bar with Phillip Space. Nor can we rule out Jackson or Phillip."

"Roger that," Raven said. She glanced at Chelsey, who stared down the street, waiting for Jackson Anders to appear.

Thomas returned to their surveillance mission. Chelsey fell silent again.

"Chelsey, about Devereux's offer—"

"Can't talk about it right now. We need to focus on finding a murder suspect."

"I just don't want you to be angry."

"I'm not angry with you. Give me time to process the news."

Raven stared at the condensation pattern on the car window, her breath fogging up the glass.

"I'm scared."

There. She'd said it. Was it the first time she'd ever admitted to being frightened?

"Of what?"

"Devereux's offer. The changes it could bring. I don't know if I can handle it."

Chelsey finally tore her gaze away from the street, looking at Raven with a mixture of concern and understanding. She sighed, her shoulders slumping.

"I've been thinking about it too. You have nothing to fear. You're a born leader, and I don't doubt you'll excel working under Devereux. But the truth is, I'm afraid as well. Wolf Lake Consulting... I don't know if I have the financial skills to keep it going. Maybe you should take the job offer. I can't guarantee you'll have a paycheck a few months down the line."

"I won't leave you, Chelsey. Not when you need me."

"Raven, you deserve this opportunity."

"We'll find a way to make it work. I won't allow your business to go under."

Chelsey smiled through the tears that threatened to spill, touched by her friend's commitment. A momentary silence settled between them, the weight of their fears momentarily lifted as they shared a rare moment of vulnerability.

Suddenly, Chelsey's eyes flew back to the street. "Look," she whispered, pointing down the road.

Raven turned in her seat. It was time to set their personal worries aside and focus on the task at hand. "That's him."

A figure made its way down the sidewalk. It was Jackson Anders, his nervousness evident in every jittery step he took.

"He looks paranoid."

The murder suspect glanced over his shoulder, as if fearing someone was following him.

"Thomas and Aguilar are in position."

Chelsey radioed Thomas and ensured they'd seen the man. "Let's go."

Both women stepped out of the car. A truck motored past as flurries drifted on the wind. Down the road, Thomas and Aguilar circled behind Jackson, coordinating their movements with practiced ease. They closed in, cutting off any potential escape routes.

The suspect shot a look over his shoulder and spotted Aguilar. For a moment, it looked like Jackson would bolt. He seemed to sense the trap closing around him, his eyes darting from one alleyway to the next as he searched for an escape.

Then he sprinted down the sidewalk—and smashed into Raven, who had moved with Chelsey to intercept him. The man bounced off her body in surprise.

"Jackson Anders," Chelsey said, grabbing his arm to prevent him from fleeing. "We just want to talk."

"Please, don't make this harder than it has to be," said Raven.

Jackson hesitated, his eyes darting between the two women and the tightening circle of law enforcement. He tugged his arm free and turned to run again.

Raven's muscles tensed as she lunged forward, her arms wrapping around the man's waist. With a grunt, she tackled him to the ground, driving the breath from both of their bodies. She could feel the struggle in his body as he thrashed and fought to get away, the fear radiating from him like heat.

"Please, Jackson," Raven panted, her voice strained with effort. "Stop resisting. We don't want to hurt you."

At the sound of her voice, something in Jackson seemed to shift. His eyes, wide with terror, locked onto hers, and the fight drained out of him. Raven seized the opportunity, pinning his arms behind his back while keeping her weight on his legs to prevent any further attempts to flee.

"Stay down," she said as Chelsey helped to hold him in place. She hoped her words would reach through the haze of panic clouding the man's mind.

Thomas and Aguilar sprinted up to them. A sudden shriek pierced the air. Elaine.

Raven glanced over just in time to see the woman rush out of her apartment, her face contorted with alarm. The sight of Jackson on the ground, captured by Raven, only fueled her distress. The screams grew louder and more frantic, each syllable carrying raw, unfiltered fear.

"Stop it! Don't hurt him!" Elaine cried out, tears streaming down her cheeks as she stumbled toward them.

"Elaine, we're not hurting him," Thomas said, moving to block her from interfering. "We just need to talk to him. He'll be okay."

But her cries didn't abate, her emotions overwhelming any logic or reason. As she continued to plead, Raven felt a pang of guilt. They were doing their job, but the cost to those involved was sometimes too great to bear.

"Trust us, please," Chelsey said. "He's off his medication and needs help. We'll make sure he's okay."

Aguilar placed two calming hands on Elaine's arms. "We're not here to hurt him. We just need some information. There's a possibility someone is setting him up."

Raven maintained her grip on Jackson as Chelsey helped keep him pinned. Jackson fell limp, exhaustion overtaking him.

With the situation under control, Thomas released the tension from his shoulders. "We know this is difficult, and we don't want to cause you any pain. But there are lives at stake, and we need your boyfriend's cooperation."

Raven watched Elaine closely, searching for any sign that

their words were getting through to her. They needed to protect the innocent and pursue justice, and taking Jackson into custody might be the best thing for him.

"Elaine," Raven said, "you have to trust us. We'll make sure Jackson is treated fairly."

Thomas handcuffed the suspect and lifted him off the ground.

"Please take care of him," Elaine said. "He's not a violent man. I know him better than anyone."

"We'll take care of him," Thomas assured her, his eyes filled with empathy. "I swear. You can follow us to the station if you like."

"Give me a second to grab my coat."

The wind continued to whip through the village. A chill Raven couldn't define crept up her back. Looking behind, she saw an empty street.

Yet she swore someone was watching and laughing.

47

The interview room lights drew shadows inside Jackson Anders' eye sockets. Thomas and Aguilar sat across from the murder suspect, whose once animated face now resembled a mask of defiance. Though he wore the expression well, his hands betrayed him. Cuffed to the table, they trembled.

Through the window, Thomas glimpsed Elaine outside the room. She fidgeted in her chair, wringing her hands, clearly worried about the treatment of her boyfriend.

"Jackson," Thomas said, "we need your help. Can you tell us where you were on the night of the murders?"

Thomas gave Jackson the dates and times.

"Sure. I was home watchin' TV. Elaine can vouch for me."

Thomas nodded, making a mental note of Jackson's alibi. He studied the man before him, knowing that beneath the hardened exterior lay a complex web of emotions and a troubled past. A schizophrenic, Jackson had struggled with his demons for years, but it didn't make him a killer.

"Did anyone else see you that night?"

"Neighbor who lives in the next apartment saw me," Jackson answered. "He was takin' out the trash. We exchanged a few words. I went back inside after."

"Can you give me the man's name?"

"Nope. I'd never talked to him before. Ask Elaine."

"We will."

As Thomas spoke, he observed Jackson's every move, searching for signs of deceit or hesitance. Though his eyes never wavered away from the sheriff's, Thomas spied the wheels turning behind them, as if Jackson were weighing the consequences of his words.

"Anything to clear my name," Jackson muttered.

Aguilar set her elbows on the table. "I'd like to ask you about the fight at the bar. What transpired between you and Phillip Space?"

The mere mention of Phillip's name ignited a fire in Jackson. His face contorted with rage as he stood, sending his chair clattering to the ground behind him.

"Phillip?" he spat, his voice seething with anger. "That bastard tried to ruin my life. He's been spreading lies about me, trying to make everyone think I'm some kind of monster."

Aguilar, ever the picture of calm, stood and placed a placating hand on Jackson's shoulder. "Easy, Jackson. We're just trying to understand what happened that night."

Thomas retrieved the fallen chair and set it in place. As he did, he noticed Elaine, still visible through the window, wincing at the commotion. Returning his focus to the task at hand, he prompted Jackson to continue.

"I'm sorry. But he said terrible things about me."

"How do you know Phillip said those things?" Thomas asked.

"It was Eddie Monroe who told me about it. That night at the bar, he said Phillip had been spreading rumors about me. Vile stuff, like I was sleeping around on Elaine."

Thomas exchanged a glance with Aguilar. Eddie Monroe, the man who had photographed the fight between Jackson and Phillip, was now also the one who had incited it.

"Did you confront Phillip about these rumors?" Thomas asked, attempting to coax more details.

"Of course I did. I stormed right up to him and demanded he tell me why he was talking trash. But he just laughed in my face, like it was all a big joke to him. Claimed he didn't know what the hell I was talking about."

As Jackson recounted the events, Thomas observed his features. The tightness of his jaw, the wild glint in his eyes. It was clear the mere memory of that night had reignited a deep-seated anger within him. Thomas wondered what other secrets were buried beneath the surface of this troubled man's life.

"Thank you for sharing that with us, Jackson," Aguilar said, her voice still embodying calm reassurance. "We understand this is difficult for you, but your cooperation is invaluable in helping us understand what transpired."

Jackson's breathing steadied, his shoulders slumping as the tension drained from his body. But beneath the veneer of compliance, Thomas recognized the simmering anger that lurked within him—an anger that might drive him to kill.

Aguilar jotted a note. "We understand you're upset, but we need to focus on the facts. Can you tell us more about your conversation with Eddie Monroe?"

"He seemed pretty eager to let me know what was going on. Are you saying it wasn't true?"

"Did you know Eddie well?" Thomas asked, shifting the conversation.

Jackson shook his head, a dismissive shrug rolling through

his shoulders. "Nah, not really. Just a guy I met at the bar. Didn't think much of him at first, but looking back, I dunno. It's weird."

"Weird how?"

"It's like he was trying to stir up trouble or something."

"Trouble?"

"Yeah." Jackson's tone turned introspective, his eyes distant as he recalled the fight. "He seemed almost excited, y'know? Like he wanted to see what would happen if he kicked a hornet's nest."

"Interesting." Thomas tucked this new information away in his mental file. It struck him how little they knew about Eddie Monroe and his motives. "So you don't think there's any deeper connection between you and Eddie?"

"Look, I've got my issues, and I've screwed up plenty; I won't deny it. But these murders you're asking me about? I'd never kill someone. And as for Eddie, like I said, he's just some guy I met at the bar."

"So there's no reason Eddie might want to make you appear violent?"

"Don't know why he would."

"Okay, Jackson. Thank you for sharing that with us. Your cooperation is invaluable."

"So can I go now?"

"Not yet. There are still a few more questions we need answers to."

There was something about Eddie Monroe that didn't add up, and Thomas knew he would have to work harder to uncover the truth.

"I'm tired."

"Sure you are. Where have you been staying, Jackson? We checked your house, and you haven't been home in days."

The suspect lifted a shoulder. "Just around."

"Like where? I saw pine needles on your jacket."

"So I slept in the forest a couple of nights. Nothing wrong with that."

"Why didn't you stay with Elaine or go back to your house?" Aguilar asked.

"Because all of you think I did it."

"Did what?"

"Killed those women. I hid because you would blame me no matter what I said."

"Isn't it cold sleeping in the forest?"

"If you know where to look, you can find a shack here or there. Sometimes I built fires. But not often. Didn't want them to find me."

"You didn't want *who* to find you?"

"The people who want me arrested. The ones who keep telling you I killed those ladies."

"Thank you for your cooperation, Jackson," Thomas said. "If it's the last thing I do, I'll find those people and make sure they stop saying terrible things about you."

"You'll stop the lies?"

"I will. Listen, if you go home or back to the forest, they might repeat those lies again, and neither of us wants that. We're going to hold you overnight for your own safety. There's a lot we still don't understand about Eddie's involvement, and we can't be sure what his intentions are. Would you like to call your lawyer?"

"I don't need a lawyer, and I've slept in a cell before."

Perhaps Thomas was mistaken, but he was certain neither Jackson nor Phillip could carry out such gruesome murders.

"We'll make sure you're comfortable for the night."

Lambert entered the room and led the suspect back to the cells. Thomas wondered how Jackson and Phillip would react when they saw each other. At least they had separate cells.

As he exited the room with Aguilar, he found Chelsey and

Raven waiting in the hallway. He took a deep breath, preparing to deliver their findings.

"I don't believe Jackson killed Patricia or Ellen. However, we still need more evidence to clear both him and Phillip."

"Then why are you holding him?" Raven asked.

"His own safety," Aguilar said. "We're concerned about Eddie Monroe's role in all this. It's clear that Eddie instigated the fight between Jackson and Phillip, but his reasons remain unknown."

"Jackson seemed to think Eddie was eager to stir up trouble," Thomas added. "We need to dig into Eddie's background, find out who he really is and what he wants. Now that we know about the fire and the compromised gas line, we have to consider the possibility Eddie murdered his foster parents."

"We'll get to work," Chelsey said. "The more we know, the better equipped we'll be to handle him."

"Let's look at the newspaper archives," Aguilar suggested as they settled at their desks.

Thomas nodded, his fingers tapping on the keyboard as he pulled up the database. "We need more information about Eddie and his foster parents."

As they sifted through the digital archives, Thomas felt a growing sense of unease. The more they learned about Eddie Monroe, the more unstable he appeared.

"Here's the article LeVar and Scout found," Thomas said, scanning the text. "Firefighters discovered the bodies of Eddie's foster parents inside their burned-out home. The cause of the fire was deemed suspicious, but no charges were filed against Eddie. The article implies he could've been responsible."

Aguilar read over Thomas' shoulder. "It says here that Eddie claimed it was an accident, but the investigators found traces of accelerants down the road."

"And the gas line tampering. Accident or not, Eddie has a history of violence," Thomas said, scratching his face as he pondered the implications. "If he's the one who killed Patricia and Ellen, we need to find solid evidence before he kills again."

"We should talk to anyone who knew Eddie back then."

"I'll tell Lambert to monitor Jackson and Phillip while we're gone. Let's hope we find something to connect Eddie to the murders before it's too late."

48

Thomas studied Eddie Monroe's residence, noting the peeling paint and overgrown bushes that obscured its facade. Chelsey and Raven climbed out of the Civic parked behind his truck. He glanced at Aguilar, who surveyed the property with wariness.

"Doesn't seem like anyone's been here for a while," he said.

Eddie's house was separated from its neighbors, allowing for a level of privacy. His eyes lingered on the dark windows.

"Something feels off," Raven said.

As the group approached the house, their boots crunched on the icy walkway that led to the steps. Thomas couldn't ignore the nagging feeling in the pit of his stomach that something was very wrong. He knew he needed to stay focused and determined. Lives were at stake, and Eddie Monroe might be a murderer.

Sunlight burned through the clouds. A car motored past, causing the group to turn and look. As they crept closer to the house, the silence grew denser, as if the barren trees suffocated any sound that dared to breach their perimeter. Thomas felt his heart pounding in his chest, a drumbeat of anticipation and dread.

"Keep your eyes open," Thomas said. "We'll split up. Aguilar and I will take the front; Raven and Chelsey, you two check the back. Stay in contact."

Chelsey pulled up the zipper on her leather jacket. "Got it."

Thomas approached the front door alongside Aguilar. He raised his hand to knock, hesitating before letting his knuckles rap against the wood.

"Mr. Monroe?" he called out, pressing his ear to the door. There was no response, only an oppressive stillness.

"Something doesn't feel right," Aguilar grumbled, glancing around the perimeter.

Thomas nodded in agreement, his concern mounting. A stench reached his nostrils and made him flinch.

"What the heck is that?"

"Smells like something died in there."

"Mr. Monroe? Nightshade County Sheriff's Department." No response. "Let's go in. We have enough cause for a welfare check."

As they entered the house, a wave of putrid odor assaulted their senses, so overwhelming that he had to fight back his gag reflex. The smell of death and decay clung to every surface, a nauseating stench reminiscent of carrion left to rot under the blazing sun.

"Good God." Aguilar covered her nose with the crook of her arm. "What is that?"

"Nothing good."

Thomas pulled out his flashlight and clicked it on, casting its beam across the shadowy interior. "Mr. Monroe, this is Sheriff Shepherd. We're here to check on you. If you're here, let us know."

There was no answer, only the sound of his breathing echoing through the abandoned space. He found a light switch on the wall and flicked it on. Outside, Chelsey and Raven continued to explore the backyard.

Aguilar removed her radio. "Raven, Chelsey, we're inside. There's a terrible smell, but we haven't located it yet. Anything on your end?"

"Nothing yet," Raven said through the radio. "We're checking out the shed now."

"Be careful. And keep us updated."

"Will do," Chelsey confirmed.

He turned to Aguilar. "I'll take the living room and kitchen. You check the bedrooms."

"Heading there now," she said.

Thomas moved across the living room. He couldn't shake the uneasy feeling that someone was watching them.

"Thomas, it's Chelsey." Her voice crackled through the radio. "We found something in the backyard shed—a rusted hook. Looks like there might be dried blood on it."

"Don't touch anything. I'll come collect the evidence."

"We'll wait for you."

As Thomas made his way to the backyard, a creaking sound caught his attention. It seemed to come from below, drawing him towards a door to the basement. His instincts screamed at him to proceed with caution.

"Heard something," he said into the radio. "I'm going down into the basement. Keep your eyes open."

"Hold up," Aguilar said. "I'll come with you."

"No. Stay up here and watch my back."

Descending the stairs, he felt the air grow colder, the stench of decay intensifying. Every step was a battle against the terror growing inside him, but he persisted, driven by the need for answers.

Reaching the bottom, he swept the flashlight beam across the concrete floor, revealing old boxes and discarded furniture.

And then, tucked away in a corner, he saw it. A plastic bag that had spilled over, concealing a grisly sight within.

"Good lord." He swallowed the bile rising in his throat. Inside the bag were three dead crows, their lifeless eyes staring into nothingness, as if accusing him of arriving too late to save them.

Aguilar's voice came through the radio. "Thomas? Come in."

"Found dead crows," he said, barely able to choke out the words. "Three of them in a plastic bag."

"We need to get this place locked down and processed. There's no telling what else we might find here."

"I couldn't agree more."

The rusted hook, the dead birds—they all pointed to a horrifying truth: Eddie Monroe was more than just a suspect in their case. He was a monster, hiding in plain sight.

He took another breath to steady himself before lifting the radio. "We'll regroup outside. I need to secure this scene before we go any further."

Aguilar met him in the kitchen. She wore gloves and carried two photo albums under her arm.

"What's that?"

"Found these upstairs," Aguilar said, setting the albums on the table. "Pictures of Eddie and his foster families."

The worn covers and yellowed pages told a story of their own—Eddie Monroe's life stitched together through photographs.

He flipped through the pages and scanned the images. One picture showed a house engulfed in flames. The fire department had yet to arrive.

"So much for Eddie's claim that he was at a friend's house," he said. The image unsettled him—a symbol of destruction and chaos. For how many decades had Eddie Monroe been a killer?

As they exited the house, the sun did little to chase away the chill that had settled inside his bones. A group of neighborhood kids stood in the next yard, watching them with curiosity. Thomas waved them over, holding up a picture of Eddie.

"Hey, have you seen this man around recently?" Thomas asked.

The children exchanged glances before shaking their heads in unison.

"Been days since we last saw him," one of the older kids muttered. Their eyes held a mixture of fear and suspicion, as if they also sensed the darkness that surrounded Eddie Monroe. Thomas gave them cards with the phone number to the sheriff's department in case Eddie returned.

As they dispersed, he turned to Aguilar, his expression grim. Several paces away, Chelsey and Raven bounced on their toes and tried to stay warm. He joined them outside the shed, where a hook hung off the wall. Dried blood and hair covered the point.

"We need a forensic team here immediately," he said.

"I'll call the county and get the medical examiner out here," Aguilar said.

Something squawked from the treetop and made their heads snap up. Thomas shielded his eyes and looked up. A black crow watched him from its perch.

"Where are all your friends?"

He didn't want to know the answer.

49

Early the next morning, Raven peeked at her watch. Devereux's deadline approached.

"Raven," Chelsey called from the next desk as LeVar and Scout bowed their heads together in concentration. "Can you pass me those files?"

"Sure." She struggled to focus on the investigation.

As they discussed the case, Raven's mind wandered to the great times she'd shared with her colleagues. If she took the job offer, all of that would end forever. But if she stayed, the money issues plaguing Wolf Lake Consulting wouldn't disappear. What would happen if the business closed and she lost her job?

"Hey, sis. Are you still with us?" LeVar asked.

"Uh, yeah. Just thinking about Eddie Monroe."

The familiar hum of Chelsey's voice discussing the investigation with LeVar and Scout served as a constant reminder of their friendship. The sudden vibration of Raven's phone jolted her back into focus. Devereux already?

Darren's name lit up the screen, and she answered. "Hey, what's up?"

"Found something," Darren said. "There's another set of fresh tire tracks near the cabin. Looks like we had company."

"Eddie?"

"The treads came from an SUV or a truck. That's as much as I can tell."

She placed the phone against her chest. "Chelsey, Darren found more tire tracks. There was an unknown vehicle near the cabin."

"It has to be Eddie Monroe," Chelsey said. "With Phillip Space and Jackson Anders behind bars, there's no one else to blame."

"Unless someone set up Eddie as well. I screwed up once. Jumping to conclusions doesn't seem like the best idea right now."

The desk phone rang.

"It's Thomas," Chelsey said. "Hopefully, he has good news."

Raven said, "Darren, Thomas is on the phone. I should see what he found. Call me if our mystery vehicle returns."

She rolled her chair over to Chelsey's desk.

"Got some news about the hook," Thomas said, his voice tense. "It tested positive for blood. I'm taking it to Claire so she can check it against the DNA of the murder victims. We pulled prints off the weapon. They belong to Eddie Monroe."

Chelsey nodded. "So he's the killer."

"Don't forget Phillip Space's fingerprints are on the other murder weapon."

"True, but I have to believe we zeroed in on the correct suspect this time. The way Eddie manipulated Jackson into attacking Phillip suggests he's our guy."

"I concur, but now we have to find him."

Raven's hands trembled as she clutched her mug. The coffee had gone cold, and every ring of the phone made her leap out of her seat. Chelsey sat rigidly at her desk, pretending not to notice. She had to fix things between them.

"Chelsey," Raven said, "I realize this isn't the best time, but I'm sorry I didn't tell you about the job offer sooner. I didn't want it to affect our partnership."

"Wait, what?" Scout asked, spinning her chair around.

LeVar folded his tattooed arms over his chest. "I didn't want to tell you until Raven decided. She received an offer to run a security team in Harmon."

"But she's not taking it, right?"

"Sis?"

Chelsey looked up from her papers, her eyes glistening with hurt. But she remained silent, waiting for Raven to continue.

"I haven't been straight with you guys," she said. "Over the last month, my finances caught up with me. Things could be better. There's no way I want to accept Devereux's offer, but I'm close to losing my vehicle."

"Then we'll all pitch in," Scout said.

"I'm not taking your money, Scout."

"But you can't leave. You're ... family."

Raven bit the inside of her cheek so she wouldn't break down in front of everyone. "Even though I'm considering it, I promise I'll prioritize this investigation. Our work together means so much to me."

For a moment, Chelsey only stared at her, her jaw clenched. Then, with a slow breath out, she spoke.

"We don't have time for personal issues right now. You need to make the decision that's best for your future. I understand how hard this must be for you."

LeVar approached Raven. "You're an integral part of this team. We all care about you, and we want you to be happy."

"Right," Scout chimed in. "If you have to leave, I'm sure we'll still see you."

Raven's heart swelled with gratitude for her friends' support. She called up Eddie Monroe's background check, a lump forming in her throat. "Thank you, guys. I appreciate it."

An hour passed with barely a word spoken. The only time banter didn't flow inside the office was after everyone left for the day. Now it felt like a morgue.

LeVar edged closer to Scout's computer screen, scanning the lines of data that seemed to stretch on forever. "Find anything yet?"

"Nothing substantial," Scout said, biting her lip. "Eddie Monroe is pretty elusive online, but I'm not giving up."

"We need something significant if we're going to figure out where he's hiding."

They needed a break in this case, and they needed it soon. Scout's fingers danced across the keyboard as her specialized AI software sifted through Eddie's digital footprint. Raven marveled at the teenager's ability to navigate the vast online world with ease, picking up on even the most minuscule details that might lead to something important.

"Wait a minute," Scout said. "I think I found something."

Raven pushed away from her desk. "What is it?"

"His IP address surfaced on a few incognito forum names. One of these forums is where he used to hang out."

Scout pulled up an old post by Eddie.

"Read it aloud," LeVar urged.

Scout paused before speaking. "'Wolf Lake's citizens are nothing but parasites, leeching off each other. They don't know what they've got coming. One day, they'll all get what they deserve.'"

"Psycho alert."

This was more than just unsettling; it was a direct threat.

"Should we tell Thomas?" Scout asked.

"I'll text him, but we need more. People say wacko stuff online all the time."

"Stay on it," Chelsey said. "There might be more where that came from."

The glow from the screen reflected off Scout's glasses. LeVar offered suggestions as she clicked and scrolled. The room was silent save for the hum of the computers.

"Hey, look at this," Scout said. She pointed to an image—a photo of Eddie Monroe standing in front of a rustic cabin, a smug grin plastered on his face.

"Where did you find that?" Raven asked, leaning in closer to examine the picture.

"Social media profile. It was hidden among his vacation photos. He rented it two springs ago."

"Check out the post. 'Got this place for next to nothing. Nobody rents this place until summer.'"

"Can you find any information about the cabin?" LeVar asked.

"Of course she can. EXIF data, right?"

"You bet," Scout said, her concentration focused entirely on the task at hand. Within moments, she extracted the information. "Got it. The cabin is located deep in the woods, past the Wolf Lake inlet."

Chelsey looked at Raven from the corner of her eye. "That's close to the state park."

Raven rubbed the goosebumps off her arms. "Too close."

"Could be our guy's hideout," LeVar said. "If the cabin is open all spring, it would serve as the perfect hideout. It's not under his name, so the sheriff's department wouldn't know he uses it."

"We need to act fast. If this is where he's living, we can't afford to let him slip away."

"I'll call the sheriff's department."

"I'll gather our gear while you notify Thomas," Chelsey said. "This might be our only shot."

As the team sprang into action, Raven reflected that despite the problems her admission had caused, it never took long for them to come together.

50

Thomas wiped the perspiration off his forehead and joined his deputies beside their desks. On the table lay the evidence they'd gathered on Eddie Monroe. The door opened and Raven entered with Chelsey, LeVar, and Scout.

"Let's get started," Thomas said.

They gathered around the table, where he directed their attention to the forensic reports. He passed copies to everyone.

"I have the results of the DNA tests from the hook in Eddie Monroe's shed. The blood matches Patricia Hudson's."

Their faces reflected the gravity of the situation. Eddie had been a person of interest, but now he was their lead suspect.

Lambert cleared his throat. "Should we release Phillip Space and Jackson Anders?"

Thomas shook his head, his blue-green eyes narrowed in thought. "No, not yet. We need to be certain Eddie Monroe is the killer. We've made too many mistakes already."

"And even if Phillip and Jackson are innocent, they're safer here," said Aguilar. "Eddie is targeting them."

Thomas studied the lab results. "Pretty bold of him to leave the hook in his shed."

"He's convinced he fooled us into believing Phillip or Jackson killed those women. We need to move quickly on this, Thomas. Eddie hasn't returned to his house in days. If he's hiding at the cabin Scout found, let's grab him before he figures out we're onto him."

"We'll move on the cabin today," Thomas said, his fingers tapping on the table as he weighed their options. The need to act was building up a pressure inside him.

Raven stepped forward with a series of photos clutched in her hand. "We used satellite imagery to capture the terrain around the cabin." She spread the photos on the table, revealing an isolated, weathered cabin surrounded by dense woods. "It's deep in the forest, about two miles from the state park. A perfect hideout for someone running from the law."

Thomas scrutinized the images, his eyes moving from the cabin to the surrounding trees. The killer would feel safe, secure from prying eyes and judgment. He glanced up at Raven. "You did well. Now we know what to expect when we locate the cabin."

"Right." Lambert tapped the first picture. "The terrain slopes away from the entrance. If we come from the west, he won't see us approach. It might be our only chance to catch him."

"Good thinking."

As they prepared to leave, Thomas could see the strain in each of them. They had to find the murderer and stop him before he inflicted more pain and suffering. He'd killed two innocent women, and it seemed he'd gotten away with murder as a boy.

The computer screen illuminated Scout's expression as she pulled up more satellite images of the cabin and its surrounding woods. With precise movements, she zoomed in on the area where the structure stood, its outline barely perceptible among the dense foliage.

"Can you zoom out?" Thomas asked.

Scout expanded the view until it encompassed several miles of terrain. "How's this?"

"Perfect. Look here." He pointed at the screen. "See the state park grounds? Eddie must have run to the cabin after breaking Darren and Raven's window. That's how he escaped from LeVar and Darren."

"Smart move on his part," Deputy Lambert admitted, squinting at the image. "He knew the way back to the hideout."

Thomas scanned the satellite image again, hoping to uncover a detail that would give them the upper hand.

"Scout, are you certain about the EXIF data? Could Eddie have tampered with it?"

Scout considered the question. "I'm sure the data is reliable, Thomas. There's no sign that he altered the numbers."

Raven stepped forward. "I don't believe Eddie Monroe has the technical know-how to manipulate the EXIF data. It's not something easily done without leaving traces."

Thomas nodded, accepting their assessments. They couldn't afford any mistakes.

"We'll proceed with the plan," Thomas said. "As soon as we gather supplies, we'll hit the cabin." He turned to Scout, his expression softening. "You've done an incredible job. But I can't let you come with us on this one. It's too dangerous."

Scout's face fell and her shoulders slumped. She opened her mouth to protest, but was cut short by the arrival of Buck Benson, Serena, and Naomi. They were here to drive Scout home, ensuring her safety as the rest of the team prepared for the confrontation.

"Hey, kiddo," Buck said gently, placing a comforting hand on Scout's shoulder. "It's time to go."

"Isn't there some way I can help?" she asked.

"You've done plenty," Thomas said. "Were it not for you, we wouldn't have found the cabin. Let us handle things from here."

As Scout reluctantly left with her mother, Thomas felt guilty. He knew how much the teenager wanted to help, but he wouldn't put her in harm's way.

Aguilar folded her arms and studied the picture. "We need to be prepared for anything. I suggest the deputies wear Kevlar vests. Eddie's history suggests he's unhinged and unpredictable."

Without question," Thomas said. "But we don't have enough Kevlar vests for the entire Wolf Lake Consulting team."

"Then we prioritize. Deputies first. The WLC team can hang back and run surveillance. We'll just have to be extra cautious."

Thomas nodded, fully aware of the risks they were about to take. He glanced around the room at his team. They all understood the stakes and yet showed no hesitation.

"Then it's settled. We'll come in from the west with Chelsey and Raven serving as our eyes and ears. LeVar, Lambert, and Aguilar—gather our vests. Everyone, stay sharp and watch each other's backs. No one goes off alone."

"Understood, Shep," LeVar said.

They discussed the final preparations. The uncertainty of what they'd find at the cabin, combined with the knowledge that they were walking into dangerous territory, ramped up Thomas's anxiety. But he knew there was no time to waste—they needed to act now before Eddie could slip away once more.

"Let's gear up and move out," he said.

With a collective nod, they prepared their weapons. As they loaded their guns and checked their equipment, Thomas allowed himself a moment of introspection.

He understood the risks involved. The responsibility rested on his shoulders to keep his team safe.

With everyone's cooperation, he would stop a killer.

51

While his deputies gathered supplies, Thomas stood in the doorway to his office and motioned Chelsey forward. It was impossible to ignore the tension between her and Raven, and as she entered the room, he scanned her face for signs of distress.

He closed the door so the others wouldn't overhear. She sat with her hands folded in her lap. Thomas returned to his seat, stacking the case files strewn across his desk. The investigation took precedent, but he couldn't shake his concern for her fractured relationship with Raven. They would have to work together to run surveillance, and he couldn't afford a lack of communication.

He looked up from his papers. "I know this is a difficult time for everyone, but I've noticed the problems between you and Raven."

She shifted in her seat. "It's complicated."

"Complicated or not," he said, filing the folders inside a drawer and leaning forward, elbows on the desk, "we need to work together if we're going to solve this case."

"I understand that, Thomas." She clasped her hands

together. "But I can't pretend it doesn't hurt when she gets a job offer and leaves without even talking to me about it first."

His eyes widened. "Job offer?"

She explained Raven's situation and told him about Franklin Devereux's proposal.

"I can see how that would be difficult for you," he said. "But maybe there's another way to look at it. Perhaps Raven felt she needed to decide for herself, with no outside influence. You know how strong-willed she can be, and she's probably embarrassed about her financial situation."

Chelsey let out a bitter laugh. "Strong-willed is one way to put it," she muttered, a hint of a smile tugging at her lips. She stared down at her hands, lost in thought, while he waited for her to speak. "Sometimes, I wonder if we're just too different. We care about each other, but I don't know if that's enough."

"Opposites can complement each other. You're both powerful, driven women who dedicated yourselves to your work. If you can build on those shared values, maybe the rest will fall into place."

She looked up at him, searching his face as she considered his words. He could see the gears turning in her head, and he hoped he had given her something to hold on to.

"Maybe you're right. I'll try to keep an open mind and focus on our common goals."

"I think it might be best if you give Raven space to decide. Pressuring her could push her further away."

Her eyes flickered with hurt, but she nodded, drawing a deep breath. "I know. It's just hard, Thomas. I care about her so much."

"Your ability to understand her position, even when it hurts you, is one of your greatest strengths. It's not only what makes you an exceptional investigator, but also an incredible person."

"I'll try to keep my distance for now. Let her figure things out."

"Trust is essential," he said, placing a supporting hand on hers. "You two have something special. It may take time, but I believe you'll resolve your problems."

"I'll keep what you said in mind. Let's get back to work. We have a killer to catch."

"Indeed, we do, but I have to ask: Do you think the issues will affect your ability to work together on this case?"

She lifted her chin. "Whatever problems Raven and I have, it won't affect our professionalism. We understand the importance of solving this investigation, and it remains our priority."

"Good." Relief washed over him. "I needed to make sure. It's crucial that we're all focused and able to work as a team."

"I love Raven. The job offer she received . . . it hurt me deeply, but I know our duty is to catch this killer and bring justice for the victims. Our issues won't get in the way."

Thomas observed her, noting the sincerity on her face and the unwavering strength in her voice. Her resilience always impressed him, not only as an investigator but as a person. She put her feelings aside to focus on what mattered.

"That's good to hear. I want you to know that I admire your determination. It speaks volumes about your character. And I mean both of you. I don't need to tell you how much I respect Raven. But isn't there a way to figure these problems out together? I'm talking about the increased costs Wolf Lake Consulting has to deal with and Raven's bank account."

"If there was a solution, I would have suggested it by now."

"There's always a solution. It will come to you. Have faith." He placed a hand on hers, offering reassurance. "We're going to solve this case together. And once it's over, I'll help you with the financial plan for Wolf Lake Consulting. We'll make sure your business stays strong."

"I don't want a handout."

"Now you sound like Raven."

"Yeah, I suppose I do."

"You're so alike, it's scary."

As they returned to the others, the team assembled around the table. Thomas cleared his throat, garnering their attention. "We have our next steps planned out. Lambert, you're best suited to handle the terrain and breech the cabin. You'll lead our team."

Lambert stood a little taller. "You've got it, boss man."

"Chelsey and Raven will be our eyes and ears, just in case Eddie makes a run for it or tries to circle around us."

Aguilar nodded, giving Chelsey an encouraging look, while Raven's expression remained neutral. The tension between them lingered, but they understood their objective: to catch the killer.

"Stay sharp, stay safe, and remember why we're doing this," Thomas said. "For Patricia and Ellen."

The team dispersed, moving with purpose. To Thomas's surprise, Chelsey placed a hand on Raven's shoulder.

"I've got your back," she said, ready for the challenges ahead.

Raven's eyes glistened. "And I have yours."

52

Eddie Monroe sat in the cabin, his eyes fixed on the fire. The dancing flames reminded him of the night when he had set fire to his foster parents' house. Their screams echoed through his memory. He tightened his grip on the whiskey glass, feeling a strange sense of satisfaction as he recalled the rage that had consumed him that night.

"Deserved it," Eddie said. He took a swig from his glass. "They all did."

It had been so easy to get away with murder. All he'd needed to do was claim he was sleeping at his friend's house. Nobody realized he'd slipped out the window after everyone fell asleep and hurried back to his house.

His thoughts wandered to Jackson and Phillip. How simple it had been to frame them for the murders. A smug grin crossed his face as he pictured the sheriff cuffing Jackson, whose schizophrenic ramblings only confirmed his guilt in the minds of those around him. And Phillip Space was sitting behind bars, accused of a crime he didn't commit.

Like taking candy from a baby.

With both men jailed, the focus would shift elsewhere. He

needed another patsy, someone to keep suspicion off him a little longer. His mind raced through potential targets. Who could it be? He swirled the whiskey in his glass.

As he mulled over the possibilities, he felt pride in his ingenuity. For years, he had hidden in plain sight, manipulating events and people to his advantage. Patricia and Ellen had reminded him so much of his foster mother. They'd deserved their fates.

He took a last sip of whiskey and set the glass down on the rough wooden table. Time was running out, and he had to make a choice soon.

A rustling jolted him back to reality. Someone was coming up the ridge.

The noise was subtle, but on a still night like this one, the forest amplified every sound. It was coming from the woods. Anyone who stumbled upon the cabin posed a threat. Was it the sheriff's department? It couldn't be. He'd been so careful.

Standing against the wall, he peeked out the window. No sign of intruders, but they were out there. His knife reflected the firelight. He retrieved the blade and tucked it into his pocket.

Whoever approached the cabin needed to die.

53

A gust of wind stirred up the snow as Thomas and his deputies approached the cabin. The wooden structure stood up the ridge and was hidden behind a canopy of trees, its weathered exterior blending into the surrounding forest. Aguilar brought up the rear, scanning the area for movement.

From a half mile behind, Chelsey and Raven surveyed the forest and radioed their findings. No sign of Eddie Monroe.

Lambert led the way forward. He scaled the terrain as if taking a casual stroll through his backyard. Thomas struggled to keep up. They broke through the treeline and came face to face with the cabin.

"Looks like someone's been around," said Lambert, bending down to pick up a crumpled food wrapper near the door. He held it up for the others to see.

"Nobody should be here. Check inside," Thomas said.

As they entered the cabin, the smell of damp wood and musty fabric filled their nostrils. A sleeping bag lay in the corner, next to a bag filled with clothes. LeVar wrinkled his nose at the smell emanating from the bag.

"Seems Eddie's made himself at home," LeVar said, examining the contents of the bag. "But where is he now?"

"Stay sharp. He could be anywhere."

The cabin was small. They searched every corner as a team. It was Lambert who noticed the false panel in the wall, running his fingers along the edges.

"Look at this," he called out, prying the panel open with a grunt.

The other officers gathered around as he pulled out a dusty box. Inside were newspaper clippings about the deaths of Eddie's foster parents and articles detailing Patricia's murder.

"I wonder if he broke into Jackson Anders' house and left those newspapers for us to find," said Aguilar, sifting through the clippings. "This confirms our suspicions about Eddie."

"His obsession runs deep," Thomas said.

Nausea rolled through his body as he imagined Eddie setting his foster parents' house afire.

"Thomas, he's not here," LeVar said. "Should we hide and wait for him to return?"

"He knows we're onto him. We need to catch him before he hurts anyone else."

Thomas snapped photographs with his phone and radioed Chelsey.

"Let's move," Lambert said, closing the box and tucking it under his arm.

They exited the cabin and entered the night. The wind howled as they searched for tracks. Every groan of the trees was a reminder that the woods held secrets—secrets that had led them to the doorstep of a killer.

Lambert grabbed his arm. "Did you hear that?"

The crackling of branches underfoot, the snapping of twigs.

Something was out there, watching them. He shared a glance with LeVar, who nodded in silent agreement.

"Chelsey, Raven," he spoke into the radio, "monitor our surroundings. We're going to check this out."

"Got it," Chelsey replied.

The deputies moved cautiously through the underbrush, their senses heightened as they followed the sound. The rustling grew louder. They came to a clearing, and there, in a shaft of moonlight, stood the killer.

"Eddie Monroe, freeze!" Thomas shouted, his voice breaking through the silence like a gunshot.

But Eddie had already spotted them, his eyes wide with fear and recognition.

Lambert cursed as Eddie bolted deeper into the forest.

"Chelsey, he's on the move," Aguilar called into her radio. "Tell us where he is."

"Copy that," Chelsey said.

Thomas wanted to order Chelsey and Raven to stand down and not chase Eddie, but they were closer and had a bead on him. What if he carried a weapon?

Adrenaline raced through his veins as he jumped over a fallen tree and sprinted after the killer. Aguilar and LeVar ran by his side as Lambert took the lead.

Eddie tore through the undergrowth, his breath ragged and desperate. He glanced over his shoulder, his eyes filled with psychosis. Chelsey and Raven pursued him, gaining ground but unable to catch the murderer. In his haste, Eddie vanished into the evergreens.

"Where'd he go?" Aguilar asked, her eyes darting around the dark woods.

Thomas shook his head, frustrated and worried. He couldn't see the private investigators anymore.

"Split up," he said. "Lambert and LeVar, follow the ridge to the right. Aguilar and I will come around the other side of the trees and cut him off."

"Be careful," Lambert said before running off.

The air grew colder, and the creaking branches seemed to laugh at them. Their shadows deepened, as if to hide the killer within their depths.

Thomas gripped the radio. "Chelsey and Raven, you are not to engage Eddie Monroe. Stand back."

No reply.

He glanced at Aguilar, who was busy contacting backup units to establish a perimeter around the forest.

"LeVar, Lambert, what's your position?" Thomas asked, his voice steady despite the rising tension.

"Closing in on Chelsey and Raven's last known location," LeVar said, his tone desperate. "I don't see them."

"Find them."

∾

IN THE THICK of the woods, Raven's breath came in gasps as she and Chelsey tracked Eddie. The ice was like grease beneath their feet, and they moved in silence, fearing any noise would give away their position. Each shadow seemed to pulse with menace, and Raven felt her skin prickle as she scanned the surroundings.

"Nothing," Chelsey said. "He could be anywhere."

"He has to be close."

They couldn't afford to lose him now.

"Backup's on the way," Aguilar said over the radio.

Thomas warned them to stay away from the killer, but Chelsey ignored the command. The sheriff and his deputies were scattered behind them. Only Raven and Chelsey could catch Eddie Monroe.

Raven sensed someone watching.

"Over there," Chelsey said, pointing to a rustle in the bushes.

They approached, muscles tensed for action. False alarm. A startled squirrel bounded away, and Raven glanced at her partner. Had they lost him? She knew the killer was close; she could feel it in her bones. But where?

"Stay on guard. He knows we're here."

As they continued their search, the wind dug into her bones. The darkness became a living thing. Still she pushed forward, driven to bring Eddie Monroe to justice.

Raven and Chelsey moved through the thickening forest, their breaths shallow and their bodies frozen. The sharp scent of pine needles filled the air. An owl hooted. The bramble grew wilder, catching at their calves and ankles as they pursued the elusive Eddie Monroe.

She looked over her shoulder to ensure Chelsey was still behind her.

"Don't worry about me," Chelsey said.

They were getting closer, but Eddie seemed to have vanished.

"Go left around that cluster of trees," Raven said, pointing ahead. "I'll take the right side. We'll cover more ground that way."

"Right."

Chelsey nodded in agreement before slipping around the copse of trees.

Raven's footsteps were light and quiet as she rounded the opposite side of the copse, ears straining for any sound. She hesitated, feeling exposed and vulnerable without Chelsey by her side. A chill crept down her spine.

"Raven, I think I heard something." Chelsey's voice crackled through the radio, muffled by the screaming wind. "Stay where you are."

"Copy that."

But as Raven rounded the bend, her foot snagged on an

exposed root that sent her tumbling to the ground with a thud. She clutched her throbbing ankle. Twisted but not sprained.

She climbed to her feet and looked behind her. It was so dark she'd lost her way.

"Chelsey?" Raven whispered into the radio. "Where are you?"

"I'm where we split up. Come back."

But she didn't know if she should head left or right. Everything looked the same in the night.

A figure lunged at her from the shadows. Hands reached for her throat.

The killer, his eyes wild and desperate.

"Chelsey!" Raven choked out as the radio fell from her hand.

She fought for her life as his grip squeezed the air from her lungs.

Chelsey's yell pierced through the chaos. But would she make it in time?

54

Chelsey slipped on the snow and ice as she rushed toward Raven's frantic cries. She spotted Eddie Monroe; his hands gripped Raven's throat.

Not her friend. She wouldn't allow harm to come to her partner. Instinct took over, and she charged, heedless of the slick conditions.

With a scream, she collided with the killer. His grip on Raven slipped away as the force of her tackle sent him sprawling to the ground.

Raven clutched her neck and rolled onto her side, gasping and gagging. Her dark braids splayed out around her like a halo, and she writhed, trying to regain her bearings.

"Chelsey," Raven croaked, her voice hoarse.

"Stay down. I got this."

But Eddie was quick to recover. With a snarl, he clawed his way back on top of Chelsey, who fought to keep him at bay. His hands found their way around her throat, squeezing. Panic surged through her as she scrambled to free herself. But he was too strong.

Several steps away, Raven struggled to regain her footing.

But would it be too late?

"Raven," Chelsey choked out, her vision blurring as she struggled to breathe. "Help...me..."

Chelsey's hands clawed at Eddie's arms, trying to pry his fingers from around her throat. The pain was unbearable. With a surge of adrenaline, she loosened Eddie's grip just enough to gasp for air.

Her thoughts raced, a torrent of memories and regrets swirling together. She thought of Thomas, Lambert, and Aguilar, wondering if they would make it in time. She thought of Tigger, her loyal orange tabby, waiting for her return. And she thought of Raven, who had become more than just a coworker—a partner, a confidante, a sister.

With a guttural cry, Raven hurled herself at Eddie, her desperation lending her superhuman strength and speed. Their bodies collided and tangled in a frenzied struggle. As Raven rolled on top of the murderer, Chelsey helped keep the thrashing man pinned.

"Hold him down," Raven said, understanding the unspoken plan. Neither could overpower Eddie alone, but together they might stand a chance.

As the killer fought to free himself, Chelsey summoned her self-defense training. She pinned one arm, while Raven held the other, their bodies pressing down on him with all their weight. Could they hold him? Where were Thomas and his team?

The sound of footsteps echoed through the forest, growing louder as Thomas, Aguilar, Lambert, and LeVar came into view. They drew their guns.

"Chelsey, Raven!" Thomas called out. "Don't let him up. We're here."

Eddie had fought his way to his stomach, but Raven held his arm behind his back while Chelsey lay on his legs to keep him still.

"About damn time," Raven smiled at Lambert, her grip on Eddie's arm tightening.

"Got you covered," Lambert said, a grin tugging at the corner of his mouth.

"Stay still, Eddie Monroe," Aguilar said; she aimed her gun at the struggling man. "It's over."

The fight was leaving the killer.

Thomas took over for Chelsey while Lambert took Raven's place.

"LeVar, cuff him," Thomas said.

"Sure thing, Shep Dawg," LeVar said, snapping the handcuffs onto Eddie's wrists with a satisfying click.

As Chelsey and Raven finally released their hold on the killer, they collapsed beside each other, their breaths ragged and labored. They had done it. Together they had stopped a monster.

Her chest heaved as she gulped air. She glanced over at Raven, who was still panting from the exertion, and saw the bruises forming on her friend's neck.

"Raven, are you hurt?"

"Been better. But we got him."

"Damn straight," Chelsey said.

Aguilar and Thomas stood nearby, their guns trained on the cuffed killer as Lambert and LeVar held him.

"Aguilar and LeVar, escort him back to the cruiser. Lambert, help me with Chelsey and Raven."

"Sure thing, Thomas," Lambert said as Aguilar and LeVar hauled Eddie away.

"Chelsey, where are you hurt?" Thomas asked, concern softening his face.

"He strangled me, but it's just bruising," she said, feeling the warmth of his hand as he helped her to her feet. "Nothing serious."

"Raven, how about you?"

"Same. It'll take more than that psycho to finish me."

"Thank you both. Had you not blocked his path in the forest, we would have lost him. Your bravery saved lives today. I promise we'll handle it from here."

"Couldn't have done it without each other," Chelsey murmured, pulling Raven into a tight embrace. Tears streamed down their faces, their love for each other stronger than ever.

"Come on," Thomas said. "Let's get you checked out and go home."

∽

THE SHERIFF'S department hummed with an undercurrent of tension as Thomas settled into his office chair. He stared at the phone on his desk, his fingers drumming a staccato rhythm against the smooth surface. It was time to make the call. Or rather, two calls. He picked up the receiver and dialed the first number.

"Hello, Ms. Ford? This is Sheriff Thomas Shepherd. I have news regarding your client, Phillip Space. We've apprehended the actual killer, Eddie Monroe. Mr. Space will be released from custody."

Thomas listened, nodding as the lawyer expressed her gratitude and promised to fetch Phillip from the holding cell. Hanging up, Thomas dialed Jackson Anders' attorney.

"Mr. Tannenbaum? I'm Sheriff Thomas Shepherd. We've captured Eddie Monroe, who we believe murdered those women. Jackson Anders is no longer a suspect and will be released."

Lambert was already heading to the holding cells to release the prisoners. A few minutes later, voices traveled down the hallway. As the door to the office area opened, Thomas looked up to see Jackson Anders enter, escorted by Lambert. A shadow of doubt lingered in Jackson's eyes, but hope tempered it.

"Am I free to go?" he asked.

"Indeed you are," Thomas said, his eyes meeting Jackson's. "I'm sorry for the ordeal you went through."

"You kept me safe and got me back on my medications. Who knows what Eddie Monroe would have done to me if you hadn't put me in a cell. Plus, it was free room and board for the night."

"That's one way of looking at it."

"I'll do my best to stay out of trouble." He paused, glancing toward the door as Phillip entered the room. The air grew heavy with unspoken animosity.

"Phillip," Jackson said, his voice low and uncertain.

"Jackson," Phillip replied, his tone equally cautious.

They stared at each other for a long moment, tension winding tight between them like a coiled spring. Aguilar and LeVar stepped forward to prevent a fight from breaking out.

"Listen," Phillip said, breaking the silence, "I never said anything about you, okay? We were both set up by Eddie."

"Seems that way." Jackson's expression softened. "And I never wanted any of this to happen."

"Neither did I."

Phillip extended a hand toward Jackson. For a beat, neither man moved, their eyes locked in silent communication. Then Jackson reached out and grasped Phillip's hand, sealing an unspoken truce.

"Let's just put this behind us, okay?" Phillip said.

"It already is. Hey, maybe you can speak to Mike for me and explain what happened. That's my favorite hangout."

"I'll see what I can do."

Thomas watched the exchange as the two men moved past their differences. The attorneys arrived, and the prisoners exchanged words with their lawyers. Elaine was there too.

In the cramped evidence room, the team sifted through the items collected from Eddie's house and the cabin. The metal hook gleamed ominously under the lights, a chilling reminder of the murders. Towers of newspaper clippings threatened to topple over, each article detailing the heinous acts committed by the man now locked away. And then there were the pictures—photographs of Phillip and Jackson, captured in moments of anger and vulnerability, intended to be used against them.

"Can you believe all this?" Lambert asked, shaking his head. "This guy was twisted."

"More than we ever realized," Aguilar agreed, her voice heavy with disgust.

Thomas organized the evidence, already planning ahead for the trial. It would be a challenging process, but he felt confident in their case.

"Jackson, Phillip," Thomas called out, motioning for the two men to join him. Their faces held a mix of relief and wariness. "Your assistance will be required during the trial. You'll both need to testify about your experiences and interactions with Eddie."

Phillip's brow furrowed, his eyes dark with concern. "But we're no longer suspects, right?"

"Correct," Thomas reassured them, a flicker of empathy crossing his face. "You've both been cleared. We know Eddie set you up. Now it's our job to make sure he never gets out of prison."

Jackson stepped closer. "We'll do whatever it takes."

"Together, we'll see that justice is done."

The two former suspects left the station with their attorneys as free men. As the team continued their work, the atmosphere in the room shifted from one of grim determination to quiet resolve.

Eddie Monroe would never kill again.

55

The door to Thomas's office clicked shut behind Raven. Chelsey was speaking with Aguilar, and the other deputies were busy building their case against Eddie Monroe. Even as Raven tried to focus on the conversation she needed to have with Thomas, she could still feel the killer's hands wrapped around her throat.

"Thomas, I need to talk to you about something important."

He looked up from his desk and closed a folder. "What's wrong? You seem shaken. Do you want to talk about what happened in the forest?"

She took a deep breath, steadying herself before plunging into the confession. "I received a job offer from Franklin Devereux. A lucrative one. But accepting it would mean leaving Wolf Lake Consulting and all of you."

Thomas leaned back in his chair, his expression thoughtful. "That's quite a decision to make. Tell me more."

She paced the room, wrestling with her emotions. "It's not just about the money. It's true I'm struggling financially." She stopped, staring out the window at the rain streaking down the glass. "My loans are piling up, and this job would help me get out of debt. But I can't bear the thought of leaving my friends—you, Chelsey, everyone. And the work we do together . . . it means so much to me."

Thomas listened, his attention never leaving her. He understood better than most the struggle to balance personal needs with a sense of duty.

"Raven, you're an incredibly talented investigator. Your contributions to this team are invaluable." He paused, taking a moment to consider his next words. "Shepherd Systems had another record quarter, thanks in no small part to your mother. If it would help, I could pay off your loan. To ease some of your burden."

Her eyes widened, and she shook her head. "No, I can't accept that. It's too much."

"I want to help. I don't want to see you struggling like this."

Her pride wouldn't allow her to accept such a generous offer. She knew the value of standing on her own two feet. It had been a hard lesson learned when her mother had thrown her out at eighteen, and she wasn't about to accept handouts now.

"Thank you, Thomas. I appreciate your kindness, but I need to find my way through this."

"Whatever you decide, know that we're here for you. You have our support, always." He tapped his fingers on the armrest. "I have to tell you that your instincts about Phillip Space were spot-on. You were right all along."

She blinked. "I just couldn't get over the feeling that something wasn't adding up."

"Your dedication to finding the truth is commendable, and it's part of what makes you such an asset. If you decide to leave, know that we'll miss you. But you need to prioritize what's best for your future and wellbeing."

Raven stared at the floor. Her dilemma had not changed. On the one hand, she felt loyal to her friends and the work they did together. On the other, she couldn't ignore the opportunity for financial stability that Franklin Devereux's job offer presented.

They sat in silence, lost in their own thoughts. The air between them was thick with unspoken emotions and a mutual understanding that their paths might soon diverge.

"Thomas," Raven said, lifting her gaze to meet his, "I want you to know how much I appreciate everything you've done for me. Your support means more than I can express."

"Likewise, my friend. You've made a real difference in this town, and in my life."

As she left Thomas's office, she knew her decision would not be easy, but she also felt reassured by the knowledge that, no matter what she chose, her friends would always be there for her.

Darren waited with concern. As soon as he saw her, he stepped forward and enveloped her in a comforting embrace.

"Hey," he murmured, his stubbled cheek pressed against hers. "How'd it go?"

She trembled in his arms, tears streaming down her face. "It was difficult," she said, her voice cracking. "Next to talking to Chelsey, that was the most uncomfortable I've felt in years. I told Thomas about Franklin Devereux's offer and how I'm struggling. He offered to help, but I couldn't accept it."

"Ah, Raven. You're so strong, but sometimes it's okay to let others help you."

She buried her face in his shoulder. "I can't bear the thought of leaving Chelsey and everyone. What do I do?"

He pulled back, looking into her eyes. "Follow your heart. I realize that sounds cliche, but it's the best advice I can give. Have faith in yourself and everything will work out."

As they held each other, Raven scanned the room through her tear-blurred vision, noticing Chelsey sitting across the room with a pained expression on her face. She felt a pang of guilt, knowing the dilemma was affecting her friends.

"Chelsey looks upset," she said, wiping away her tears.

"Give her some time. She'll come around."

LeVar approached. "Hey, sis. I thought about that job you're considering. I want you to know whatever you decide is cool with me."

"Thanks, LeVar," she said, forcing a small smile. "That means a lot."

Chelsey stared at a half-empty mug of coffee. She rose from her seat and crossed the room.

"Hey," Chelsey said. "Can I talk to you?"

"Yeah, anytime."

They stepped away from the others, finding a quiet corner near a bookshelf filled with case files and mementos of past investigations.

"I wanted to say that I'm worried about you. I know how hard this decision must be, but I need you to know how much our partnership and friendship mean to me."

Raven looked into Chelsey's eyes, seeing the pain and fear hidden beneath the surface. She swallowed hard, feeling a knot tighten in her throat. "Chelsey, I—"

"Please," Chelsey interrupted. "Just let me finish. I'm afraid of losing you. You're more than just my partner. You're my family. And the thought of not having you by my side . . . it terrifies me."

Raven felt a surge of emotion well up inside her, touched by Chelsey's honesty and the depth of their connection. She reached out and took Chelsey's hand, giving it a reassuring squeeze. "You're my family too. And no matter what happens, nothing can change the bond we share. I promise I will weigh all options and make a decision that takes into account my personal and professional goals, as well as our friendship. I owe you that much."

"That's all I ask."

"No more procrastinating. I'll give you an answer in the morning."

Raven walked away from her colleagues, retreating to the solitude of the kitchen. She sat in a chair, her fingers drumming against the cool plastic of the tabletop.

"Hey," said Darren, poking his head inside the doorway. "Mind if I come in?"

"Join the party."

He entered and leaned against the wall, watching her intently. "I saw you talking to Chelsey. You've got a lot on your plate."

"Understatement of the century," she said, running her hands through her long braids.

"Devereux's offer is tempting. But I know you're worried about Chelsey and her business."

"I can't deny that the money would change my life. But it feels like I'm betraying my family."

"Take the night to clear your head. Then trust your instincts. They've never steered you wrong before."

Raven laughed without mirth. "Easier said than done."

"Nothing worthwhile ever comes easily. Listen, I need to blow out of here. Do you want me to drive you back? We can pick up your vehicle in the morning."

"Nah, I need to decompress."

"Don't be long, okay?"

"I'll be home soon."

As he left the kitchen, she wandered the hallway and scanned the framed certificates on the wall. Each represented years of hard work and dedication. She closed her eyes, trying to picture her life without her friends at Wolf Lake Consulting and the sheriff's department.

As the clock struck midnight, Raven knew she had to make a

choice, one that would shape not only her own destiny but also Chelsey's business. And as the station cleared out and gave way to the graveyard shift, she braced herself for the inevitable moment when she would reveal her decision to those who mattered most.

56

Thomas's silver Ford F-150 cut through the darkness, its headlights showing him the winding road that led to the A-frame house beside Wolf Lake. Chelsey gripped the steering wheel of her Honda Civic, following his truck. It was almost one in the morning, and she could hear the distant sounds of the ice melting on the lake, a reminder of the gradual transitions of nature.

They pulled beside each other in the driveway.

"Listen," Thomas said, rolling down his window. "You can hear the ice breaking up."

Chelsey shivered at the chill but smiled at the sound. "It's beautiful."

Stepping out of their vehicles, they stared at the expanse of the lake illuminated by the pale moon. The rain had ceased, and the once-solid ice was now fractured and shifting, its edges surrendering to the relentless lapping of the water.

"Nature always finds its way," Chelsey said.

"Right when you least expect it."

As they entered the A-frame, Jack bounded over to greet

them, his tail wagging. Chelsey bent down to ruffle his fur, feeling a surge of warmth and affection for the loyal pup. Tigger sprawled on the couch, snoring softly. The cat's presence also brought her comfort, despite his perpetual indifference to everything but food.

"Hey, buddy," she said, scratching Jack behind the ears. "Missed you."

Thomas hung up their coats and kicked off his boots. "I don't know about you, but I'm exhausted."

"Me too." She rubbed her eyes. "But it's good to be home."

Surrounded by the familiar scents and textures of their shared life, she felt a sense of peace she hadn't experienced in days. In the presence of their pets and the constant ebb and flow of nature just outside their door, her worries seemed to recede. Somehow, she would save her business. The answer was out there, and she would find it.

She sank into the cushions of the living room couch, one hand stroking Jack's fur as the other clutched a steaming mug of chamomile tea. The warm liquid soothed her throat and nerves.

"Thomas, I've been meaning to talk to you about Wolf Lake Consulting."

Thomas looked up from a book, concern flickering in his blue-green eyes. He closed it gently and set it aside, giving Chelsey his full attention. "What's going on with the firm?"

"Business has been great, more clients than ever before. But despite the success, we're struggling to stay profitable. Costs are rising faster than revenue, and I'm not sure what to do about it."

"You're an amazing leader, and I'm confident you'll figure this out. But have you talked to your staff about this?"

"I told Raven," she said, her fingers tightening around her mug. "Sometimes I wonder if I'm cut out for this. Running a business is so much harder than I ever imagined."

His thumb brushed reassuring circles over her knuckles. "We all have our doubts and fears, but you can't let them define you. Remember when you first started Wolf Lake Consulting? You had nothing but your determination and drive, and look how far you've come."

Chelsey's eyes misted over with unshed tears. Thomas was right. She'd come a long way since the early days of her fledgling business. But the road still seemed fraught with uncertainty, and a dead end loomed ahead.

"I don't want to let anyone down. My clients, my team, you. I want to make this work."

"Chelsey, you won't let anyone down. You're strong, resourceful, and resilient."

"I'm scared of losing Raven. Her departure could be the final nail in the coffin. I think I need to hire someone to run the financial side of Wolf Lake Consulting, but I don't have the funds."

He wrapped his arms around her, pulling her close. She could feel the steady beat of his heart against her back, a comforting rhythm that made her feel safe, even as her world seemed to crumble around her.

"Let me tell you a story," he said. "When my father was building Shepherd Systems, things were tough. Really tough. He struggled to keep it afloat, and I remember nights when he'd come home looking so defeated. But he never gave up. He believed in what he was doing, and he fought like hell to make it work. Now Shepherd Systems is a regional powerhouse."

"Wow. I always figured your father had things figured out from the beginning. But how do I know I can do this? What if I fail?"

"You've already proven yourself capable of overcoming obstacles. You'll find a way."

She knew he believed in her, and that meant everything. In

the dim lighting of the living room, she looked into his eyes. He meant every word.

"I appreciate what you're saying, but it doesn't change the fact that I'm not sure I can do this."

"What if I talked to Naomi? She has Shepherd Systems running in beast mode. I could ask her to take a few hours off from work and help Wolf Lake Consulting."

"That wouldn't be right. You need her."

"I've seen you overcome so much already. You're too strong to cave now. Are you sure you won't accept my help?"

Chelsey bit her lip, considering his offer as she looked out the window at the lake.

"I can't."

"Then you'll solve the problem on your own."

She shook her head. "Not on my own."

"Explain."

"It's weird, but I sense the perfect answer is coming. Maybe if I sleep on it, the answer will come to me in the morning."

The stillness of the water reflected her newfound calm, as if nature were telling her to accept the situation for what it was. The seasons represented constant change, the inevitability of life's challenges, and rebirth.

"That's the spirit."

"I just need to keep the business afloat without Raven. It feels impossible."

"Nothing is impossible when you put your mind to it. Besides, she hasn't taken Franklin Devereux's offer. Not yet."

For a moment, they sat in silence. She mulled over his words, drawing strength from his faith in her abilities.

"Your belief in me means everything."

As the night deepened, she felt a renewed sense of determination.

"Let's get some sleep," he said, wrapping an arm around her shoulders. "Tomorrow is a new day."

Chelsey nodded, leaning into his embrace. They climbed the stairs toward the bedroom, pausing once more to look out at the lake. The ice continued its retreat. And as they watched, she hoped the challenges they faced would melt away too, leaving behind the clear and steady waters of a brighter future.

57

Raven sat at her desk inside Wolf Lake Consulting. The lights highlighted the financial records she'd spread out before her like an intricate puzzle. She rubbed her temples, feeling the effects of a sleepless night. As much as it pained her, she had decided to accept Franklin Devereux's job offer. But she couldn't leave Chelsey and the business they both loved without doing everything in her power to save it first.

"Okay, my friend," Raven said to the empty room. "Let's see what we can do."

She studied the numbers on the spreadsheet, her mind processing ideas. Her fingers tapped on the desk as she formulated a plan to increase revenue and cut costs for the private investigation firm. If she could find the right combination of strategies, she might pull Wolf Lake Consulting back from the brink.

As the morning sunlight filtered through the blinds, she dove into the numbers. Her muscular arms tensed as she leaned in closer to examine the figures. Every detail mattered, and she was determined not to miss anything.

"This much is obvious," she said, thinking aloud. "We need to improve our online presence. That's a start."

Raven considered various tactics, such as revamping their website and increasing their social media presence. She also entertained the idea of creating a price structure to attract new clients and retain existing ones. Chelsey wouldn't like it, but she needed to make changes if she wanted to survive.

As the minutes passed, she brainstormed ideas on cost reduction. She rifled through the files on her desk, searching for any overlooked opportunities to trim expenses. She even contemplated using Devereux's network to introduce new clients to the firm, hoping fresh business would breathe life into their dwindling revenue stream.

"Maybe LeVar knows someone," she whispered. Her brother had his own connections through the sheriff's department and the community college.

Her determination grew stronger as eight o'clock approached; Chelsey would arrive soon. She refused to abandon the business that had been a second home to her. Wolf Lake Consulting deserved a fighting chance, and she intended to give it just that.

When the top of the hour arrived, she rocked back in her chair and studied the financial plan she had crafted. She exhaled, satisfied with the result of her hard work. The documents laid out on her desk were the culmination of hours spent dissecting Wolf Lake Consulting's finances and devising strategies to save the business. Chelsey needed to see this, but the thought of presenting it made her heart race.

The front door opened. Sunglasses framed Chelsey's face as she entered the office, surprise registering at the sight of Raven. "What are you doing here so early?"

"Hey, Chelsey. I've been working on something for the business. Can we talk?"

"Sure, I suppose."

Chelsey took a seat across from Raven, her eyes never leaving the stack of papers on the desk.

"I spent all morning going over your financials." Raven held up the papers for emphasis. "I've come up with a plan that I think could really help you turn things around."

"Really? What do you have in mind?"

"First, I think you should hire Scout to manage your online presence. She has a knack for that kind of thing, and it could bring in more clients."

"Scout's good with computers. That might work. What else?"

"I identified some areas where you can cut costs without affecting your productivity. For example, you can renegotiate contracts with your suppliers and reduce overhead by switching to more energy-efficient equipment."

Chelsey listened, her eyes flicking from Raven to the financial plan. "This is impressive, Raven. You put a lot of thought into this."

"Also, you should get rid of the antiquated heating and cooling system and replace it with an air pump."

"That sounds expensive."

"I worked out the numbers, and the loan payments are lower than the cost savings."

"Wow."

"I just want to do everything I can to help save the business. You've worked too hard to let it fail now."

"Your suggestion here," Chelsey said, tapping her finger on one page, "about targeting businesses who won't balk at our rates is a great idea. I love that you suggested bulk rates for multiple tasks."

"I thought so too." Raven shifted in her seat, hands clasped. "It would show your appreciation for their loyalty and encourage them to continue working with you."

Chelsey nodded, slowly lowering the document onto the desk. Her eyes met Raven's and filled with gratitude. "I can't thank you enough for all of this, Raven. You've gone above and beyond to save the business."

Raven felt warmth spread through her chest at Chelsey's words. "I couldn't stand by and watch the business crumble."

Tears welled up in Chelsey's eyes and her lower lip quivered. She blinked, trying to hold them back, but a few escaped and trailed down her cheeks. "This means everything to me. Your friendship, your dedication. I don't know what I would do without you."

"You'll get through this."

Chelsey wiped away her tears with the back of her hand, taking a deep breath to steady herself. "You're right. I will." She paused, hesitating before continuing. "There's something else I wanted to talk to you about."

"Go ahead."

"Once we implement these changes and get our finances back on track, I want to take on more cases," Chelsey said, determination in her voice. "I think we can handle a bigger workload."

"Absolutely. With this plan in place, you'll be more than ready for that."

"Anyway, I've been thinking about how to make this business more sustainable in the long run. I realized I need someone by my side who truly understands the financial side of things. Someone who can help guide us through rough patches and ensure we keep growing."

"Like a financial officer of sorts?"

"Kind of."

Raven squinted, her curiosity piqued. "Who are you thinking of bringing on board?"

Chelsey hesitated, her fingers tapping the edge of the desk. "Well, I was thinking I'd like it to be you, Raven."

"Me?" She fell back, stunned by the sudden proposal. Her heart raced as she tried to process the unexpected turn of events.

"You've proven time and again how much you care about this business, and your work today only solidifies that. I trust you, Raven, and I think we could achieve great things together."

"What are you saying?"

"That Wolf Lake Consulting deserves two owners, not one."

She stared at Chelsey, speechless. The possibility of co-ownership had never crossed her mind, and now it dangled before her like a tempting prize. This could change everything.

"I don't know what to say." Raven's voice trembled slightly as she spoke. "This is a lot to take in."

"I need someone who gets this business, someone who cares for it like you do. We've been struggling, but together I truly believe we can turn things around."

Chelsey gestured at the piles of papers and the financial plan. "Your financial savvy, combined with my investigative skills—we'd be unstoppable."

The offer was unexpected, yet it presented an ideal solution to Raven's predicament. She could help save the firm she loved while securing her own financial future. It felt like fate.

"Chelsey," she whispered, her eyes glistening with unshed tears, "you don't know how much this means to me."

"Take your time and think it over. I want you to be sure before making such a big decision."

But as Raven looked around the familiar office, at the photographs of their past cases pinned on the walls, and the pet beds nestled in the corners, she realized she didn't need to think about it. This was where she belonged.

"I don't need to think it over. I accept."

"Really? You're sure?"

"More than ever," she said, her confidence growing with every word. "We'll make this work. I promise."

In that moment, Chelsey moved from behind her desk and wrapped her arms around Raven, pulling her into a tight embrace. The warmth of their friendship filled the room.

"Thank you," Chelsey murmured into her friend's shoulder. "I know we'll face challenges, but with you by my side, I'm ready for anything."

"Me too." Her heart swelled with gratitude.

They held each other for a moment, united in their commitment to the future of Wolf Lake Consulting. There was work to be done, challenges to overcome, and yet they faced it all with renewed resolve. Together they would succeed and forge a path for themselves and the business they cherished.

58

After contacting their high-profile clients to offer a loyalty discount, Raven glanced over at Chelsey, who was busy typing away on her laptop. She knew what she had to do next, though every fiber of her being tried to make her procrastinate.

Inhaling, she picked up her phone and dialed Franklin Devereux's number. Her head throbbed as she listened to the ringtone.

"Ms. Hopkins," he answered, his voice smooth and confident.

"Mr. Devereux, I've given your offer some thought, and I wanted to let you know my decision."

"Go ahead."

"I'm staying with Chelsey and Wolf Lake Consulting," Raven replied, her voice steady despite the conflict within her. "I appreciate your offer, but my loyalty lies here."

There was a pause on the other end, and she could feel his incredulity through the line. "You're rejecting my offer?" he asked, disbelief coloring his words.

"Yes," she confirmed, her resolve unwavering. "I believe in what we're doing here, and I can't walk away from that."

"I don't understand." Franklin sounded almost hurt. "My firm is the best in the region. You'd have access to resources and opportunities you could only dream of at Wolf Lake Consulting."

"Perhaps," she said, acknowledging the truth in his statement. "But I've grown attached to this place, to the people I work with. Money and prestige aren't everything."

"Clearly, we have different priorities."

"Maybe we do. I'm sorry to disappoint you, but I know I've made the right choice."

Desperation crept into his tone. "I'm willing to make you an even better offer. I'll increase your salary by another twenty percent, provide comprehensive life insurance benefits, and throw in a substantial sign-on bonus. You'd be a fool not to accept."

She paused, considering Franklin's generous proposal. It wasn't every day that someone was offered such a lucrative opportunity. However, loyalty and personal connections meant more to her than financial gain. The team at Wolf Lake Consulting had become a family to her, and she couldn't abandon them.

"I appreciate the offer, truly. But my decision remains unchanged. I've chosen to stay with Chelsey and become co-owner of Wolf Lake Consulting."

"Co-owner? Are you certain? You're walking away from a life-changing opportunity."

"I am." She looked at Chelsey, who was working diligently at her desk. "We've built something special here, and I believe in our team. We may not have the same resources or prestige as your firm, but we have heart, dedication, and a strong sense of camaraderie."

Franklin let out a heavy sigh, the sound of defeat audible even through the phone. "Very well. I can't say I understand your choice. You're wasting your talent there. You could do so much more with us."

"Is that why you want me, Mr. Devereux? To add another trophy to your collection?"

There was a pause on the other end of the line before he spoke again, his tone subdued. "No, it's not like that." He released a sigh. "Our firm has been struggling with security issues, and none of my previous hires have been able to handle it. I need someone like you."

Guilt tugged at her. He'd made her several generous offers and remained patient, and she'd led him into believing she would accept the position. Heck, she'd assumed the decision was a forgone conclusion until Chelsey made her co-owner of the business.

She tapped a pen against her chin, considering his words. "How about this? Let me meet your current head of security. Maybe there's something I can do to help without abandoning my team here."

"You're willing to do that?"

"Give me thirty minutes," she said, already gathering her things.

As she hung up the phone, Chelsey shot her a questioning look.

"Everything okay?"

"It's complicated," Raven said, slinging her bag over her shoulder. "But I think I just found a way to help Franklin Devereux and still stay true to Wolf Lake Consulting."

As she drove to Harmon, her thoughts raced. Franklin Devereux was a powerful man, and turning down his offer had put her in an unenviable position. In the center of the city, she pulled into the parking lot and checked her hair in the mirror. She hoped that by offering her expertise to help their head of security, she could not only salvage their professional relationship but also create an opportunity for Wolf Lake Consulting to collaborate with his firm. If she played this right, she might help Chelsey too.

Raven walked through the lobby, her sneakers squeaking against the polished floor as she approached the receptionist. "I'm here to see Franklin Devereux."

"Of course, Ms. Hopkins," the receptionist smiled, guiding her to Franklin's office. "He's waiting for you."

Devereux stood as she entered the room, his expression a mix of relief and apprehension.

"Are you sure about this, Ms. Hopkins?"

"It means a lot to me that you wanted me to lead the security team. The least I can do is say thank you."

"As you wish."

He led her down the hall to another office where a man in his early forties waited, looking out of place in a suit and tie.

"Raven, this is Oliver Morris, our current head of security," Devereux said. "Oliver, meet Raven Hopkins, the woman who just might help us out of this mess."

"Nice to meet you, Raven," Oliver said, extending his hand. "I've read great things about your work."

Mr. Devereux took a seat.

"Pleased to meet you, Oliver. Mr. Devereux tells me there have been some security issues here."

"Understatement of the year." Oliver chuckled grimly. "I'm used to dealing with life-and-death situations in the field, but managing security for a corporation like this is a whole different ballgame."

"Life and death situations?"

"I'm a military man."

"I see. Tell me more about your experience in the military," she said, sensing that Oliver's background held the key to unlocking his potential.

"Did two tours in Afghanistan," he began, rubbing the back of his neck. "Learned how to improvise and adapt to any situation. But when I came back, I struggled to find my footing in the civilian world. That's when Mr. Devereux offered me this opportunity. I should be thankful. Well, I *am* thankful, except that I'm in over my head. Too much to overcome."

"Sounds like you've overcome a lot already. But let's be honest, Oliver. You've never worked in security before, have you?"

He sighed, his shoulders sagging under the weight of his admission. "Never have. But I'm not willing to give up. I just need a few months working under someone who understands what needs to be done. That's why I suggested Mr. Devereux hire you."

"You suggested me?"

"Yep. I read all about your accomplishments and knew you were perfect for the job."

Raven studied Oliver's earnest expression, taking in the lines of determination on his face. He was a man searching for guidance, and she wanted to provide it.

She leaned against the edge of the corner table. "I can see you're intelligent and capable, but you need someone to show you the ropes. You weren't trained?"

"Thought I could figure it out on my own. But this isn't like the military."

"First off, thank you for your service."

His face reddened. "Of course."

"Anyone with your qualifications is more than ready to run the security team. You just need guidance. Which is why I'm here."

"Are you offering to train me?" Oliver asked.

"That's correct. I won't leave Wolf Lake Consulting, but I

propose that Mr. Devereux hires my company as a security consultant for your firm."

Mr. Devereux raised an eyebrow, skepticism creeping into his features. "And how does that benefit our companies?"

"By allowing us to work with your crew," she explained, maintaining steady eye contact, "Wolf Lake Consulting will have a stable income while we train Oliver and your security team. Your firm gets the expertise it needs, and we ensure our survival."

Silence engulfed the room as Devereux weighed the proposal. Oliver's gaze flitted from one to the other.

"You've convinced me," Devereux said. "We'll give it a shot. But if this arrangement doesn't deliver results, we'll need to reevaluate."

"Fair enough," she said, extending her hand to seal the deal. Franklin grasped it, the tension dissipating as they shook on their agreement.

"Thank you," Oliver said, excitement shining in his eyes. "I promise I'm a fast learner."

"I don't doubt that for a second."

They stepped into the lobby, which was filled with employees and clients alike. As Raven observed the organized chaos, she couldn't help but feel a renewed sense of purpose. The marble floors beneath her feet felt cool and solid, grounding her. She had made the right choice.

"Ms. Hopkins," Devereux said, his tone more amicable than before. "I must admit, this wasn't the outcome I expected, but I believe it's for the best."

"Sometimes the unexpected path proves to be the most rewarding," she said.

"Your loyalty to your team is commendable. It's a rare quality these days."

"Thank you again for offering to bring me aboard. I look forward to working together and seeing what we can achieve."

"Likewise." He offered her a genuine smile before turning to Oliver. "Oliver, I expect you to give this opportunity your all and learn as much as you can from Raven."

"Absolutely, sir," Oliver said, standing straighter, his determination clear. "I won't let you down."

Raven watched the exchange, feeling the beginnings of camaraderie between them. They were a team now, bound by their shared goals and aspirations.

"Then it's settled," she said. "We'll call you by the end of the day and set up a training schedule."

The stage was set for success, and Raven was more than prepared to lead both firms toward promising futures.

59

Raven cruised up the hill that led to Wolf Lake State Park. The last light of day dipped behind a curtain of trees and spread an amber glow on her face. The temperature was just warm enough to lower the window without freezing. She inhaled, taking in the scents of pine, melting ice, and earth that permeated the air. Her heart raced with anticipation, a mix of pride and excitement swirling within her as she drove back to the ranger's cabin.

She couldn't believe the gift fate had given her. She was staying at Wolf Lake Consulting, and it felt right. The day had been long and eventful, a hive of activity as they sorted through new cases. She felt a renewed sense of purpose now, knowing she was integral to the business's success. Co-owner. It seemed impossible, but it was true. Things were about to get interesting.

As the cabin came into view, she spotted Darren waiting outside, his dark hair ruffling in the breeze. A smile spread across his face as he saw her approach. The feeling of peace and belonging cradled her.

"Hey there," Darren called out as she stepped out of the car.

"Hey."

She hurried towards him. He wrapped his arms around her, pulling her into a tight embrace as she closed her eyes, lost in the warmth of his touch.

"Missed you today," he said, his breath tickling her ear.

"I missed you too," she murmured, pulling back just enough to meet his gaze.

"So everything worked out?" he asked, curiosity glinting in his eyes.

"My instinct tells me this is the start of something amazing."

They stood for a moment, still wrapped in each other's arms, as the sun continued to set and the shadows grew longer. The future stretched out before them like an open road, full of possibilities and the promise of adventure.

"Let's go inside," Darren suggested, releasing her from his embrace. "We can celebrate this new chapter together."

The sound of gravel crunching under tires alerted them to another arrival. They turned to see LeVar's black Chrysler Limited pulling up beside her Nissan Rogue.

"Hey, there's the woman of the hour," LeVar said, striding over to join them. "Word around town is you made quite an impression on Chelsey today."

"More than that," Darren said with pride. "She landed a contract to train Franklin Devereux's staff."

"Really?" LeVar clapped Raven on the shoulder. "That's amazing. But what did you say to Chelsey? She's been a bundle of energy since your talk."

Raven chuckled and shook her head. "That's between me and her, little brother."

"Fair enough."

"Hey, why don't we make the most of this evening?" Darren asked, gesturing to a nearby grill. "It's cold, but we can have ourselves a little cookout to celebrate."

"Sounds like a plan."

LeVar rubbed his hands together in anticipation. They hurried into the cabin to grab jackets, then carried food and charcoal out to the grill, braving the biting March wind. Raven felt the cold air nip at her cheeks as they set everything up, but the excitement of the gathering heated her from within.

"Darren, you got the grill under control?" Raven asked, watching him ignite the charcoal.

"I promise not to burn down the forest," he said. "That would be a bad look for a ranger. Just give me a few minutes, and we'll have ourselves a feast fit for champions."

LeVar looked around at the serene park, then turned to her. "You know, sis, I'm proud of you. You're changing lives."

She smiled at her brother's words. With Darren by her side, and LeVar supporting her every step of the way, she knew the future held great things for them all. "Get used to having me around. And now that I'm a half-owner, I'll be watching you like a hawk. Don't slip up, newbie."

LeVar chuckled and helped her collect everything they needed for dinner. Darren flipped the sizzling steaks. Tendrils of smoke spiraled upward, kissing the cold air. Inside the ranger's cabin, Raven and LeVar gathered plates and silverware, setting the table.

"LeVar, I'm really excited about what we can achieve at Wolf Lake Consulting. I've been thinking about ways to expand our services, maybe even expand to support law enforcement across the county."

"Sounds like you got a plan in mind."

"I do," she said, arranging a stack of napkins on the table. "It's not just about growing the business. It's about making a lasting impact on the community and helping people find answers and justice."

He leaned against the counter, arms crossed as he listened. "You know, sis, I gotta say that since you became an owner,

Chelsey has this insane energy around her and the business. It's like you two are unstoppable together."

"It's not just Chelsey and me. You're part of this team too. Your skills, your knowledge—it all makes a difference."

"Like a family," he added, his words echoing the sentiment rooted in their hearts.

"Couldn't have said it any better," she agreed, a soft smile playing on her lips.

As they finished setting the table, Darren appeared in the kitchen with a platter of steaks. The aroma wafted through the cabin, inviting and intoxicating.

"Feast your eyes on this," he announced, placing the platter on the table.

"Darren, you've outdone yourself," she said. "Medium-rare?"

"You know it."

"Let's eat before the cow comes back to life," LeVar said.

They took their seats around the table, each aware of the significance of the moment, not just for themselves but for the future of Wolf Lake Consulting. The clink of silverware against plates and the low hum of conversation filled the air as they savored the flavors.

"Before we go any further," she said, placing her fork down and raising a glass, "I'd like to propose a toast." Her eyes met those of her companions "To friendship, love, and pursuing our dreams."

"Hear, hear," LeVar agreed, lifting his own glass. Darren joined in, and the three glasses clinked together, the sound ringing out with a promise of better days to come.

With the toast complete, the conversation shifted to lighter topics. Laughter punctuated their stories and jokes, a balm for their weary souls.

"Who knew you were such a prankster, Raven?" Darren said, recalling an anecdote about her antics at Wolf Lake Consulting.

"Hey," she replied, grinning mischievously, "I have to keep things interesting somehow. Otherwise, life would be too boring."

"True," LeVar chimed in. "And speaking of interesting, have I ever told you two about the time I accidentally locked myself out of the office in nothing but my boxer shorts?"

"Wait, what? Okay, LeVar, you have to tell us that story."

As the laughter continued to flow, the trio took advantage of the blue gloaming. Donning their jackets, they ventured out into the crisp air, embarking on a stroll along the ridge trail. The beauty of nature enveloped them as they walked, its serenity soothing any lingering worries or doubts.

As they reached the edge of the lake, the stars came out to greet them. They paused in their journey, admiring the water's surface as it mirrored the sparkling light. In that moment, the future seemed infinite, filled with potential and promise.

60

Bright-eyed and excited to get started, Raven sipped her coffee. The warm bitterness was a welcome contrast to the frost outside the office window. She glanced at Chelsey, who pored over documents.

Chelsey pushed a lock of hair behind her ears as she looked up. "We need to come up with fresh ideas for marketing our expanded services and attracting those high-paying clients."

"Hundred percent. We have the skills; we just need to make sure people know about them. Perhaps we can start by revamping our website, adding more case studies and success stories."

"You bet, but I know nothing about web design." Chelsey scribbled a note. "Let's find out if Scout can help. And we should definitely target local businesses, but also look into reaching out to potential clients in surrounding cities. Maybe even hold some workshops or seminars to showcase our expertise."

"I hadn't thought of that. That's an amazing idea."

As they discussed their plans, the front door of Wolf Lake Consulting opened and Oliver Morris stepped inside. He stood tall, his expression eager as he approached Raven and Chelsey.

"Morning, ladies," Oliver greeted them, extending a hand to each. "I'm here to learn from the best."

"Welcome, Oliver," Raven said. "Let's get started. By the end of the week, you'll have Mr. Devereux's firm in tiptop shape."

Over the next two hours, Raven introduced Oliver to the world of security management and investigative techniques. He listened attentively, asking questions and absorbing every detail. His enthusiasm and aptitude for learning didn't surprise her.

"Okay, so when you're doing a background check," Raven explained, "you want to verify employment history, criminal records, and any relevant financial information. You'd be surprised at how many people try to hide their past."

"Got it," Oliver said, jotting notes on a pad. "And when conducting surveillance, what's the best way to remain inconspicuous?"

"Blend in with your surroundings. Dress appropriately, use a nondescript vehicle, and avoid direct eye contact. If you look like you belong, people don't notice you."

As they worked through various scenarios and techniques, Raven experienced a sense of pride. By sharing her knowledge with Oliver, she was not only helping him grow, but also contributing to the success of their business.

"Thanks, Raven," he said as their session ended. "I learned so much today. I can't wait to put these skills to use."

She shook his hand. "You're doing great, Oliver. Just remember to stay focused and trust your instincts. Your background puts ours to shame, so it's only a matter of time before you run laps around us."

"I don't know about that."

"Trust me. I have faith in you."

As he left, Chelsey looked up from her work and caught Raven's eye. "You did good with him," she said, a smile playing on her lips.

The women continued their planning, envisioning a future of growth and success for Wolf Lake Consulting. They were deep in discussion about their upcoming networking event—an opportunity to showcase their skills and connect with other local businesses.

"Let's make sure there's a good mix of professionals," Chelsey said. "Private investigators, security experts, law enforcement."

"Great idea. And we should have a couple of case studies to present. Nothing too detailed, but enough to show our range and expertise."

"We want them to remember us when they need help."

As they continued to strategize, they heard the arrival of Scout, who had an early release from school today. With her glasses perched on her nose, the teen scanned the organized chaos before her.

"Hey, Scout," Chelsey said, beckoning her over. "You're just in time to help us plan our big event."

"Wow, this is amazing," Scout breathed, her eyes darting between the two women. "I can't believe how much you've accomplished in one morning."

Raven took a seat. "It's hard work, but we're proud of what we're building."

"Definitely," Chelsey said. "But we couldn't have done it without the support of people like you, Scout."

"Speaking of which," Raven said, turning her attention back to planning the event, "what do you think would draw the biggest crowd? A panel discussion or a workshop?"

"Uh . . . a workshop, I guess?" Scout said with uncertainty.

"Good call," Chelsey said. "Interactive is always better."

"Maybe you could do something on digital forensics with Claire Brookins," Raven added, looking at Scout. "You're really skilled in that area."

"Me?" Scout mumbled, her cheeks flushing. "I'd be happy to help if you want me to, but would anyone take a teenager seriously?"

"You'd be surprised."

"Scout, we have a proposal for you," Chelsey said. "We need someone to manage our web presence, and we think you're the right person for the job."

"Okay. I'm happy to add that to the work I do as an intern."

Raven shared a knowing grin with Chelsey. "You have the skills, and we've seen your dedication firsthand. But we don't want you to work on our web presence as part of your internship."

Scout's fingers fidgeted with the hem of her shirt. "I don't follow you."

"We're not asking you to do this as a favor. We'd like to pay you for your services."

Scout's eyes widened. "Pay me? You mean this would be an actual job?"

"Yes. A professional position that you can add to your resume and build on for your future career."

The girl stared into space, taking a moment to process the implications.

"Wow. I never expected this. To have you trust me with something so important . . . I don't know what to say."

"Take your time," Chelsey said. "We know it's a big decision."

The teen closed her eyes, as if gathering her thoughts. "Like I really need to think this over. I'll do it. Thank you for believing in me."

"We know you'll do great things."

"So this is real? I'm hired?"

"You were always part of the team. This just makes it official."

Raven's throat tightened as tears trickled down the teenager's cheeks. "Congratulations. You deserve this."

"Oh my God. I need to call Mom."

As Scout dialed her mother's number, Raven wrapped an arm around Chelsey's shoulders. "We did well."

"Hit it out of the park."

After the call, Scout hung up and turned to face them, excitement lighting up her eyes.

"Mom's thrilled," she said. "She's so proud of me. But most of all, she says thanks to both of you."

"Let's celebrate," Raven said, reaching for a bottle of sparkling cider. The cork popped, and fizzy liquid filled three glasses, bubbles dancing like Scout's eyes.

"Here's to our new partnership and the bright future ahead," Chelsey toasted, raising her glass. Raven and Scout followed suit, their glasses clinking in unison.

"Cheers," said Scout, taking a sip.

Raven leaned against the edge of the desk, sipping her cider. "We're excited to have you on board. Your skills are going to be invaluable to us. Tell us. What do you feel we should do first?"

"Improve our online presence. Maybe redesign the website, optimize it for search engines, and create engaging content to drive traffic."

"Sounds promising. We could use a fresh perspective."

Chelsey said, "And your knowledge of cyber security will be a great asset as well."

Scout's eyes lit up at the mention of cyber security, her passion evident. "Yes, I can help set up secure systems for our clients and provide consultations on best practices."

"Perfect. We'll discuss a plan of action in more detail tomorrow. For now, let's just enjoy this moment."

"Yeah," Raven said, finishing her drink. "Let's celebrate like Kool & the Gang at a cheesy wedding."

This was only the beginning, but it marked a pivotal step in their journey. As long as they were together, nothing would stand in their way.

GET A FREE BOOK!

I'm a pretty nice guy once you look past the grisly images in my head. Most of all, I love connecting with awesome readers like you.

Join my VIP Reader Group and get a FREE serial killer thriller for your Kindle.

Get My Free Book

www.danpadavona.com/thriller-readers-vip-group/

SUPPORT YOUR FAVORITE AUTHORS

Did you enjoy this book? If so, please let other thriller fans know by leaving a short review. Positive reviews help spread the word about independent authors and their novels. Thank you.

Copyright Information

Published by Dan Padavona

Visit my website at www.danpadavona.com

Copyright © 2023 by Dan Padavona

Artwork copyright © 2023 by Dan Padavona

Cover Design by Caroline Teagle Johnson

All Rights Reserved

Although some of the locations in this book are actual places, the characters and setting are wholly of the author's imagination. Any resemblance between the people in this book and people in the real world is purely coincidental and unintended.

❦ Created with Vellum

ACKNOWLEDGMENTS

No writer journeys alone. Special thanks are in order to my editor, C.B. Moore, for providing invaluable feedback, catching errors, and making my story shine. I also wish to thank my brilliant cover designer, Caroline Teagle Johnson. Your artwork never ceases to amaze me. I owe so much of my success to your hard work. Shout outs to my advance readers, including Mary Arnold, Deanna Stotler, Marcia Campbell, and Ted Browne, for catching those final pesky typos and plot holes. Most of all, thank you to my readers for your loyalty and support. You changed my life, and I am forever grateful.

ABOUT THE AUTHOR

Dan Padavona is the author of The Wolf Lake series, The Thomas Shepherd series, The Logan and Scarlett series, The Darkwater Cove series, The Scarlett Bell thriller series, *Her Shallow Grave*, and The Dark Vanishings series. He lives in upstate New York with his beautiful wife, Terri, and their children, Joe, and Julia. Dan is a meteorologist with NOAA's National Weather Service. Besides writing, he enjoys visiting amusement parks, beach vacations, Renaissance fairs, gardening, playing with the family dogs, and eating too much ice cream.

Visit Dan at: www.danpadavona.com

Printed in Great Britain
by Amazon